Never Say Never

Timber Falls, Volume 7

Fiona West

Published by Fiona West, 2022.

This is a work of fiction. Similarities to real people, places, or events are entirely coincidental.

NEVER SAY NEVER

First edition. April 4, 2022.

ISBN: 978-1-952172-39-7

Written by Fiona West.

PROLOGUE

Ruth

The first time Ruth Zane found Charlie Miller in her thinking spot, she turned around and left. She wasn't supposed to talk to him, and it really wasn't that urgent that she sit there right this minute; her younger brother Wyatt had gotten into her Halloween candy stash and decimated it. Just a walk through the woods would be good enough to calm her down.

The second time she found him in her thinking spot, she watched him for a while. He was just sitting on the tire swing, looking out at the river. After a few minutes, he got up and left, tromping off into his side of the woods. He kicked at a decaying log on the way by and whacked at a low pine branch but obviously, that was none of her business, even if he was infringing on her property. When she sat down on the swing, she had the oddest feeling that someone was watching her, and she decided if it was her brother Ranger, she was going to hide all his Magic: The Gathering cards under the washing machine where he'd never find them. Life had been a lot lately, and she just needed the sound of the river to wash away her worries. The adults around her didn't seem to think that twelve-year-olds could have serious worries...but she did.

A few weeks went by, and she didn't see him. It was just as well; she still wasn't supposed to talk to him, and things at home weren't getting much better. Her mom hadn't even come to her choir concert, even though she'd promised. She just apologized over and over, dark circles under her eyes as she used the curling iron on Ruth's hair.

So, the third time he was in her spot, Ruth just waited again.

"I know you're there!" Charlie shouted. "You might as well come out." She didn't think it was wise to ignore an older kid who was yelling at her. He was still facing toward the river when she stepped out of the tree line cautiously. "What do you want?"

"You're in my spot," she said meekly, and Charlie sneered, looking more like a man than a boy of sixteen.

"This is my land. Get lost."

"How do you know?" She came around the front of the swing to face him.

"What'd you mean, how do I know? It's on our side!"

Ruth crossed her arms. "Prove it."

"Wha—how—are you kidding me?" the young man sputtered. "Everyone knows it's on my side!"

"Not me. I've been coming here for years."

"Well, so have I, and I've never seen you until lately."

"Probably because you knew this is my side."

His face darkened. "Look, my dad has really been on my case lately, so just lay off."

"You think you're the only one with problems?" Ruth shot back. "My mom can't get out of bed!"

His eyebrows lifted in confusion. "How does that work? Are her legs broken?"

"No, she's just...tired all the time. I think someone put a curse on her." She hadn't told anyone else that, and the moment it left her mouth, she regretted it. Charlie Miller was popular; if he started telling people what she'd said, they'd have ammunition to tease her. Her speech impediment gave them reason enough already; it wasn't fair that she couldn't even say her own name correctly. But her fears eased when a smile ghosted across his face.

"That's not likely."

"How do you know? You're claiming a tire swing that isn't even yours."

"Well, it sounds like we both need it. Maybe we should share it."

Ruth frowned at him. She didn't think her dad would like that. But Charlie seemed to realize she was wavering. "I'll give you a push when I'm here, and I'll leave if you need it more than I do. But only because of your sleeping mom thing."

"Fine."

He climbed out of the swing, and Ruth climbed in. Charlie pulled her backward by the dangling rope, then let her go. She flew out over the bank of the river, much higher than she could usually go, and it felt good. It felt...freeing.

"What's your dad so mad about?"

"I got a B on my history paper."

"That's pretty good."

"He said it wasn't good enough. He said I have to redo it, even if she won't grade it again."

"Wow." Her own father mostly made sure she was going to school. He didn't seem to worry about how she was doing until report card time, and by then, there was nothing she could do about it. He seemed happy with C's, anyway.

"Yeah. You know anything about Mesopotamia?"

She shook her head. "I've only been to Washington, Colorado and Nebraska."

"Did your parents drive?"

"Yeah."

"Then you've been to some other states, too, because those don't touch."

"Oh." She hadn't noticed those; there had been a lot of wheat fields and corn fields in between, a blank counterpoint to the layered magnificence of her own woods. "Well, it doesn't count if I didn't get out of the car."

"Says who?"

"Says me."

Charlie huffed in annoyance, then started toward the trees.

"Where are you going?"

"Home. I've got a baseball game."

"Don't tell anybody about our deal, all right?"

Charlie gave her that momentary smile again. "I'm not stupid, Ruth. My dad would kill me if he knew I'd made a deal with a Zane."

The swing was slowing down now, and she dragged her feet on the dirt. "Why'd you do it, then?"

Charlie shrugged as he kept walking. "You seem nice enough. A little weird, but nice."

"Gee, thanks," she called back, kicking off to go higher, and she watched his red windbreaker until it disappeared into the dappled shadow of the woods.

CHAPTER ONE

Charlie

Fourteen Years Later

"I'm not eating that."

Charlie sat forward over the dinner table. "This is what's for dinner, Aiden." It was dark outside the large windows behind the boy, so Charlie could see his own annoyed reflection, as well as the smirk his brother and sister-in-law were sharing. They were a safe audience for his children's antics. At least Dahlia was asleep; three-month-olds were predictable that way. That was one less person to wrestle with.

"I don't want it, either. I'll just have a glass of milk," Emily announced. Despite being told about six hundred times that her dolls were not allowed at the table (on account of their creepy vacant eyes), Emily was brushing the hair of the one she called Samantha. Or June? No, this one was Samantha. Probably.

"This is what's for dinner," Charlie repeated evenly, even though he could feel his calm fraying. "If you are hungry, you can eat the curry. If you're not hungry, you can leave the table. But there will be no snacks later. This is it, you two." He dug into the chicken and vegetables with fake enthusiasm. It wasn't the worst curry he'd ever had...but he could taste the freezer burn still on it. He should've made them something they'd like better, but he couldn't live on tacos every night. Thankfully, Em had finally outgrown that phase.

If he didn't see another package of tortillas for a decade, it would be too soon.

"I think it's pretty good," his brother Jason piped up, shoveling the mediocre food down. "Don't you think, Lace?"

His wife nodded as she tried to urge their own child to eat the puffs she'd brought. Iris sat in Dahlia's new high chair, banging on the tray with both hands, and Charlie winced at the noise. At least they backed him up with this foolish parenting endeavor.

"I'm going to make myself a sandwich," Aiden announced, pushing back from the table with a brash confidence that matched his eleven years. Charlie didn't take the bait.

"If you do, there will be consequences," Charlie said, wishing there was a way to subtract salt from pre-made food. "Probably relating to screens."

Red-faced, Aiden sat back down hard in his chair, scraping against the floor in protest. "This is the worst thing I've ever eaten."

"You're lucky then," Lacey commented, trying to entice Iris with a spoonful of something soft and orange. "When I was a kid, my mom used to give us canned carrots." She stuck out her tongue at the memory, and the rest of them laughed, except for Aiden.

"Oh—Charlie, do you remember that weird potpie Mom used to make? With the big onion chunks?"

"Ugh, yes. She was obsessed with that recipe for the longest time. And always when we had people over, so we couldn't even complain!"

"I think I fed most of mine to Brownie."

"Great idea," Aiden snarked. "Maybe we should get a dog."

"Not happening. Have you even taken a real bite, Aid?"

"I'm done," Emily said. "May I be excused?"

"Em, you didn't try it, either." Her tactic was a little different from Aiden's—she just ignored the food she disliked, then cried about being hungry right at bedtime so he'd cave to get her into bed. Well, not today. Audience or no, these kids were going to eat.

"I ate a little." She gave the doll's hair another stroke. "I gave it one star."

Jason and Lacey chuckled before he glared at them.

"This is not a restaurant. You don't get to give stars. Please eat your food or there will be no dessert."

Both children sat up straighter.

"What kind of dessert?" Em asked, as Aiden slumped down in his chair, trying too late to pretend he wasn't interested.

"Well," Charlie said slowly. "We don't know. Something yummy that Aunt Lacey brought. If you want to find out, you'll eat some curry."

"I mean," Emily said, going back to her hair-brushing, "I'll find out either way." Sometimes his kids were too smart for their own good. Why had he procreated with such a brainiac? Starla had always been too good for him. And if he hadn't been such a jerk, she'd probably still be with him instead of happily remarried to the surgeon who lived up on the mountain.

"But your opportunity to eat will be gone then," Charlie reminded her. "So you'll have to watch all of us eat that yummy stuff while you don't get any."

Em cocked her head to one side in thought. "I'll just go to my room."

"Sounds like you've got it all figured out," Lacey said, smirking, and Charlie elbowed her.

"Just you wait. These battles are coming to you sooner than you think."

"I know, and I'm taking notes, believe me."

"You're gonna need them if she's anything like Jase."

Lacey smiled fondly at her husband, who was obliviously chatting with Aiden, wholly focused on their conversation about video games. That was the funny thing about ADHD: there was no deficit of attention, but he did struggle with where to put it. And right now, animatedly talking with Aiden, they could probably yell *fire* and Jason wouldn't be phased at all. He likely wouldn't even hear them.

"A handful, was he?"

"You could say that."

"I guess he's still a bit of a hurricane, so that shouldn't surprise me."

In his private thoughts, Charlie usually likened him to a river: this massive wall of energy blasting into things and sometimes flooding them unless kept within his banks, but ultimately a source of life and blessing to the world.

"I couldn't ask for a better brother." *Geez, Miller, way to get maudlin.* His emotions were out of control lately; he wasn't sure why exactly. He stabbed another few bites of the curry, resolving to look at the package closely so he wouldn't buy this brand again.

"But you're a good brother, too. You make him take his meds. You keep him on track."

This was getting uncomfortable; he didn't do that for the praise. And outside of their parents, Lacey and Starla were the only people who knew about the role he played in his brother's life.

"Let's just agree that there's good mutual support."

Lacey spooned another bite for Iris. "Agreed."

"May I be excused?" Emily asked again, and Charlie sighed.

"Fine. Go. Good luck with your empty tummy." Em skipped off toward the bonus room, no doubt to find more dolls.

"And do something scientific while you're at it!" he called after her.

"Still on that kick?" Lacey asked.

"It is not a kick. It's not a crime to want my daughter to know that the sciences are accessible to her. As a female scientist, you should appreciate that."

"I do appreciate it," Lacey said slowly, like she was chewing on the thought, "but only if it's something Emily wants. There's no sense in pushing her toward something that's not an interest."

"It should be an interest," he mumbled, stabbing at the food again. "The world runs on science."

"An interesting assertion from a man who sells cars for a living..."

Charlie laughed mockingly, and Lacey grinned.

"Where's my dessert, woman?"

"It's in the freezer. Store-bought cheesecake. Being a woman of science, I have better things to do than bake."

"We'd better let it warm up," Charlie said, wiping his mouth with his napkin as he rose from the table.

"I hate cheesecake," Aiden interjected. "So I'm done." He was out of his chair and fleeing the room before Charlie could take a breath to bellow at him. All he could do as he went into the kitchen was shake his head.

CHAPTER TWO

Ruth

Mr. and Mrs. Donovan looked truly chagrined as they sat across from Ruth at their kitchen table. Out of habit, she smoothed down the laminated placemat she'd made with Nina and Wes, then made herself stop.

"We really wish we could keep you on. I assure you, it's not personal whatsoever," Mr. Donovan said. "You've been a great addition to the family." *Not exactly, sir. Families aren't supposed to get fired.*

"But since I'll be working from home, it just doesn't make sense to have a full-time nanny. We're so sorry to let you go. The children love you, and we'd love for you to come back for date nights sometimes or..." Mrs. Donovan sighed. "I'm sorry, Ruth."

"It's fine," she assured them softly. "I'd make the same choice." But she couldn't stop staring at the basket weave placemat. Nina had been so proud when she finished it, her little tongue sticking out in concentration as they worked on it over Fall Break in anticipation of Thanksgiving. Now it was only January, and it was already time to say goodbye. She didn't mean to fall in love with the kids; it just made her life harder. Maybe she'd pick a new job, something simple, like scooping ice cream or selling bait. There was good money in that when it was tourist season in Timber Falls. Still, knowing her, she'd find a way to feel bad for the worms she was digging up in the woods.

"Would you like to say goodbye to the kids?"

Ruth nodded. It took her a second to actually stand up from the table: it felt so final, leaving the place where she'd fed them and colored with them and played with homemade play dough, scented with lemon essential oil. Sudden partings were always the hardest.

She gave them both hugs; Nina seemed the most confused, so she gave her a little kiss on the head to let her know everything would be all right. After she said a more distant goodbye to the Donovan adults, she left.

The winter sun had mostly set, and the filtered light that was left cast long shadows on the tree-lined highway. Ruth drove toward town with no real destination in mind. She soon found herself in the little grocery store her dad referred to as "the Stop and Rob" to buy an individual serving of instant macaroni and cheese. It had become kind of a ritual: whenever she said goodbye to a family, she'd go buy mac and cheese and toast the good and bad of the experience. Even Damon seemed to know her ritual by now.

"Can I cook this for you?" he asked, tossing a thumb over his shoulder toward the microwave behind him.

"No, thank you. I should go home." But as she considered the amount of housework waiting for her at home, she changed her mind. "Actually, that'd be nice, if you don't mind."

Ruth drove up to the falls and parked where she could watch the water. Her mac and cheese was the perfect temperature; at least something was going right today.

"Pros," she said aloud. "They were kind people. Their kids were pretty well-behaved. The pay was good." She paused to take a bite, savoring the cheesy goodness. "Cons. Their dog was annoying. They often changed their plans last-minute, and I couldn't go to Audubon Society meetings because of the hours." She really had missed her birding friends. Maybe this wasn't all bad. "Disappointments: I won't get to go to Nina's ballet recital. We didn't make borax crystal snowflakes yet. I promised them breakfast for dinner next week and their parents are sticks-in-the-mud who probably won't let them do it." She speared the last bit of food out of the container and licked it off her plastic fork. "Opportunities: now I can spend more time with my brothers." They were on her last nerve lately, so she wasn't sure whether that was an opportunity to reconcile and improve things or to knock some sense into them. Either way, it was probably needed. With another sigh, she opened her truck door, which emitted a loud squeak, and she tossed her empty cup into the nearby trash can.

When she pulled into their looping driveway, there were already four other cars there, so everyone was home. *Probably wondering where I am.* She was a little surprised no one had texted her. Then, just as she was gathering up her bag, her phone vibrated.

Ranger: Ruthie, is there more crushed red pepper somewhere?

When she came inside, all four of her brothers plus her dad were sitting in the living room. It was on the seam of the doublewide, so it was bigger than it usually was in a manufactured home, but it still appeared quite full with the big black sectional full of guys. Her dad was the only one who noticed her. The brothers were too busy stuffing their faces with the pizza she'd made earlier.

"You okay, kiddo?"

"I got fired."

With a frown, her father got to his feet and started out of the maze of couches.

"What'd you do," Wyatt joked, "forget one of the kids at school?"

"No, Mrs. Donovan is going to work from home, so they don't need me anymore. They're still paying me through the end of the month."

Her dad wrapped her in a hug. "I'm sorry. It's never fun to say goodbye."

"Nope." She squeezed him back. At least someone cared.

"More time to do laundry," called Levi. "Speaking of which, did you do my uniforms?" He was the oldest of the boys, and he'd been working as head chef at Annie's restaurant for a while now, but still seemed concerned with making a good impression. Ryan was still in college. Wyatt worked construction, and Ranger worked at the insurance office with their dad for lack of interest in anything else.

"They're in your closet," Ruth called back, still in her hug. "Did anyone put the laundry in the dryer?" She thought it was a reasonable question, given that seven adults lived here, not just one, but no one answered. She hated the question for another reason: the word dryer. It was one of the words she just couldn't master. Two r's in the word made it twice as hard, plus the r at the end was always a problem. Thankfully, her dad had never allowed her brothers to tease her about the way she spoke, and mostly, they didn't. So no one batted an eye at the way she said it now at age twenty-six.

"No one? Hello? Earth to Zanes."

There were some mumbled denials of knowing it needed to be done before they all went back to their movie. Ruth sighed.

"I better go do that before it smells weird." Her dad gave her one more tight squeeze before he let go, but his voice stayed low, under the roar of the racing cars and explosions on the screen.

"I know it just happened, but do you have any leads on a new job?"

She cast her gaze down to the scuffed floor. "Not yet."

"That's fine," he soothed. "I'm sure you'll find something."

"Yeah," she agreed, though she wasn't at all sure. Most families hired on help at the beginning of the school year, and this was January. "I'm gonna go check on her."

"She's having a good day." And when she checked, the glow that always overpowered his worn features when he talked about her mom was there, just as she knew it would be.

"Awesome." Ruth gave him a peck on the cheek before slipping down the hallway into the quiet back part of the house. "Hey, Mom."

The dark-haired, middle-aged woman was sitting up in bed, dressed in a T-shirt and pajama pants, and she smiled. "Hey, kiddo. How was your day?"

"I've had better," she said, pulling a floral folding chair up next to the bed. "I got fired."

"Oh, no!" Her mom set aside the novel she was reading. *Man, sitting up and reading? She **is** having a great day. And I'm ruining it.*

"It was nothing I did, they just don't need me anymore."

"That's still disappointing." Her mom held out her hand, and Ruth took it gently. "I know you liked Nina and Wesley."

Ruth let herself tip over and rest her cheek on the back of her mom's cool hand. "I did. Thank you for understanding."

"I do, Ruth. I'm sorry."

She rested in the care her mom showered over her for just a moment, but the laundry was still nagging at the back of her mind. She'd had her pity party, now it was time to put away the metaphorical obnoxious party horn and pointy hat and get back to work.

"On the upside," she said, sitting up, "I've got your favorite sheets clean. Or rather, I will, once they get into the dryer."

"Those boys." Her mom shook her head, obviously disappointed. "They're running you ragged, kiddo."

"Nah, I'm fine. I don't mind taking care of you." She leaned over to press a kiss to her mom's head. Did she feel too warm, or was it just her imagination? "Did you eat?"

"I wasn't hungry. They offered."

"Okay. I'll be back with your sheets soon." They had pink peonies on them; Ruth had found the fabric at the antique store and fallen in love with it. Then, through the magic of YouTube, she'd made her mom a set of sheets. It had not been without challenges: dreadfully tangled bobbins and pricked fingers and forgetting to push in that infernal button when she wanted to backstitch—but she'd done it. And the joy on her mom's face had been worth every minute of cursing and frustration. Of course, that was a few years ago, and they were getting faded. But when you spent most of the day in bed, it was the little things that mattered.

"Might close my eyes for a bit," her mom said with a yawn.

"That's fine. I'm not going anywhere."

"Thanks, Ruth."

She closed her mom's door quietly as she snuggled into the big bed, then just stood there for a minute. Without her income, it wasn't going to be easy to make ends meet. She'd get on the internet and find something...hopefully sooner rather than later.

CHAPTER THREE

Charlie

When Charlie arrived at work on Monday, a white woman with dark wavy hair was waiting for him with a large purse clutched under her arm. He forced his gaze away from her legs and up to her face. But that was even more painful, because she reminded him of his ex-wife.

"Can I help you?" he asked, forcing a charming smile even though he hadn't finished his coffee yet.

"Yes, I'm here to fill in for the receptionist."

"Oh." He dropped the act. "You're early."

She blinked in surprised. "The agency said 8:00."

"It's 8:30. I'm not paying you for an extra half hour. You can take an hour for lunch to make up for it."

"All right," the woman said quietly as he unlocked the door and turned on the lights in the office. He heard her quiet gasp once she could see the chaos. Yeah, he felt horrified, too...but her reaction wasn't helping his bad mood.

"The desk is here. See if you can organize it a little, but don't throw anything away. I'll be in my office if you need anything."

"All right. And your name is Charlie?"

He bristled. "Mr. Miller."

"And I'm Gwen," she said, putting out her right hand. He shook it, but also shook his head. "Something funny?"

"Oh. No." *I just have no interest in getting to know you, so your name is irrelevant.*

Her glare had him looking toward his office door longingly. "I beg your pardon?" she asked, an edge to her voice.

"Nothing. Let me know if you need anything."

Still scowling a little, Gwen moved to the desk and sat down, stowing her purse underneath. Satisfied that she was actually going to work now, Charlie went to his small office. It, too, overflowed with paper—invoices, contracts, receipts, budget paperwork, advertising estimates...so much paper. With a sigh, he checked his email first—that was overflowing, too, but at least it was contained to the screen.

A few hours later, he decided to stretch his legs and check in with his brother, who he could hear getting coffee in the small conference room next door. But there was no one sitting at the reception desk when he passed by.

"Where's what's her name?"

Jason was looking at his phone, typing out a message so fast that Charlie had trouble focusing on his thumbs.

"Left."

Charlie looked around the cluttered front office. "Like, took her lunch break?" It was only 11:15, so it wasn't likely. And he hadn't sent on her any errands. It did not bode well for the answer to his question.

"Nope. After you talked to her, she just picked up her purse and walked out. Said something about a hostile work environment."

Charlie cursed. It didn't even make him feel better his kids weren't around to hear him, because he was doing it plenty in front of them, too. If Aiden didn't get detention for cursing, it would be a genuine surprise. Then again, vandalism seemed to be more his style lately.

"Can you call the agency for a new one?"

Jason finally looked up. "I'm pretty sure that was their last one who was willing to come."

Charlie crossed his arms. "Meaning?"

Jason looked around the disaster zone. "Meaning that you're not nice to them, Charlie. They don't want to work here because you're gruff, harsh and just plain rude with everyone all the time."

"With everyone all the time?" Charlie said, but even he could hear that he was just proving Jason's point by the acerbic way he said it. His brother didn't acknowledge his question.

"If I didn't love you, I'd have been out of here months ago. I know Starla hurt you, man. I get that. But you're not gonna feel better by hurting all of us, too. That's not healing, that's just...revenge on the wrong people."

Charlie stared at him. It wasn't easy to hear his little brother casually lob such opinions at him, when he'd been the one taking care of Jason and trying to keep him on the straight and narrow all this time. Setting up reminders for his meds. Making him eat or go home when he lost all track of time. But looking around the trashed office, he realized that he maybe wasn't in a position to offer anyone help at the moment. He realized he was maybe more on the other side of the equation. Maybe.

"Can you help me find the invoice for Mrs. Fisher?" He swallowed hard. "Please."

Jason smiled at him like he'd said something funny. "I can try. But you know I'm allergic to paperwork."

"Is that why it's everywhere?" Charlie joked gently. "Did you sneeze?"

His brother's smile got bigger, and the tightness in Charlie's chest eased a little.

"No, I didn't sneeze, thank you very much." Jason held up a piece of paper by its corner, much the way Charlie had seen him dispose of Iris's diapers. "Is this it?"

Charlie peered at it. "No, but I've been looking for that, too. I need to call them about replacing those defective shocks we bought."

"Oh right. Wait, that was months ago."

"Now you see my point." He sighed. "And things are no better at home."

"Yeah," Jason said, glancing up at him, "I kinda noticed when we were over for dinner."

"Oof, if you noticed, it must be bad."

"Well," Jason said, recycling a stack of outdated forms, "I just don't want to see the same thing happen to you at home that's been happening at work."

"Thanks." Charlie swallowed his pride as he went on. "And thanks for sticking around."

"What other work place is going to want a space case like me?" Jason joked.

"You're a talented mechanic. I'd have a terrible time replacing you."

"Not to mention how awkward Sunday dinners would be."

"Truth. Speaking of which, don't forget to buy Aiden a birthday present."

"Lacey's on it, I think. She got him a book or something."

"Good. He already spends most of the day staring at scree—ah HA!" Charlie cried, triumphant. "Found it!"

"Does that mean I can go back to the shop?" Jason was already edging toward the door, wiping his hands on his coveralls as if to get the paper's ickiness off them. Ironic considering how much grease he had under his fingernails.

"Absolutely. Thank you for your assistance. Go forth and fix machines."

Jason gave him a brief salute at the door, then disappeared into the shop. Rock music crescendoed as the door opened, then faded as it swung gently shut again. Charlie sat down in the quiet office and put his head in his hands.

Jason wasn't wrong about the pain. Seeing Starla with Sawyer ate away at him, opening up his old wounds every time they exchanged kids or spent holidays together. Being at their wedding last month, having to hold in his tears as he kept track of their kids, had been one of the most gut-wrenching experiences of his life. But he'd done it. For the sake of peace, he'd gotten through the day. Dahlia had helped by being fussy and needing someone to walk with her outside until she fell asleep. On the steps of the church where they'd gotten married, where they'd attended every Sunday, Charlie had looked up at the stars and wondered how he'd let things get so bad, how he'd screwed up his life so much.

He hadn't married her with the intention of making her life miserable; he'd cared about her. He still did. But caring hadn't been enough. He hadn't loved her with the kind of love Pastor Kellan talked about spouses needing, the kind that's self-sacrificial and patient and seeks to serve rather than be served. He'd done for her what was convenient for him. And he'd gone to other women with what should have belonged to her.

Thoughts about their pastor had him pulling out his phone. When he and Starla had separated initially, Kellan had offered to meet with him for support. Charlie had laughed off his offer at the time; Starla couldn't really leave him. She wouldn't. It had felt unfathomable then, like someone asking when he was going to voluntarily amputate his leg. She'd been unhappy with him before...and no, she'd never gone to stay with Ainsley for more than a night when she was mad. But this wasn't different, he'd told himself. It was the same game they always played; this time it was a little more public than he'd prefer, but a game nonetheless. He hadn't realized she was really leaving him until that awful moment in the library, when she gave him that horrible letter. The one asking if she could move away and take their children with her.

It had been like finding out he had a terminal illness; he'd felt his life was over. Ainsley had taken pity on him, even though he hadn't deserved it and she didn't like him much. He and Aiden had crashed on her couch that afternoon, watching some pointless TV show and eating snacks, and Charlie had felt far more immature than his thirty years. Had she baked for them? Probably. His ex-wife's best friend had always been an overachiever.

But he'd thought about calling Kellan after that, several times. Sawyer had suggested it, too. The thing was that it didn't look good, going to the pastor for counseling. It didn't inspire confidence...he needed a certain image to be considered a reliable resource for one of the biggest purchases people make in their adult life. And he'd been honing that image since high school: the winning smile, the sense of fashion, the casual, open demeanor no matter what was going on inside. But that was just the problem: what was going on inside had gotten out of control, much like the mountains of paper on the desk in front of him. He didn't think it would take much to make it all go sliding off the edge, literally and figuratively.

And if that happened, his kids would be the ones who suffered. Charlie already carried guilt like a yoke across his shoulders, weighing him down. He'd broken their home; as much as he hated that expression, it felt accurate. If he let himself break, too...He just couldn't. He needed to face this; it was time.

As he spoke to the chipper church receptionist, he prayed for two things: that no one he knew would find out he was getting counseling...and that it would help.

CHAPTER FOUR

Ruth

On Monday morning, Ruth stumbled into the kitchen in search of coffee and groaned. It looked like someone had robbed the place: open jars of peanut butter, dirty knives sitting precariously on the edge of the counter, spinach on the floor from someone's green protein smoothie. There was half a cup of coffee left in the pot, and she counted herself lucky that they'd even left her that much.

She poured it into the only clean mug in the cabinet, even though it proclaimed her the champion trap shooter of the Linn County Shooting Range, 14-21 Division. She'd shot a gun a few times, out in the woods, aiming at pop cans, but she'd never win a prize for such a performance; it was Ryan's mug, but she'd been there, cheering him on when he won. Ruth found some milk in the fridge...or rather, she thought she had, but the carton turned out to be empty, and she settled for coffee creamer, even though it was hazelnut.

Seeing the gigantic mess had made her appetite wane, so she took her coffee into the living room, her computer under one arm, ready to take this job thing seriously. Everyone else was gone except Mom, and the house was quiet. Today was the day she'd try to find a new family to partner with. The Donovans had sent her a nice letter of recommendation, describing her capability and responsibility; whenever she parted amicably, she tried to collect them, since she wanted parents to have the utmost confidence in her abilities, even though she'd been doing this for eight years now. They were, after all, leaving their most vulnerable treasure in life in her hands. She felt the weight of that.

She checked two different websites, neither of which had any openings within twenty miles of Timber Falls. They lived on the western edge of town, so going to Salem wasn't unthinkable, but a long commute just meant more time away from her mom and all the work that needed to be done here. She did drive into Salem to go to the gym sometimes, and she knew that they sometimes needed childcare workers. There were closer gyms; there was one in Mill City that had a nice martial arts place attached, but it just didn't appeal to her. She couldn't put her finger on why. Logically, it was more sensible. But she just kept driving to Salem, kept paying her dues at the more expensive place. In the back of her mind, she was looking for something...or maybe someone. But that felt like a pipe dream. She'd had two significant relationships when she was in high school, but both had ended in polite breakups. Still, she wasn't eager to go through that again. And yet, the gym reminded her that there was more to life than cleaning and working and reading. The symbolism of going out into the world and conquering something soothed her restless soul, even if it was just the fifth level on the rowing machine.

It upset her brothers, she knew. They were just sure men were ogling her, and they weren't there to glare at them. But that felt rather nice, too. It didn't matter, anyway—half the time, if she did get up the courage to talk to someone, the minute she opened her mouth, his face changed into something like pity, twisted into a disappointed grimace that her graceful outsides didn't fit with her maladapted tongue. Her mom told her it was a blessing, that it would chase away anyone shallow who didn't have her best interests at heart, and Ruth wanted to believe that. But she didn't.

She opened another site and expanded her search again, but this one was thirty miles away and only two days a week...it just didn't pay enough. She wasn't some college kid looking to make a few extra bucks; she was a professional.

She glared at the empty chip bag and empty pop bottle on the coffee table. It felt hopeless, but she had no other option. Maybe she'd call the geriatric care lady that Martina Carpenter used to work for. She sometimes got requests for childcare. Maybe she should see if the PTA needed people for after-school care.

Too many maybes.

Frustrated, Ruth got to her feet and gathered up the cups and glasses, then grabbed the trash can and swept the chip bags and candy wrappers into the trash. After a little more work with the vacuum, she got a text.

> **Mom:** Stress cleaning or regular cleaning?
> **Ruth:** Did I wake you? I'm sorry.
> **Mom:** No, I'm awake because I'm hungry.
> **Ruth:** I'll be right there.

She felt her pocket buzz again on her way into the kitchen, but she ignored it. Mom's meals were pre-packaged into her bird-sized portions. Too much, and she slept all day.

Too little, and she was hungry and grumpy. It was a pickle. Sometimes literally; the woman loved pickles.

Ruth knocked softly at her door and waited for a response. When her mom answered, she was frowning.

"I could've gotten it," she protested as she took the half an apple and tiny portion of peanut butter.

"And yet, here I am," Ruth replied. "How was your night?"

"You never answered my question..."

Ruth sat down. "Stress cleaning." Then, on second thought, she crawled into the bed on her dad's side.

"No luck with the job search?"

"No, but I haven't looked very hard. I'm going to, though." She had to; the guilt was eating away at her. Her mom's hand on her head felt nice.

"You'll figure it out. I know you're trying."

"I just need to get over myself. There's stuff in Salem I could apply for. I told myself it was too far away, but it's really not." She wasn't usually so forthcoming about her own sacrifices, but she was down right now.

Her mom combed her fingers through Ruth's hair slowly; with hair so straight, she didn't know how she still managed to get so many tangles in it overnight.

"Knowing your own limits is not the same as getting over yourself. Why don't you want to work in Salem?"

Ruth shrugged one shoulder. "It's a long drive, so I pay more for gas. And I have less time at home, and there's so much to do here. And I usually can't do Audubon Society meetings when I do."

"Those all sound perfectly reasonable to me. But you could ask your brothers if they're willing to cover some of the household chores. Lord knows they depend on you far too much."

"That's a good idea," Ruth said, sitting up. "I'm gonna go do that. I should do it anyway. Thanks." She gave her mom a gentle kiss on the cheek, then scooted off down the hall to let her eat in peace. Too much noise and activity could easily wear her out for the day, and she wanted her to be able to take advantage of the quiet part of the day to sleep.

Ruth: I'm looking at some jobs in Salem; can you guys cover dinner?

Ryan: For how long?

Ranger: If you want delivery pizza, sure.

Wyatt: who's paying for that.

Ryan: Not me.

Ruth: It doesn't have to be fancy. Spaghetti or something. Surely one of you can boil water and open a jar.

Ryan: Water boiling...that's in the oven, right?

Speaking of boiling...she didn't truly have much of a temper, but these four were certainly testing her patience at the moment. She'd go and work out to burn off some of this frustration, and then drive around and put in applications.

Ruth: Fine. Forget it.
Ranger: Ruthie, he's just kidding.

She put her phone on silent. If no one would help her, she'd just figure it out herself. Maybe she could batch cook on the weekends...whatever. She grabbed her backpack out of her half of the closet. Ranger kept his side tidy, which was more than she could say for Ryan or Wyatt...they were lucky, really. They could be in the three-bed room with those guys. The doors locked, so that helped with privacy. But locking doors didn't help with cleanliness. Their room was the one place in the house she didn't dare touch, for her own safety. Of course, her own room also housed Ranger's pet ferret.

Ruth texted her mom goodbye as she got in the car. She'd time the drive to the YMCA. If she could get a discount to work out there, it might be worth it. And yet, another sigh billowed out of her as she started her truck.

On Highway 22, she saw two red-tailed hawks hunting in the barren fields and a Cooper's hawk sitting on a post, just watching. A large black bird evaded her view; it couldn't be a turkey vulture. It wasn't the right season for them, but she thought it was too big to be a crow. As the forest and fields thinned out into suburbs and city, all she saw were house finches and chickadees. The gym was fairly empty, since it was the middle of the day on a Monday. She smiled at the front desk guy, Tad. He looked like a Tad: huge biceps, wavy blond hair cut longer on the top, and a tank top. She'd never seen the man wear anything with sleeves.

"Hey, Ruth. It's been a while. Everything okay?"

She just nodded. He wasn't flirting, just being friendly. He lowered his voice so only she could hear.

"Let me know if anyone gives you trouble today, all right?" He glared in the direction of the weight room. "I've got a couple of repeat offenders I'd like to kick out permanently."

Ruth snorted. "You're worse than my brothers."

"Oh, I don't think that's possible. But at least I know no one's going to mess with you while they're here."

"Not if they know what's good for them," Ruth said, rolling her eyes. "I know where to find you." Usually, a stern glare and one-word answers had them fleeing, but a few times, she'd had to text Tad about the really stubborn ones. She tucked her phone into her sports bra just in case; hopefully, it wouldn't pop out. She was somewhat busty for her size, and more than one phone had been forced out. This would not be a good time to replace it.

She'd been on the elliptical about twenty minutes, listening to a podcast about how climate change was affecting migration patterns, when it suddenly paused and the phone rang. She slowed down as she looked at the screen.

Starla Devereaux? That was odd. Did she have overdue library books? Calling about them seemed rather aggressive for Starla, but hey, maybe she was just a cog. Ruth knew better than most that people sometimes had to play a role they didn't ask for.

"Hello?"

"Hi, Ruth, this is Starla Devereaux. I heard through the grapevine that you might be available to nanny. Is that right?"

Her heart was already thumping from the exercise, but it picked up another tick.

"Yes, I was just let go by the family I was nannying for." Aiden and Emily were nice kids. And Starla had always been kind to her...she'd even waived the fees when Ryan lost their only copy of *Treasure Island*, the graphic novel edition, even though it had been super popular. She should've never let him take it on their hunting trip.

But Charlie? It was going to bring a hailstorm of negative opinions down on her if she associated with Charlie in any way. There was some kind of long-standing feud between their families—she was fuzzy on the details, but the guys seemed to know them all...in fact, the details seemed to get bigger and more injurious every time she heard the story.

"Would you be willing to meet our kids? They're very sweet, and I know you'd enjoy them. Aiden's ten, Emily's seven and Dahlia—"

"I'm sorry to interrupt. Would this be just for you, or would I be splitting the time between you and Charlie?" Ugh, his name was hard to say.

There was a long pause.

"You'd be working for both of us."

"And you're aware of the long-standing feud between the Millers and the Zanes?"

"I am aware." Starla seemed to choose her words carefully. "It isn't a problem for me if it isn't a problem for you."

"And your co-parent?" Ruth could just picture how this would go...movie-star handsome Charlie Miller shouting at her to get out of his house. He was charming enough that he was intimidating even if he hadn't been tall, dark-haired, and delicious. But that added piece just made it even more difficult.

Starla hesitated again. "I think I can bring him around. He's a good father. He'll want the best person for the job." Ruth had her doubts about that; not him being a good dad, but him being willing to work with her. She'd seen him with his kids at church: he was tough but fair, and they had a great rapport and an obviously warm relationship. But if he took the feud as seriously as the men in her family did, she didn't think he was going to be fine with this at all. But the money would be excellent, she was sure.

"I'll be honest; I'm not optimistic. But I'm willing to give it a try if you are."

"Wonderful. Oh Ruth, thank you, thank you so much!"

"You heard me say I'm not optimistic, right?"

She could hear Starla's smile. "That's all right. I'll bring him around. He's a good dad. That will dominate his other concerns."

"Very well. When would you like to meet?"

They set a time for Wednesday and after more gratitude from Starla, Ruth hung up. She stared out of the big windows onto the strip mall. Now she just needed to figure out how to handle her own family.

CHAPTER FIVE

Charlie

On Wednesday afternoon, Charlie drove up the gravel forest road toward Starla's house. She and her new husband lived way out of town. He felt no shame in resenting that; even though he also lived way out of town, at least his house was on the side closer to civilization. And yet, sometimes the drive through the woods helped him sweep away the frantic feeling that he always had at work these days. It was quieter out here—until he got inside, anyway. But not today. Today, it felt ominous. Foreboding. Like when his kids had been playing quietly for too long. He called it Miss Clavel Syndrome from the book *Madeline*: that calm, collected French lady had a sixth sense that he envied. His wasn't nearly as good. A chipmunk sprinted across the road in front of him, and Charlie touched his brakes. Emily didn't like it when he hit the rodents, and even though she wasn't with him, he'd have to listen to her cry about it if she saw it lying smashed in the road on the way down.

Charlie pulled into the driveway; they were interviewing nanny candidates today, but there was only one truck out front. That was odd. Not only was there only one, but he knew who it belonged to: Ruth Zane. The kids she nannied for must have had a playdate with Aiden and Em; they were about the same age, he thought. That was the only logical explanation. That or he'd gotten the day wrong. Charlie pulled in next to Sawyer's mechanic shop and pulled out his phone to check his calendar. There was a text from Starla.

Starla: The candidate's here. Where are you?

No. Impossible. There was no way, knowing their family history, that she would put the two of them in a room together for a job interview. Surely she knew him better than that.

Charlie: I'm outside. But if your candidate is Ruth Zane, then we're done here.

Starla: You're not even going to meet with her?

Charlie: There's no reason to. No Zane is going to watch my kids. It will not stand.

Starla: Seriously?

Charlie: Can you send the kids out, please?

A tap on his window made him jump. Starla's long-haired husband, Sawyer, stood next to his Tahoe, wiping his hands on a red rag. Charlie pushed the button to restart the car and rolled down the window.

"Yes?"

"Did you forget where the front door is?" Sawyer asked with a grin.

"I assume it's in the same place it was, unless you've done some major construction since I was here last."

Sawyer cocked his head. "Why are you sitting out here in the cold, then?"

"There's a Zane inside."

Sawyer shook his head. "For what it's worth, I told her this wasn't going to work." His light Southern accent softened the directness of his words.

"You know I hate saying this, Devereaux, but you were right. I can't believe she's considering it."

"I guess her mama's still unwell. She needs the money."

"Deborah Zane has been unwell since I was in high school. It may make her offspring pitiable, but it hasn't made them better people." Well, not Ruth—as far as he knew, she was still the same shy girl she'd been back when they'd shared the tire swing. But he wasn't supposed to know that.

Sawyer grunted, and Charlie couldn't tell if it was agreement or chiding at his harsh words. "I'm no stranger to feuds, but it seems to me that y'all are taking this to an unhealthy level."

"Respectfully, you have no idea what you're talking about. No Miller will do business with a Zane. Haven't you ever wondered why I recommend everyone go to Salem to get their insurance?"

Sawyer stared at him for a long moment, then chuckled. "No, I can't say I have. Are you really that spiteful?"

"You know I am," Charlie huffed. His phone dinged in his hand and he glanced at it.

Starla: I will not send them out. You may come in and fetch them if you'd like.

"Your wife thinks she can bait me into interviewing this woman."

"She seemed nice to me. Quiet. A bit uneducated, maybe; she said she'd never been to college. But the kids took to her right away. She kicked Aiden's butt at the frisbee game on the video game box."

Charlie knew the game he meant; Sawyer was still getting the lingo for all the kid stuff, but Charlie tried not to laugh to his face when he messed it up. He may or may not have texted Jason to laugh about it privately.

"It doesn't take a college degree to watch my kids, but playing video games also doesn't make her qualified to care for my children. And it provides no reassurances that she's not going to act the same way her family has in the past, making baseless accusations."

"Y'all were fighting about land or something, right?"

Charlie glared at him. "In 1921, Ephraim Zane and Charles Miller, for whom I am named, were neighbors. There was a stand of apple trees between the two properties; Ephraim falsely believed it was his and began bottling and selling apple cider from the orchard. When Charles confronted him about his unethical actions, Ephraim not only refused to concede that the land was his, he also refused to share any of the profits with Charles."

"And you've been enemies ever since."

Irritation barbed at Charlie. "I don't think you understand what these people are really like. They try to get away with everything they can. I've lost count of the number of times they've scratched my car or cut me off or bumped my cart at the supermarket. They're antagonists."

"I do remember the trouble Mrs. Sadiq had with Ruth's brother Ranger a while back...something about him bullying her over her head covering. Ainsley got herself involved, I think." They were cousins, which probably explained in part why she'd sided against him with Sawyer. But maybe not entirely.

Charlie pointed at him. "Exactly. Racist, xenophobic nonsense."

"But you can't put that on Ruthie."

"Can't I? Apple doesn't fall far from the tree."

"I would think apples were a painful subject for you."

Charlie gave him a winning smile. "I'm bigger than my family history. But thanks for thinking of me."

"Seriously. You should give the lady a chance."

Charlie didn't think of Ruth as a lady. He still thought of her as the same girl who used to bother him when he was trying to sulk. "How old is she, anyway?"

"It didn't come up in the thirty seconds I met her."

Charlie peered into the garage through his windshield. "Working on anything good?"

"MTT Turbine Streetfighter." Sawyer was a strange man—he was surgeon originally, but because of an illness, his hands shook too much to keep operating. He still worked at the hospital, training the new doctors, but he also fixed motorcycles.

Charlie whistled. "That must have set you back a pretty penny."

"Nah, got a good deal on it because the engine needed an overhaul."

"Got a buyer for it?" Not that he could help or even cared. He just really didn't want to go inside.

"Not yet. Mike came up to look at it, but I think it's more power than he really wanted. And more money."

"Mmm." Charlie cast a glance toward the front door. No children appeared. He cursed internally. Starla could be so impossible sometimes...and it was just getting worse.

He hit Starla's name on the contact list and put the phone on speaker. Sawyer leaned a hip against his car, and Charlie bristled. But he was parenting with the man now. He'd have to have more patience with his intrusions.

"Hello?" Starla sounded as amused as Sawyer looked.

"Can you please send the kids out?"

"You're late for our meeting. Can you please come inside?"

"Not going to happen."

"Hi Charlie, Ruth here." Okay, so apparently, they were on speaker phone, too. "I apologize; I thought your co-parent had told you about the situation." That was interesting; most people referred to Starla by her name or as his ex. *Co-parent* sounded like something a counselor would come up with. He still hadn't met with Pastor Kellan; he'd been surprisingly booked up.

"I'm sorry she wasted your time," he replied frostily.

"It's fine. We had a good time. You have delightful kids. I would've enjoyed working with them."

There was the scrape of a chair, and a moment later, the front door opened. A curvy woman with straight dark hair shook Starla's hand in a business-like manner, and he had to admire her demeanor. He thought of people who worked with children as being sort of sticky and experts in nothing more than runny noses. But she was wearing a suit. Not the kind that was in style these days, but she looked nice.

He body slammed the thought into the wall of his mind. He was permanently single now; there was no point in admiring her hips or the silky fall of her hair. Women were not for him. He couldn't be trusted. He'd proven that over and over.

Ruth climbed into her ramshackle truck and carefully turned around. He got out of his SUV, but she didn't acknowledge him.

"What the heck, Charlie?" Starla fumed, storming down the front steps. "Do you know how incredibly *rude* that was?"

He shrugged. "You should've known better. This is on you."

Starla threw up her hands in frustration. "She's got a list of references as long as my arm, all of them glowing. Everyone in the area who's worked with her was sorry to see her go. All three of the kids took to her immediately."

"*Aiden* took to her immediately?"

Starla glared at him. "*Yes.* That's what I'm saying. He was quiet, but she made him laugh. And she knew all about *City of Ember.* And she braided Em's hair while we were sitting there, a French braid. And when Dahlia fussed, she just picked her up and did this weird arm hold, and Didi went back to sleep in her arms and Charlie, I love her. I want her. It has to be her."

Disturbed, Charlie turned to Sawyer.

"She hasn't had a lotta sleep lately," was the only explanation the man offered.

"Absolutely not," Charlie said. "According to our divorce decree, we have to agree. And I will never allow this woman to care for my children."

"Charlie," she started, and he knew that tone. It was her *kind of breaking down but trying not to* voice. "If you don't want Ruth, that's fine. But I don't have time to do all these meetings. So you figure out who your top two candidates are, and I'll meet with them. How does that sound?"

"I don't have time for this, either, Star. That's why I want to hire a helper."

Starla groaned and let her head fall back. "Charlie. Please. Be reasonable for once."

"I'm very reasonable. Hiring my enemies is unreasonable."

"Top. Two. Candidates."

Charlie held up his hands. "Fine. Top two. But you have to bring your top two."

"Fine. But Ruth will be one of them."

"Whatever." He lifted his voice. "Kids, get your stuff, let's go."

"They can't hear you. They've all got headphones on."

"Even the three-month-old?"

When she rolled her eyes that hard, he felt like he was seventeen again. It hurt.

"You thought Dahlia was going to come running? Boy, you did miss out on the infant stage with the first two."

Sawyer turned back to the garage as they climbed the stairs.

"How's he doing with the kids?"

Starla waggled her head as she opened the front door. "He maxes out on their noise sometimes. But that's why we haven't rented out the cabin yet."

"Good solution."

"Thank you," she replied, but her voice was cool. It was a reminder that he was still rebuilding her trust, even if it wasn't as his wife.

"Aid, Em, get your stuff. It's time to go home."

They ignored him.

"I wish you wouldn't say it like that," Starla mumbled.

"Like what?"

"Like this isn't their home, too."

Charlie looked around the large log house. There was classroom art on the fridge, made of string and glitter. Books and games littered the family room. Dahlia was asleep in her bouncy seat, sucking softly on her pacifier. Spilled cereal was stuck to the table and someone's underwear was hanging off the banister. This was no longer a vacation rental or a bachelor pad.

"I stand corrected," he muttered. "Kids, get your stuff. It's time to go to my house."

As if they were rousing from sleep, they stirred slowly and gathered up their things. Charlie bent to scoop up Dahlia, unbuckling her.

"She ate a lot, but a lot of it came back up," Starla said, as she handed Emily her coat. "It's kind of weird."

"I'm sure it's fine," Charlie said. He just wanted to leave. The sooner he left, the sooner he could get them fed, into bed, and get back to work in his home office.

Oh, and find them a nanny.

CHAPTER SIX

Ruth

"Ooh, blonde brownies," Perry Helsing cooed, leaning over the pan Ruth had just set on the table.

"That's not keto," his wife called from the other side of the room, and Perry's shoulders drooped.

"But..."

"No buts. You promised the doctor."

Perry turned his attention to Ruth. "Why do you have to make such delicious things for our meetings, beautiful?"

Ruth shrugged. "Because this way, I actually get some."

"Atta girl," he chuckled, squeezing her into a side hug. "We sure have missed you around here."

Her heart squeezed, too. "I've missed you too."

"Did you see my Cassin's vireo on eBird?"

"For the last time, it was a warbling vireo," Jean said, coming over to join the conversation.

Perry sniffed. "I know what I saw."

"It didn't have the spectacles around the eye!"

"You didn't hear its song," he said. "It sounded nothing like the warbling."

"I heard it," Hattie said, strolling up to the group and helping herself to a blonde brownie. Ruth really made them for her; Hattie was their unofficial mayor in town, and she'd done plenty for her family over the years. The woman had an irrepressible love of sweets. "I thought it was warbling, too, Perry," Hattie went on. "Sorry."

"They're all ganging up against me, Frank," Perry called to the older man who'd just walked into the VA hall. It seemed silly to use such a sizeable space for just the six of them, but that was a small town for you. They didn't have a ton of other options, and this one was free. Ruth was fairly sure Hattie had a hand in that.

"Ganging up on you?" asked Frank, angling around the folding chair with his cane. "About the vireo? It was definitely a Cassin's."

"See?" Perry said emphatically. "I told you." And when his wife turned her back, he quickly took a brownie and shoved it into his mouth while Ruth suppressed a giggle. They rarely bothered sitting down. It was too dark tonight to go out birdwatching, but they'd usually stand around and chat and share their finds from earlier in the week until someone got tired and wanted to go home. But tonight, Hattie had brought a documentary called *Birders: The Central Park Effect*, and Ruth was excited to see it. It was a rare evening that she actually watched something she wanted to see; her brothers outvoted her a lot, and she didn't enjoy streaming things on her computer by herself.

"Is this the lady with breast cancer?" Perry asked, and Jean elbowed him.

"Spoilers."

That subdued the room a bit; several of these families had been touched by cancer recently, even though both women were in remission.

"I want to get to New York City this year," said Frank. "I want to see the snowy owl in Central Park. Did you hear about that?" The group chattered about what they'd heard, and Ruth's heart just sang, almost like a bird itself. There was something about being with people who just *got* you, who spoke your language and cared about the same things. Her work tended to be low on adult interaction and her family looked at her blankly when she mentioned a peregrine falcon or a Cooper's hawk. They listened politely enough, but there was no resonance for the enthusiasm. It felt like she was calling into a canyon expecting an echo, but only got silence in return. But here in the VA hall, the echoes were so loud, she could barely hear the movie.

"Pale Male is still alive, thank you very much," Frank asserted. Ruth knew of the famous red-tailed hawk that lived in New York, but she doubted very much that he was still kicking...er, flying.

"Wasn't he hatched in 1990?" she asked, and Jean nodded.

"Frank, don't go all the way across the country to see a dead bird. That's weird."

"He's not dead!" Frank insisted, but the others shushed him when they realized the movie had started.

Someone sat down next to her, and Ruth startled.

"Hi, what did I miss?" Jennie Wallace asked, breathless.

"Perry's cheating on keto and maybe saw a Cassin's warbler; Frank's going to New York to see the snowy owl; opinions differ strongly on whether the hawk known as Pale Male is still alive."

"Ooh, we should do another owl walk at the falls," Jennie said, "in the spring. Don't you think?"

"I'd love that," Ruth said, whispering, "but do you really want to take them out in the dark? There's a lot to trip over out there."

Jennie seemed to consider this, even as her eyes stayed fixed on the screen. "Maybe I could light it with lanterns or something. I'll brainstorm."

Ruth smiled. Jennie was certainly a doer. And she seemed to have a lot of free time. That was certainly enviable. But Ruth had lots of good things going in her life...she just didn't have time to count them.

Ruth sat back and watched the movie. They weren't particularly good at being quiet; at one point, they had to pause for a discussion about all the types of warblers in the film. Really, it was a wonder they ever saw birds, but there was something about being outside that calmed them down. Their trail walks and field time were more whispery than this.

Ruth got up to use the bathroom partway through, and she found Jean trailing her.

"Have you found a job yet? I think my niece is looking for someone. She's in Corvallis, though." That was almost an hour away. It was a cute college town, but devoting two hours a day just to travel plus the cost of gas felt prohibitive for what she was getting paid.

She shook her head. "Ryan does that drive four days a week for his night classes at Oregon State, but I think it's just too far for me."

"We'll keep our ears open," Jean assured her as the door swung closed behind them, and both kept silent as they entered the stalls. As they washed their hands, Ruth asked, "The doctor was bad news, huh?"

Jean nodded, but as she turned toward the paper towel dispenser, Ruth could've sworn she saw her tear up.

"Jean? Are you okay?" When she put a gentle hand on her back, the woman turned to her with a watery smile.

"I'm fine. It's fine. I just wish he would take this more seriously."

"It's hard to hear news like that, isn't it?" Ruth thought back to when her mom had been diagnosed with myalgic encephalomyelitis. Even after so many tests and so much waiting for appointments and specialist approvals, she hadn't been ready to hear it. She'd been holding out hope that her mother's fatigue was some kind of strange bacterial infection or hormonal imbalance. She'd wanted so desperately for it to be temporary. The news that it wasn't had been devastating. They had a kind of rhythm now, a routine. It was tolerable. She was grateful, actually—she often saw articles about people whose quality of life was much worse than her mom's. They were lucky, in a strange way, that she suffered less than some.

"We're trying the keto thing," Jean sniffled, "but one of us is trying harder than the other." They both chuckled a little.

"Well, I'll see what I can do about a treat for him next time. I think I've got a peanut butter cookie recipe tucked away somewhere that would suffice."

"Thank you, Ruth," Jean said, wiping her tears. "I mean, you really don't have to..."

"I want to," Ruth assured her. Taking care of people was kind of in her blood now. Their family's insurance company had been taking care of Timber Falls for twenty-five years, and she'd been taking care of her mom and the kids in the community for over a decade. Ruth gave her a squeeze meant to make her feel less alone as they both went back to the movie.

CHAPTER SEVEN

Charlie

The next morning, Charlie looked over the hot-pink resume in his hand.

"And you went to...dental school?"

The woman giggled. "Just for a little while. It didn't take. But I love kids, and I have lots of brothers and sisters."

That was true. Anja's siblings seemed to be all over Timber Falls—Charlie saw one brother often as he picked up the kids at the library, another when he picked up a pizza. And there were more siblings still in high school. Anja herself was only nineteen.

"So you don't have any experience working for another family?"

"Nope, just mine." She fidgeted in the chair, gazing out the window.

"Hmm." He looked at her resume again. "And what's this about the church nursery?"

"Oh. Well, that was kind of a misunderstanding."

Charlie resisted the urge to raise one eyebrow. "What kind of misunderstanding?"

"I had Bailey in there, and I just looked at my phone for a minute to see if church was almost over, and she snuck out the door to go find her mom. They didn't really want me in there after that."

This was not the person to watch his kids. Aiden would exploit the heck out of distractibility like that.

"Okay. Well, thank you for your time, and I'll let you know." He rose from the table. Normally, he would shake an applicant's hand, but he was trying to avoid contact with women in general. Plus, he didn't think she expected it—a hot-pink resume didn't exactly scream professionalism.

"Thank you," she cooed as she gathered up her purse and left. He sat back in his seat; he didn't know why he'd had them come to his office. It would've been much more helpful if he'd been able to see them interact with his kids, especially Dahlia. Some of these people would be fine with older kids, but babies were a different matter. And even for experienced people, Dahlia was *not* an easy baby. His own mother had said she wouldn't take her anymore unless it was an emergency...not that she'd ever been a kid person. She hadn't said as much, but his impression was that she'd had her fill of babies with Aiden and Emily and found Dahlia's almost out-of-wedlock conception embarrassing; they hadn't signed the papers yet, but they'd both had a weak moment on Valentine's Day. It wasn't like he was thrilled about it himself, but he wasn't going to take it out on the poor kid. He loved her just as much as the other two.

"Mr. Miller?"

Charlie looked up. A thin young white man stood in the doorway, rolling a piece of paper in his hands. "I'm here for the interview."

"You must be Henry. Please, have a seat." He gestured toward the chair across from him. Henry shook his outstretched hand, then made himself comfortable. Charlie looked over the resume, which was blessedly printed on white paper.

"You've been babysitting for six years?"

"That's right. Always liked kids. My experience is mostly summer camps and stuff."

Charlie felt the man was downplaying his experience; he'd been a counselor as well as an administrator for the camp, involved in training others in safety and how to handle tough kids. That was certainly appealing.

"Are you willing to do any cooking or cleaning?"

Henry tilted his head. "Yeah, that's a possibility. But I'd prefer if my main priority was the kids."

"Sure, I understand. Of course, you'd have Dahlia most of the day."

He looked confused. "My aunt said you have two school-aged kids."

"And a baby."

The man's shoulders slumped a little. "I'm not sure I'm up for all that. I thought this was a babysitting job."

"Yes, you'd be watching the kids after school, maybe a few evenings if I have to work late..."

Henry shook his head. "What you want is a nanny, not a babysitter."

"What does that mean?"

"Let's put it this way: babysitters let the kids stay up late and eat junk food. Nannies put them to bed on time. Nannies make them do their homework and make sure they actually become good people. And they'll do stuff like babies and cleaning, if you arrange for it and pay them extra."

Maybe that was his problem; he'd been putting out the wrong feelers. He wanted to crumple the papers in front of him in frustration.

"Do you know of any nannies who are available?"

He shook his head. "Most of the nannies get snatched up at the beginning of the school year. But I heard the Donovans let Ruth Zane go, though I can't imagine why. I'm sure someone's hired her by now."

"What's so great about her?"

"Oh, Ruth's just so creative."

Charlie tried not to show his confusion. "Creative how?"

"One time, I was babysitting for the Benson kids on a day off school, and she'd set up this whole dinosaur day for their playdate with her kids. We made realistic fossils out of salt dough and then buried them, and then we made these dinosaur silhouette lanterns and took them out into the dark. Dinner was mac and cheese with dinosaur-shaped pasta, and the broccoli was amazing. It was like lemony and garlicky. I thought for sure my charges wouldn't eat it, but they totally did. Every bite. And then, for dessert, she let them press plastic dinosaur feet into sugar cookies and decorate them with green and brown sprinkles. I think even the mac and cheese was healthy. It had, like, butternut squash in it or something. My charges did not want to go home. I think they would've moved in with Ruth if they could. I was a little infatuated with her myself. But of course, I didn't ask her out."

"Why not?"

Henry stared at him. "Well," he faltered, "you know. The speech thing."

"The what?"

"Her—she talks funny. She doesn't say things right."

Now it was Charlie's turn to stare. When was the last time he'd had a full conversation with Ruth Zane? Had he just not noticed? And why should he care that this young buck had dismissed her out of hand based on something that had nothing to do with her actual sense of humor or interests or talents? Nothing to do with the way she treated others or made them feel?

Maybe it just bothered him because it was exactly what he would've done at Henry's age, and looking back, it made him feel like a fool. Then again, he was the one who'd rejected her just a few days ago based on nothing more than her family name. So maybe he was still a fool. But based on this new information, he knew what he had to do.

Charlie stood up. "Henry, thank you for your time."

"Oh, sure. And if you hire in the shop, let me know; I used to turn wrenches for my uncle."

"Good to know. Thanks." Charlie walked him out to the front door and found Jason eating corn chips in the office.

"Was he the winner?"

He shook his head. "Nice man, though. He even knows some things about cars."

Jason looked thoughtful as he watched Henry drive away. "Could always hire him for the front desk...nothing saying it has to be a woman."

Charlie stared at him. "That...makes sense, actually."

"Thanks?" Jason tipped the rest of the bag into his mouth and spilled crumbs everywhere. "You gonna keep looking for a nanny, then?"

Charlie sighed. "No. I think Ruth really was the right person for the job."

Starla was going to gloat about this forever.

CHAPTER EIGHT

Ruth

After a mildly uncomfortable group call to iron out some details and ask some questions, they hired Ruth on a trial basis. Charlie still seemed skeptical, and she wasn't sure what had brought him around on the idea of her (besides parental desperation). But on Saturday, as agreed, she drove over to the Miller estate for her first day on the job. She had to go out to the main road to get to his driveway, which took about two minutes; there was plenty of room for an access road between the two properties, but that was clearly never going to happen. Perhaps it was just in her blood to be contrary. Speaking of which, she was ignoring a number of texts from her brothers.

Ryan: I can't believe you're doing this.

Ranger: If you need anything at all, just call and I'll come over.

Wyatt: He tries anything with you and he's a dead man. We all know his reputation. Everyone does.

Dad: I think what the boys are trying to say is good luck on your first day.

Ruth: Thanks, Dad. Shut up, everyone else.

Mom: Proud of you, sweetie. Those kids are going
to love you.

Her mom had been asleep when she went to say goodbye, so it meant a lot to get a bit of encouragement from her
now, as she climbed the wooden steps to the large Crafts-
man house. Charlie's parents lived on the eastern edge of the
property, she thought. She'd never actually been over here
before. Nerves had her stomach doing flips, but she pushed
her shoulders back and rang the doorbell, hoping this wasn't
going to be a *Sound of Music* situation where she ended up
getting pranked.

Ruth heard Charlie's voice on the other side of the door
faintly, and then Aiden's voice louder. The large wooden
door opened.

"Good morning, Aiden. Happy Saturday."

"If you say so." *Ah, nothing like a dose of pre-teen attitude
to kick a weekend off right.* Ruth grinned.

"Haven't had your pancakes yet, hmm?"

"We just got up. Dad wasn't expecting you until later."

She closed the door behind her and looked around the
downstairs for a few stunned moments before she murmured, "I believe you may be right about that." A large playroom overflowing with dress-up costumes, art supplies, mag-
netic blocks, books and video game controllers sat just off
the entryway. The hallway was also littered with clothes,
lunchboxes, and backpacks. She peered down the hallway into the kitchen, where Charlie appeared to be frantically trying to put dishes in the dishwasher while holding Dahlia on
one shoulder...dinner dishes, if she wasn't mistaken.

"Good morning," she called as she put down her back-pack in the laundry room. "Am I too early?"

"No, no, of course not," Charlie called back. "I was just..." His voice trailed off as he bent over the open dishwasher again. "Come in."

She took in the open floorplan—the door to an office was on her right. She could see stacks of paper piled on a dark wooden desk through the open door, one of those sliding barn doors. The TV stood next to it, and she walked between it and a large sectional to a kitchen table and chairs that were on the far side of the large room near French doors leading out to a deck that seemed to be trying to swallow what little grass there was. As she wandered over to the table, she realized she could see the river through the trees out the big windows in the nook; they'd removed a lot of the woods between them and the view, but left what was between her property and the house. The deck was some kind of manu-factured material with a bench running around the outside.

"What can I do to help?" she asked, already starting to clean the crayons and coloring books off the table. "I can make breakfast if you want." He was standing in the kitchen with a large quartz island between them, rubbing Dahlia's back. The kitchen itself was smaller than she would've ex-pected, but it did have shiny appliances she'd enjoy using.

"No, that's okay, I can..." He was muttering again. It was odd; the handful of times she'd interacted with Charlie, he'd always seemed much more comfortable than this, charismat-ic even. How odd that he seemed this uneasy in his own house. *Does my presence really bother him that much?* "Take off your shoes, please."

Ruth hurried to comply, placing them in the laundry room. "How about cleaning, then? I can start upstairs..."

"No!" The man looked terrifyingly guilty, and Ruth guessed that it was even worse than the downstairs.

"I could hold Dahlia for you. Give her a bottle?" Based on the baby's plaintive lip movement, she was definitely hungry.

"That's okay, I've got her."

Ruth crossed her arms and let one hip rest on the messy counter. "Can I inquire what you imagined I would do today, then?"

"I don't know," he grumbled. "Play with Emily?"

"She's still in bed," Aiden offered from the couch where he was using a tablet.

"It's not screen time," Charlie chided from across the room, and Aiden tossed it onto a couch cushion with an exasperated sigh.

"Why don't you give me the ten-cent tour, Aiden?" Ruth asked, and he looked up at her, deadpan.

"Will you actually pay me ten cents?"

"Sure!"

"You don't need to do that," Charlie said, sticking a bottle in the warmer. "Aiden, can you please show Ruth around?"

"Sure," he snarked, "I'll show our new servant the ropes." She ignored Charlie's shocked look; if he jumped in now, Aiden would take twice as long to learn to respect her.

"If I'm the authority while your parents are unavailable, and I'm a servant, what does that make you?"

Aiden scowled at her as he got off the couch. "Another servant, I guess?"

"I think your metaphor is breaking down," Charlie said evenly, "and I've heard enough of that talk, thanks. Please speak to Ruth with respect." Ruth followed Aiden out of the family room and across the hall.

"This is Dad's study. I don't know what happens in here, but it's bad enough that we can't go in without permission."

"Nothing bad happens," Charlie called. "I just don't want you messing up my paper piles."

"Who's giving this tour, you or me?" Aiden called back, and when there was no answer, he smiled. *Likes to have responsibility, but wants autonomy. Check.*

"This is the laundry room. It has definitely gone downhill since Mom left." Ruth stared at the mountains of dirty clothing piled on the floor on either side of the narrow room.

"Agreed. I'll work on it."

"Get some better detergent; this one smells weird," he said, tapping the open bottle that sat neglected on the washer.

"Again, not your servant. But if you ask politely, I'd be glad to purchase something better."

"Miss Ruth," he said, his voice dripping with false sweetness, "would you please get some detergent that doesn't smell like a field of lavender?"

Man, this kid is angry. It was understandable, but he was going to be a challenge. She hoped she was up for it.

"I'd be glad to. And this must be the bathroom?"

"What tipped you off, the toilet?"

"I like the colors in here." The dark wood shelves above said toilet held family pictures, a candle, a fake plant. The walls were a teal that felt calming.

"My mom did that. My mom did everything good here."

Interesting. Mom's clearly the victim in his mind.

"How often do you get to be with Mom?"

"We trade off weeks. They're going to trade you off, too. Like a servant."

Ruth crossed her arms and leaned against the bathroom doorframe. "Your dad asked you to stop saying that. Also, plenty of professions work in different places depending on the day. Construction workers, temps, forest rangers, scientists..."

Aiden rolled his eyes, but tramped down the hall toward the stairway. Just beyond it, she could see a formal living room that looked like it hadn't been dusted in months, and beyond that a dining room with boxes stacked up along the walls. She couldn't imagine that they were moving; Charlie had built this house just a few years ago. The noise of construction had given the Zanes many months of discomfort, especially her mom.

At the top of the stairs, Aiden gestured to the right. "That's my mom and dad's room. Well, my dad's room now, I guess."

"And that's my room—" he pointed straight "—the guest room, the upstairs bathroom and Em's room."

She peered down the hall. "Is there another room down there?"

"Oh yeah, and the bonus room."

The sheer size of other people's houses was always a shock. They crammed twice as many people—and more of them adults—into a space half the size. She let herself daydream for just a second about what it would be like to *not* share a room with her younger brother and his ferret. Duchess was a nice enough creature, but she did not smell great, no matter how many baths Ranger gave her with that tea tree shampoo. She'd drawn the line at animal care. She could barely keep all the human needs met in the house.

"So?"

Ruth blinked at the boy. "So...what?"

"So aren't you going to start cleaning?"

This button-pushing routine better not be permanent. Lots of kids wanted to test the boundaries at the beginning, she reminded herself.

"I think I'll go check in with your dad..."

"Ugh. Whatever." Aiden trotted back downstairs.

"What's all this noise?" A grumpy Emily emerged from her room, rubbing her eyes.

"Sorry. Your brother was just giving me a tour."

The girl's eyes lit. "Ruth! You're here! Can I have pancakes?"

"If it's okay with Dad, sure."

"He won't care," Emily said, adjusting the stuffed koala she held under one arm. "He just doesn't like making food."

"Who's this?" Ruth asked, touching the koala's soft gray head.

"Coleman. We got him at the zoo with Daddy's secretary."

Oh dear. He really had not used discretion at all, had he?

"That sounds like a fun day. Would you like to go to the zoo again?"

"Aiden says he's too old for the zoo," she sighed as she started down the stairs.

"Then maybe we'll leave Aiden with Mom and go just the two of us."

In the kitchen, there was no sign of Charlie or Dahlia, so she poked her head into the office. He sat at his desk, which was indeed piled with paper, cradling Dahlia in one arm crosswise while he scrolled on his computer with the other. The bottle was balanced against her mouth with his chin. It made a very amusing picture.

"Emily has requested pancakes. Is that okay with you?"

"Yeah, uh…" He moved to hold the bottle rather than balance it. "That's fine. Weekdays we try to do healthier stuff like non-sugar cereal. But on a weekend, that's fine."

Ruth was glad to hear that, as sugared-up kids were harder to manage.

"Shall I make enough for you as well?"

"I had coffee," he said, his gaze falling back to the computer screen.

"Oh, is coffee a food now? I didn't know."

Charlie's gaze snapped to hers, and there was a surprising amount of annoyance there. "I don't eat breakfast."

She held her hands up. "Fine. Just checking."

"You're just here to take care of the kids; I don't need caring for."

She gave him a nod. "Check. You going to give me that cute baby, then?"

"No, she's fine." It appeared it was going to take a crow-bar to get Dahlia away from him. She felt a fair amount of annoyance herself.

"Okay. Pancakes and bacon for two, coming up."

Ruth washed her hands and subtly replaced the dingy dishtowel with a clean one. Emily had made herself comfort-able at the kitchen table and started playing a game on her tablet.

"Is it screen time?"

Em gave her an innocent look as Ruth started exploring the cabinets. "Huh?"

"I know you heard me," Ruth said, keeping her voice even. "Please put it away."

With a frown, Emily slammed it down on the granite counter.

Ruth gave a sympathetic wince. "Ooh. I hope it didn't break. Do you like blueberries in your pancakes?"

"No." The death glare of a seven-year-old was not to be underestimated.

She could see that both of these kids were going to take some warming up. She bypassed the cheap mix and went for the flour to make them from scratch. She was going to blow these kids' minds. Ruth scrounged up baking powder, sugar, salt, vanilla, and eggs from all over the kitchen and started to follow the *New York Times* recipe on her phone.

"I thought you were making pancakes," Emily asked, her voice still a bit sulky.

"I am," Ruth assured her. "Would you like to help?"

Em nodded, then began to drag a chair over to the counter. Ruth gestured to the expensive-looking step ladder with railings that sat by the dishwasher.

"You don't want that?"

"That's for babies," Emily informed her, and this time, Ruth hid her smile.

"Oh, I see. All right, can you fill this measuring cup with flour?"

Ruth put some kid-type music on her phone, and Emily gasped.

"My mom plays this for us in the car!"

"Oh, does she? That's neat." It was the beginning of an unthawing with Emily as they egg-mixed and flour-flicked and milk-sloshed their way toward breakfast. By the time they finished, Charlie and Aiden were both shuffling into the kitchen, drawn no doubt by the delicious smell.

Dahlia was asleep on Charlie's shoulder, so Ruth turned down the music.

"It's okay. She can sleep through anything."

"Would you like my sling?" He didn't seem to want to be far from the baby, even now. Charlie stared longingly at the plate of bacon.

"No, I can't stand all that fiddly stuff."

"It's pretty simple," Ruth said. "Why don't you just look at it?"

"Isn't it yours?"

"Yes, but my boss won't let me use it, so..."

Teasing Charlie was too easy. She chided herself; she shouldn't be so sassy. But the comment won her a hint of a smile. Without another word, he carefully passed the sleeping baby to her, and Ruth cherished the way Dahlia curled into her chest. Stooping to her backpack, she pulled out the linen sling and nestled the baby into it, then tightened the rings with one hand still on her bum. Charlie watched her with silent interest. *So guarded, just like his son.* This family's love would not all be bought with simple carbohydrates, clearly.

"See? Not so complicated."

Charlie grunted, but he stole a piece of bacon before he went back to his office. Ruth was so busy watching his back, she almost didn't catch the syrup bottle as Emily knocked it off the island with her elbow. Dahlia stirred at the sudden motion, and Ruth bounced lightly on her toes for a minute until she settled in again.

She didn't see him again until it was time to feed Dahlia.

"She spits up a lot. Like, bring an extra change of clothes, maybe."

"Oh, I'm used to babies," she said, but twenty minutes later, she was regretting her confidence. The volume of what came up was far more than she anticipated, and she ended up wearing her foolishness like a badge on her shirt.

And even worse, every time he came into the playroom, Charlie seemed to be staring at it. When the kids started screentime, he came up to her...sort of. At arm's length, as if it were a snake, he held out a large white T-shirt.

Ruth took it, confused.

"For the..." He gestured to the wet spot as if it were on his own chest.

"Oh. Thanks."

Charlie muttered something unintelligible, then abruptly turned and left.

Toward the end of the day, she got a text from Starla.

Starla: So how did it go?

Ruth: Just fine on my end. Kids seem happy.

Starla: Great! I talked to Charlie, and he said he's good to move forward with you using the schedule we initially discussed.

Whew. She'd passed inspection. That was a relief. Ruth wondered if she should ask him about Charlie's attachment to Dahlia, but decided against it. She'd figure it out, eventually. It didn't feel right to go behind his back to his co-parent; she didn't want to kick an anthill accidentally. And if Charlie didn't trust her with Dahlia yet, that was his problem.

Ruth: Wonderful. Thanks, Starla. I'm really looking forward to working with your family.

She peeked into his office, where he was still working. "I'm heading out." Either Starla had worked her decorating magic in here too or he'd hired a professional decorator. Yeah, they seemed like the type. He looked up at an obscenely large wall clock, as if he didn't believe it was that late. "Fine."

"I'll see you Monday for school drop-off, then."

"Here." He scribbled something down onto a piece of paper. "Alarm code."

"Oh, great. Thanks." Apparently, she was dismissed, because the moment she took the paper, he went back to his screen. Ruth didn't think of herself as a needy person, but given his lack of enthusiasm for the situation initially, she needed a little reassurance.

"May I ask a question?"

He looked at her, and she figured silence was acceptance.

"Do you actually want me here?" She hated the way the last word sounded in her mouth because of the r, but she couldn't think of another one on the fly, so she rushed on. "Because if you don't, it's fine. I can help you find someone else. Someone just as good."

His eyes narrowed. "The word around town is that you're the best. Is that not true?"

"It depends on what you want. If you want a good nanny, I'm happy to help. But I won't be resented."

Another clanger. She hated her tongue sometimes, but she tipped her chin up and said it with as much conviction as she could. Charlie gave her an assessing look, and she'd already decided that if he tried to pity her, she'd shut that down quick.

"Fine," he said curtly. "You won't be. I'm just...adjusting."

"That's logical. I just wanted to check."

"Okay." His gaze slid back to the computer. "I'll see you Monday."

"Sounds good, Chuck." Ruth backed out of the office slowly, said goodbye to the kids, and got into her truck as fast as her legs would carry her.

Which then would not start. Ruth sat at the wheel for a moment, considering her options. There was a deer path between the two properties that she could walk home—she hadn't wanted to get dirty walking over on her first day, but getting muddy now was acceptable. Anything to get away from here; that had been a very uncomfortable conversation. She pulled out her phone.

Ruth: Sorry to bother you, but my car won't start. I'll have one of my brothers come look at it. Hope it's not in the way.

Charlie: Jason's coming over today. I'll have him take a look at it.

Ruth: Oh. Okay.

Ruth: well, thanks.

Charlie: no problem. Have a good weekend.

Well, that's nice of him. And Jason would likely know more than her brothers, who could barely change their own oil.

Charlie: and don't call me Chuck.

Nope, spoke too soon.

CHAPTER NINE

Charlie

The next week, Jason's casual suggestion during his snack had come to fruition: Henry arrived for his first day of work at the front desk. Charlie came in early to make sure he had clear in his mind what he wanted to teach him, and also to check on Ruth's truck. It had some bad spark plugs, but also needed a new fuel filter...that was often the case for people who went as long as they could before filling their gas tank. It was a quick job, but it wasn't done yet, and he wasn't sure why.

"And this is Jason's office," Charlie said, opening the door from the garage carefully. It was important to open it carefully because the stack of papers on the filing cabinet behind the door was exceptionally precarious, and more than once, Charlie had gone in there in a hurry and regretted it.

"Should I try to clean it?" Henry asked, pencil poised over the yellow legal pad he was using to take notes.

"No. Never. He does actually know where almost everything is. But I tried to organize it once and threw him off for weeks. I'd just let it be." Charlie paused. "But maybe keep the door closed when we have clients or vendors in the garage."

"Got it." The young man scribbled something down.

"In general, try to batch your questions for Jase. He's got ADHD, so staying focused on a task isn't easy. If you can only bother him once, he'll be more productive..." Charlie trailed off as he watched Jason standing on a chair, peering onto a high shelf. He walked over to him, Henry trailing.

"Jase."

"Hmm?"

"What were you doing before you started doing this?"

"I'm trying to decide if I should organize this shelf alphabetically..." *That* was almost certainly a waste of his time.

"I'll make Henry do it. Can you please finish Ruth's truck?"

"Oh, right. Yes, I can..." He mumbled something else as he wandered back toward the car, rubbing at his hands.

"Hey." Jason turned back. Charlie motioned his brother over, then remembered that Henry was still standing next to him. He groped around mentally for a reason to get rid of him.

"Henry, I'll meet you in the main office in just a minute. Can you get started on the desk?"

"Check." Henry scurried off just as Jason arrived.

"Did you take your meds today?" Charlie asked quietly as the swinging door closed.

"Oh. You know what? I don't think I did. Because I didn't eat breakfast. Lacey and I were..." He grinned. "Never mind. But I was running late." It was something about the gleam in his eye, something more tender than simply remembering his morning, that made Charlie ask his next question.

"Are you two trying for another kid?"

Jason grinned again. "Yeah. Don't tell Mom. She'll have advice. Lacey hates her advice."

"Lacey's a smart lady. I don't think she needs it."

"I think she'd agree." He looked toward his office. "I used to have some extra meds here..." He looked back at Charlie. "Could you please ask me in twenty minutes if I took it?" Charlie nodded, then set a timer on his phone. "Thanks, Chuck," Jason said, pulling him into a hug.

"Don't you start that, too. It's bad enough that Ruth does it." He had no idea why she'd called him that on her way out the other day or why he'd mentioned it to Jason.

"It's funny, though," Jason said. "I like her."

"She's something, all right."

Jason let him go. "She's exactly what you need. We're just charging her parts, right?"

"What my kids need," Charlie corrected, "and yes, just parts." Jason just smiled and went toward the car with the hood up, whistling. "Go take your meds." Jase changed directions abruptly to go toward his office. With the state he was in, excited thinking about another baby and naturally distractible, Charlie wouldn't be surprised if Jason forgot why he was going to his office before he got there. And when he stopped in the doorway...

"Meds!" Jason gave him a thumbs up over his shoulder, then went inside. He probably shouldn't have said it so loud, but Henry would probably be responsible for asking him at some point, so maybe it didn't matter. Still, he wanted to preserve his brother's privacy. He owed him that. Charlie ducked back through the swinging door to find Henry looking very baffled, standing over the desk with a myriad of piles started.

"How's it going?"

"Uh..."

"Yeah, that's okay. Let me show you how to invoice." Showing him on Ruth's truck was a mistake, because he wasn't going to give her an itemized invoice, or she'd know he'd given her a discount. But at least Henry got to see the software. Why was it so much easier to be patient with him than the temps? Was he a misogynist? He didn't think so...it felt more like fear than hatred. He didn't hate Starla, either, but he didn't want to go through that again. And the safest way to avoid that was to avoid women.

After the phone tutorial, it was filing and processing payments, and Henry's eyes were kind of glazing over. "I think that's enough training for today. I have a meeting this afternoon in town. Do you think you can cover the phones?"

Henry nodded slowly. "I...think so?"

"If you don't know the answer, just take a message and email it to me, and I'll call them back tonight."

"Tomorrow?" Henry was scribbling again.

"Tonight."

"Your brother said you're not supposed to work at night. He asked me not to send you messages during off-work hours." Charlie shot a glare toward the garage, where he could see Jason through the small window, bent over the engine again.

"Tonight," he repeated firmly.

"Okay."

He stewed about that for an hour until he left for his appointment. Jason didn't understand the customer service side of things. If Charlie didn't answer people's calls, they'd go elsewhere. They'd built their reputation by being available, friendly, and consistent. If he didn't get back to them right away, it'd be bad. Really bad. And more than that, he didn't need his brother policing his work hours. A little thought nudged him in the ribs: *But isn't that what you do for him with his meds?* It wasn't the same, though. Charlie was helping him be *more* productive, whereas Jason seemed unhappy Charlie even carried a cell phone. *Everyone works like this. That's how success happens.*

He was early, but he went inside anyway. The church receptionist greeted him warmly, and it chafed. He hadn't chased this one away—she'd been working here for years—but he often encountered women who'd worked his front desk at other offices, and it bothered him. *Whatever.* Maybe Henry would be a great fit. He sat in the foyer until Kellan came out.

"Hey man, great to see you."

Charlie shook his hand firmly and wished he could say the same. This was going to be awkward. And painful. But it was for his kids. It'd be good to do...better. He followed him back to his office down a long hallway. Inside, it had two small couches flanking a bookshelf with books stacked on top of the typical rows about everything ranging from theology and poverty to classic literature and the kind of pulp fiction he took to the beach. A large leather journal sat on the corner of his neat oak desk, and a bonsai tree basked in the rare winter sunshine on the windowsill between two vining plants that nearly reached the low-pile brown carpet below.

"So why are we here?" As a master of negotiation, it bothered him to see Kellan going straight for the point like this. *No warm up at all? Ugh. He needs to reread that copy of* Hamlet *if that's how he thinks he can get secrets out of people.*

"Well, my divorce might have something to do with it."

Kellan cocked his head, giving him a steady gaze, and it made the snake tattoo on the side of his neck stand out more, like it was staring at Charlie.

"I know your divorce was a big event in your life. But you don't have to be here because of that. It could be something else."

Like what? Charlie wanted to ask. *Why else would I come here unless my world was literally imploding?* Charlie gave him a smile, even as he felt the sweat pooling on his back. "Nah, it's just the divorce. I'll save my shoplifting for another day."

Kellan didn't smile back. "What are you feeling about your divorce?"

Rage. Shattering, soul-crushing rage.

"I mean, I'm not a fan, if that's what you mean." He paused, trying to edge closer to the truth while staying in control. "Still kind of can't believe it, I guess."

"In the classic stages of grief, denial is stage one." That wasn't great news.

"Out of how many stages?"

"Five."

Charlie held back a curse. "How long does each stage take?"

"Grief's not linear, Charlie. You may do each stage several times. In Narcotics Anonymous, we work the steps as many times as we need to."

Charlie fumed. "I'm not an addict, and I'm not *grieving*. Nobody died."

"Your marriage did. Your relationship with Starla will never be what it was." Based on his tone of voice, Charlie guessed Kellan thought he was being kind in pointing this out. But it felt like cold water dumped down his back.

"I know that," he snapped. "I just wish..."

I wish I hadn't acted that way. I wish I'd been honest with her. I wish I hadn't hurt them. Regret clogged his throat, and he struggled to clear it. "I feel angry."

Kellan nodded slowly. "With whom?"

"With her, for leaving me. With me, for giving her reasons to."

"You think you did some things wrong?"

Charlie snorted, even as a tear escaped. "I think I did everything wrong."

"That's probably not true, but confession is a good place to start. We can't undo the past, but we can try to learn from it. And we can ask forgiveness."

Charlie wiped the tear as though he had an itch on his cheek, rubbing it off with his shoulder. "I probably need to do that."

Kellan sat back, just watching him for a minute that felt like an hour. "I'd really like you to come to our divorce support group, Charlie. It's a good group of guys. You should walk through this together. You're not alone in how you're feeling. I'm not a licensed counselor; I can offer you some help, but they can tell you what they've been through and what they've learned. Being a book about a patriarchy at its core, there are no divorced couples we can look to in the Bible as a model. But there are people we can look to in real life, and these are men I'd trust with that responsibility.

They're walking through it transparently and humbly and with as much grace as they can. I think it'd help you a lot more than just meeting with me. Will you do that for me?"

That was absolutely the last thing he wanted to do. Sitting in some stuffy, brown room that still smelled like jelly beans from last Easter's egg hunt baring his soul held zero appeal. But Kellan didn't have kids. He'd never been married. Maybe he had a point about not being the best person to advise him...even if it meant putting his private problems out to strangers.

"Yes. I'll come." They talked for a few more minutes about nothing of consequence, and Charlie felt himself relaxing. Kellan asked some questions about motorcycles, and Charlie was glad to answer them. Apparently, he was looking at one Sawyer had, but wanted a second opinion about it.

"You gotta know what you're really looking for," Charlie said, crossing one ankle over his knee. "Some people want speed, some want power. Some want to be able to put their partner on the back, some want to be able to go to Sturgis and back on one tank. There's a lot to think about."

"Knowing what you want is important," Kellan mused. "In so many areas of life. Speaking of which, how's Ruth working out?"

Charlie gaped. "How do you know about that?"

"Oh, people are talking. And her mom Deborah put a praise in the bulletin." That gave him a sudden urge to leave, but he recovered as quickly as he could.

"It's going fine. She's great with the kids. She doesn't focus too much on being friends with them, you know?"

"She sounds like a catch."

"Definitely." Charlie wrapped things up and drove home, trying not to think about anything, especially not being the answer to Deborah Zane's prayers. When he got there, he put on the TV to make sure the trend would continue.

CHAPTER TEN

Ruth

Wednesday afternoon, Ruth picked up her truck from the garage; it was nice to have it back, and she'd been pleasantly surprised by how cheap the repairs were. Her dad made a funny face when she told him how much it was, though, and when she asked him why, he just kissed her on the forehead and said he was going to bed.

"Hello, Miller family," she greeted the bigger kids as they got into the vehicle. "How was your day?"

"Fine," muttered Aiden. Em said nothing. Ruth pivoted in her seat.

"Everything okay back there, kiddo?"

Emily finished buckling, then crossed her arms and glared at Ruth. *Oh my.*

"She said she had a bad day. She didn't get to be the line leader, even though it was her job," Aiden put in. "Can we go now?"

Ruth turned around and put it in gear. "Aw, that sounds disappointing. I'm sorry to hear that, Em." Ruth connected her phone and started some music, hoping it would help Emily out of her funk. But the funk persisted all the way home, the four of them riding in silence.

The minute they got into the garage, both kids were unbuckling and tearing off.

"I don't have homework," Aiden threw over his shoulder.

"I don't, either," Emily said, and Ruth had a sinking feeling in her stomach that Emily had forgotten what her dad had said yesterday.

"Emily, can I talk to you for a minute?" She had no wish to incite Aiden's love of drama.

Emily stopped on the top step and turned. "What?"

"Did you remember that your dad asked you to clean your room before you had screen time today?"

Her eyes went wide. "No, he said by dinnertime. It's not dinnertime."

Ruth shook her head slowly. "I can check with him, but I'm sure he said screen time."

"No, he didn't!" Emily shouted. "I know he didn't. I'm not doing it."

"Would you like me to check with him?" Normally, she would sit down to help a sense of calm in the room, but that would put her on the cold concrete floor, as well as several feet below Emily.

"No, I know he didn't!" She sounded on the verge of tears. "He didn't, Ruth!"

"Well, I'm happy to check, but that's how I remember it. Do you need me to help you start cleaning?"

Emily muttered something under her breath, then threw down her backpack and slammed the garage door. Ruth lunged forward—it wasn't locked. That was lucky. She breathed a sigh of relief, then turned back to the car to grab Dahlia.

By the time she got inside, Emily was nowhere to be found. Aiden sat on the couch, already engrossed in something on YouTube, eating a large bowl of chips, having ignored the baby carrots and ranch she'd prepared for him before she left.

She settled onto the couch across from Aiden with Dahlia, who was greedily sucking down the breast milk Starla had sent for her. Then Ruth's gaze fell on something she hadn't noticed before: a chess set.

"Whose is that?" Ruth asked, nodding toward the game.

Aiden glanced up. "My mom's."

That didn't make a lot of sense. Surely she would have taken it with her when she left. It was a polished wood set, intricately carved, with dark mahogany pieces paired with cream pieces opposite it. The board appeared to be granite.

"Do you play?"

"I used to." And the wistfulness of his words pierced her twice: once with amusement, because he made himself sound ancient; and once with sadness, because he'd clearly lost something here.

"Why don't you now?"

Aiden didn't answer. Dahlia's soft sucking sounds filled the room. It was quiet.

Too quiet.

Dahlia dropped off to sleep, still drinking halfheartedly, and Ruth got off the couch smoothly so as not to rouse her. She carried her upstairs to Charlie's room. It felt strange being in this room; he'd been clear that he didn't want her to clean it. But the scent of him was stronger here. She didn't want to notice it, but she couldn't help it. Her fingers itched to quickly make the bed after she placed Dahlia into the crib in the corner of the room, but she resisted. Barely.

What was in that cologne he wore? Was it designed to charm people? It was kind of working. *A magic potion.* Too bad his prickly personality negated it for her. Still, she'd rather he treat her like he treated everyone else than pity her or treat her like she was slow because of her speech impediment. She'd gotten that from some of her teachers over the years—not being able to pronounce r's didn't mean that she needed things explained at half speed.

Ruth paused at the top of the stairs as cartoon noises floated to her...from Emily's room. Ruth walked into the room without warning, and a startled Emily looked up guiltily from the tablet she was using.

"Busted." She held out her hand for the device, but Emily shook her head and clutched it tighter, holding it to her chest.

"He said tonight," she insisted loudly. "I don't have to do it now."

Ruth stood still, simply holding out her hand. Most kids would give it up within a minute or two, seeing that they couldn't win. But she could tell Em was not in that kind of mood. Ruth sat down on the edge of her bed.

"Let's put it this way: I can tell Dad you disobeyed, but gave it up when you got caught, or I can tell him you not only disobeyed him, but me as well. It's your choice. Fairly sure you're going to have consequences either way. But the second one might make it worse."

Emily's gaze was conflicted, cast down to the flowered quilt. The tablet continued to play fun, bouncy music, and she glanced down at it longingly. Then she handed it over.

"Thank you. Would you like some help to get your room clean?" Ruth shut it down, if only to save her from having the annoying song stuck in her head later. "I bet it won't take long if we work together."

Emily crossed her arms over her belly and looked out the window pointedly.

"All right. Well, feel free to come downstairs if you want a snack. I made you ants on a log."

"Does that have celery? I hate celery."

"Celery is pretty weird," Ruth agreed. "That's why I make mine with carrot sticks. You can come try it if you want."

Em said nothing, so Ruth quietly left her room with the tablet.

The afternoon passed easily: she folded the morning's laundry, putting Charlie's in a stack on his unmade bed. She ventured into his closet to hang his shirts; only the right side of the walk-in closet had anything hanging in it. The urge to organize hit her again, strong. It appeared he just hung whatever clothes he was holding at the front: polo shirts were mixed with khaki pants and pieces of suits that weren't hung together, dress shirts on the bottom rack. It was like something out of a nightmare. She avoided the top drawer—that was too invasive—but she peeked into his middle drawer: it was a muddle of socks and T-shirts. Ruth shuddered. She wasn't a neat freak by any stretch, but there was absolutely no system to this. And something inside her did rebel at the idea of a systemless household.

Fine. She would compromise: she'd organize the hanging stuff, but not the drawer. That wasn't going too far. She wasn't even 100% sure he was going to be okay with her putting the closet to rights, but it was her job to keep the house clean, right? By no measure could this closet be called clean.

It didn't take her long: casual shirts first, followed by dress shirts, then sweaters and suits. On the lower level, she lined them up similarly. *There.* Ruth breathed a sigh of relief. And she hadn't touched his underwear. It was fine. Totally fine. She checked on Dahlia again on her way out, then got dinner started. But she was feeling less fine about what she'd done by the time she finished chopping the onions. As she sliced the mushrooms, she started imagining a myriad of re-actions that didn't start with "Thanks, Ruth..." He'd been clear that he didn't want her cleaning his room. But this didn't count, did it? She didn't vacuum or dust or change his sheets. She didn't even make the bed. But she was downright jumpy by the time she heard the garage door go up.

If the pasta had been done boiling, she would've booked out of there the moment he got home. But it still had six minutes to go.

"Hi." The word sounded defeated from his beautiful lips. "How was their day?" Ruth took a breath to answer, but he interrupted. "Wait, let me get out of these clothes first. I'll be right back."

Her heart seized. "Emily had a rough afternoon." Maybe if she could delay him downstairs long enough, she wouldn't have to be here when he discovered her very invasive deci-sion.

"Hang on, I'll just..." His voice trailed off as he toed off his shiny shoes and headed up the stairs. "I'll be right back."

Ruth cringed as she turned back to the stove. The beads of sweat at the edge of her hairline had nothing to do with the steam coming off the pot. *Cook faster, darn it.*

"Ruth," Charlie said from the top of the stairs, and she cringed harder, somehow. "Could you come up here, please?"

She put on as regretful a voice as she could. "Actually, the pasta is almost—"

"Ruth. Please come up here. Now."

She turned off the gas in an effort not to overcook the pasta, then made her way slowly to the foot of the stairs. She felt his gaze resting on her all the way up, but she staunchly avoided it, using that emotional energy to come up with a game plan—and fast. She really could not afford to get fired. When she reached the top, he turned and went into his bedroom, and when she hesitated, he motioned for her to follow.

As expected, he marched her into the walk-in closet. But there was a saving grace she'd forgotten about: the sleeping baby in the same room.

"Ruth," he said quietly, though the word was packed with severity. "Do you want to tell me what happened in here?"

"Looks like the Organization Fairy visited you." She smiled at him much more placidly than she felt inside.

He rocked back on his heels with a slow nod. "The Organization Fairy, huh?"

"Yes. This definitely looks like her work." She touched one sleeve of a dress shirt reverently. "She even color-coded. You're lucky."

Charlie was staring at her, and she couldn't tell if that quirk in the corner of his mouth was a smile or a frown. "Please inform the fairy that I can organize my own clothes."

"I tried to tell her," Ruth sighed. "She's not a very good listener, I'm afraid."

His gaze narrowed. "Try harder."

"Are you sure? I didn't let her touch your underwear."

Charlie was staring again. Then he let his arms drop and massaged his temples. "I'll see you tomorrow, Ruth."

"Do you want me to text you about Emily's day?"

"Sure."

When he took off his tie, Ruth assumed she was dismissed for the day. She jogged back downstairs and dumped the pasta, which was only slightly mushy, and got the heck out of there before he could change his mind and fire her.

CHAPTER ELEVEN

Ruth

The next Monday, Ruth was at Starla's house. It was a longer drive, but she liked the area. She had an aunt who lived close to here, further up the road. "You two want to go hiking today?" she asked as they got out of the truck.

"Why would we want to do that?" Aiden asked, making a beeline for the porch.

Sawyer opened the front door. "I think a hike is a grand idea," he said, catching the boy in a clothesline hug as he went by. They lingered there a moment, and Sawyer spoke quietly into Aiden's ear. The boy nodded, and Sawyer let him go. "How's my Emmy Lou?" he asked.

"Pretty good," the girl chirped. "Mrs. Gardener showed my art to the class and said it had good perceptive."

"Aw, sugarplum, that's great! I'd like to see your perspective. Can you bring it home?" It was hard to believe Sawyer had just become their dad; he seemed like a natural, and Ruth found herself smiling at their interactions as she hauled Dahlia's car seat up the stairs. "And I would be remiss if I didn't say hello to you, too, little miss," he said, leaning over the car seat. "How's your day going?" Dahlia blew spit bubbles and kicked her feet. "Oh, is that so? Well, thank you for the update, sweet pea."

Ruth was startled, though, when he turned to her. "And how's your day, Ms. Zane?"

"It's going fine, thanks. How about you?"

"Just trying to get this machine out here to cooperate. Took a break to clear my head."

"Sorry it's giving you trouble." She stepped into the house, if only for warmth.

"Well, it's easier than fixing people, so…"

Ruth snorted. "I hear that." She thought the conversation was over when she walked over to a kitchen chair and put down the car seat to take Dahlia out.

"Charlie giving you any trouble?"

She brought the baby up to her shoulder as she considered the question. "No more than I expected."

Sawyer frowned. "Well, if he's not being polite, please let us know. He has a tendency to—"

"I know all about his tendencies," Ruth interrupted. "I'm not concerned. If I have a problem, I'll take it up with him directly."

He frowned harder, but stepped toward the front door. "You do seem like a lady who can take care of herself." Ruth counted in her head and figured it was more like nine people she was taking care of, but decided not to mention it.

"I'll take that as a compliment. Enjoy your work with the motorcycle."

"I will, thanks."

"I'm going out with Sawyer," Aiden announced, and when Ruth glanced at Sawyer, he gave a nod of assent. "Just give me a call if I need to come get him," Ruth murmured.

"Ah, he's no trouble. Just can't watch all three while my hands are greasy," he said with a grin. Ruth settled down on the couch with Dahlia to give her a bottle while Emily pulled out her homework. The baby patted her breast, as if to say, "I know where this came from." She watched Emily practice her subtraction skills...then noticed something. Ruth pushed the paper aside a bit. Someone had carved "AM" into the coffee table.

"Do Mom and Papa know about this?" She didn't think it had happened on her watch; it was lightly done, like someone had used a paperclip rather than a proper knife. But it was definitely a scratch, not a pencil mark.

"I don't know." Emily had her concerned drama llama face on, so Ruth sat back.

"Okay, I'll take care of it. Ten minus five is..."

"Four."

"Try again." Emily held up her fingers and started counting backwards, and Ruth took a subtle photo of the scratch. Dahlia was almost done with her bottle, and Ruth moved to the kitchen—this kid always spit up. Always. She moved her to her shoulder with one hand and sent the photo to Starla with the other. She got back an angry face emoji.

> **Ruth**: Sorry. I just noticed it. It didn't happen today, he's been outside with Sawyer.

> **Starla**: No, it's not your fault. He's been doing this all over. Sawyer's been making him sand it out and refinish it in some parts of the house, but that's clearly not enough of a consequence.

> **Starla**: Sigh.

Ruth: That's a bummer. Please let me know how I can support your discipline plan.

Ruth started up the creaky stairs to put Dahlia down in Starla and Sawyer's room when her phone buzzed again.

Starla: Do you have any suggestions?

She couldn't deny that it warmed her heart to be treated as a professional. She thought for a few minutes as she patted Dahlia's back.

Ruth: Maybe more of a healthy outlet for the impulse? You could get a wood-burning kit and let him make a sign for his room.

Starla: Hmm, that's a thought.

Ruth: Though you might just be exchanging one form of defacement for another.

Starla: LOL

Starla: I wonder if he'd have an interest in art

Ruth thought it was unlikely, but didn't want to say that. It seemed more likely to her he was trying to find his place in this new house; Charlie hadn't mentioned it happening at his place.

Ruth: Worth a try, maybe
Starla: Thanks for the brainstorm and the photo

Ruth sent her back a thumbs-up. She really did like Starla; she could see why Charlie missed her. Ruth turned on the baby monitor and went downstairs. But no sooner had she gotten to the landing than she heard Dahlia coughing, choking. She raced back up and turned her to her side, patting her back, fear spiking into her. Dahlia was still sputtering, crying, but seemed to get her breath back after a moment. Then it hit her: Dahlia hadn't spit up downstairs. Ruth picked her up, rocking her, trying to lull her back to sleep, kicking herself all the while for being so forgetful. Despite helping Emily and Aiden both with homework and cooking a frozen lasagna, she hadn't stopped feeling bad about it by the time Starla got home.

"Oh, that's happened before." She didn't seem concerned, and the thought that this wasn't normal weighed on Ruth. But it wasn't her kid, and Starla had two others. Maybe it wasn't a big deal? She couldn't shake the concern that followed her out to her truck, but she'd forgotten about it by the time she pulled up out front at home. The driveway was so packed with cars, she couldn't get within twenty feet of the house. Ruth let out a groan; her brothers must have friends over. She pulled out her phone and found the sibling group chat.

> **Ruth**: What's going on?
> **Ranger**: Dad took Mom to the cabin, so we're having a boys' night.
> **Ryan**: Come on in, the water's fine!
> **Levi**: By water, he means beer.

Ruth: And no one thought to mention this to me?

Wyatt: You were busy

Ruth: I'm always busy!

Ryan: Yeah, you should work on that.

Anger gave way to despair as she leaned forward and rested her forehead gently on the steering wheel. She wanted food and to curl up somewhere quiet with her phone. eBird was calling and she must go. But since Mom being gone was a rare occasion in which the boys didn't need to control their noise...yeah. The impossibility of a peaceful evening was a foregone conclusion. And she certainly wasn't going to crash her parents' evening by the river. Ruth scrolled through her phone contacts. She could call Jennie, but she'd want to socialize. She hadn't talked to Patricia or Grace in a long time...and frankly, they'd never been her favorites. With a grunt of displeasure, she threw open her door and got out. How hard would it have been to give her a heads-up? Or even—God forbid—*invite* her instead of doing their own thing and leaving her to deal? The long walk to the front door did not improve her mood.

"Hey," Ranger greeted her. "Saved you some pizza."

She looked down at the plate with disdain. "I don't like black olives."

"You could pick them off?"

"No, thank you." *If you can't be bothered to care about what I think, I'm not going to make this easy on you.*

"Ruthie, come on," he said, setting down the paper plate. "Just join the party."

"Not interested. Good night." She had an energy bar from her last bird hike in her backpack, she thought. That would do for tonight.

"Why aren't you interested? There's a bunch of guys here..."

"All of whom you've made swear they won't even look at me. How is this fun for me?"

His face reminded her of when he was little and he'd tracked muddy footprints across the floor by accident. "Fine. Have a good night hiding in your bedroom."

"I will, thanks." She surged by him, ignoring the loud music and video game noise (they *knew* she didn't approve of *Grand Theft Auto*), and went down the hall to their room. Slamming the door never felt so good.

CHAPTER TWELVE

Charlie

On Saturday morning, Charlie pulled up in front of his parents' house: they were waiting for him. His mother waited until his father opened the door for her, then she got into the back seat.

"Hello, darling," she intoned, patting him on the shoulder. "How are you?"

"Just fine. How are you?"

"Oh, fine. I think I need new glasses, though."

"Old ones out of style?" he teased.

"No, as a matter of fact, which makes it all the more annoying. Where is your father?"

Charlie looked out the windshield instead of looking at his mom in the rearview.

"He appears to be checking out my grill." His dad was bent at the waist, running a hand along the front of the SUV. Charlie bopped the horn, and he jumped. Glaring at his son, he finished his route to the other side of the car to sit in the back next to his wife.

"What was that for?"

"We're in a hurry. Quit worrying over scratches and dents."

"Why hasn't your brother touched that up?"

"Because I didn't tell him about it. Seat belts." He heard them both pulling out the inertia reels simultaneously...if he didn't remind them, they didn't bother. He'd never understood it. When pressed, his mother had once offered an excuse about wrinkling her clothing.

"Thank you for picking us up," his dad said as he pulled back onto the highway.

"Dad, we live on the same property."

"Even so. We appreciate it. How's work?"

"Work is good. Sales are up five percent this quarter."

"Just five? Did you look into those billboards I told you about? My guy can get you a good deal."

"I looked into it, but it's still pretty pricey." He also wasn't sure he wanted his face on a billboard. He wasn't an ambulance chaser.

"No, no, you gotta talk to my guy. Here, I'll send you his info again."

"James, he doesn't want to talk to your guy. Let the poor boy run his own business. You're retired, remember?" She turned her attention to Charlie. "Who's going to be at the party?"

"Just family."

When she looked at him expectantly, he elaborated. "Star and her folks, Sawyer, Rhea, Paige."

"Oh, is he family now?" James muttered.

"Dad, don't start. He's part of Starla's family, so he's part of Aiden's."

None of them had exactly gotten used to Sawyer and his clan yet.

"Look at the bright side, James: they're not Zanes."

"That would be worse," his father agreed, and Charlie glared at them in the rearview mirror, but said nothing. He didn't need to defend how smart or capable Ruth was; it was none of their business.

"I mean, can you imagine us mixing with those people?" His dad chuckled, and his mother joined in.

Not my business, not my business, Charlie chanted in his head, but he felt his restraint weakening like a bad cell signal the further he drove into the woods. He felt staticky inside. Charlie tried to drive the disconnect between what he'd observed about Ruth and his family's opinions about all Zanes out of his mind.

"What a disaster that would be. You know sooner rather than later all those boys are going to have little trailer trash—"

"Stop it," Charlie snapped. The silence that filled the car made the static worse. "Let's just talk about something else. No need to make the car ride unpleasant."

"Fine." His father's tone had gone gruff, and internally, he sighed.

"What'd you get Aiden for a present?"

"A dirt bike."

Charlie groaned. "Dad, he's *twelve.* You can't just get him a dirt bike. You gotta talk to Starla and me about a big purchase like that. We've talked about this before."

"You said you wanted the boy to spend more time outside. Now he will."

"But it also requires us to take him somewhere he can drive it. And he'll need safety equipment, instruction..."

"Well, it's too late now. It's being delivered to your house tomorrow."

Charlie drove the SUV down the long driveway and parked in front of the house. "We'll talk about this later. I'm not going to tell him he can keep it without talking to Starla. She's still his mom."

The dark mood of the car shifted abruptly when the kids burst through the front door.

"Hey, there's my grandkids! How are you, birthday boy?"

"Hi, sweetheart," his mom cooed to Emily, who gave her a big hug. "Are you all right?"

Are you all right? What kind of question is that? She acts like she's being held hostage here or something.

Starla came out on the porch with Dahlia in a sling; Ruth seemed to have converted her to the device. It made him feel a little better that Starla seemed to like Ruth. But the sling was also annoying, because it made it harder to grab his girl without Starla noticing.

"Hey, Star."

"Hi. You know this starts at 3:00, right?"

Charlie checked his phone. It was 2:55.

"So we're right on time, is what you're saying?"

"Well, I don't expect the rest of them until 3:30, just so you know."

"Millers know how to show up on time, Starla dear," his mother said, patting her arm. "Remember that, Emily. Being on time is a sign of respect to your hosts."

Starla's wince was brief, but Charlie caught it. She was always late for everything.

"Come on in." Starla gestured to the open door. "Sawyer's working on the burgers out back if you want to keep him company." Sawyer was naturally not his favorite person, but at the moment, he'd take him over his own parents.

Charlie strode through the living room, noting the paper streamers and silver birthday banner before pausing at the back door. Sawyer was bent over, trying to discern if he'd successfully lit the charcoal.

"Need some help?"

He looked up with a grimace. "I guess so."

Charlie laughed. "Don't you have a chimney?"

"Just on my house. Is there another kind?"

"Yeah, it's this—" Charlie made a cylinder shape with his hands. "—metal thing. I think I've got two for some reason. I'll bring you one. But for today..." Charlie scooted closer to the grill and peered inside. "I think you just need oxygen." He picked up the lid of a trash can that held the briquettes and started fanning the coals. In no time, they were crackling with flames.

"Thanks, man."

"Yeah." They stood in silence, watching the fire. The noise from the house pushed against the quiet, so despite the cold, Charlie was in no hurry to go back in. The trees were huddled around the weathered cedar deck, spreading their pine needles and cones generously over the large area.

"What do you think of Ruth?"

Charlie blinked at Sawyer. "How do you mean?"

"How's she working out?"

"Good. It's been good. I think she does more cleaning for me than for you, but there's two of you, and I discussed it with her before she started, so..."

"Good, good."

The silence felt less comfortable than before, and Charlie looked up at the canopy of towering Douglas fir trees above.

"Did she say something?"

"Well, she mentioned you were a bit...unfriendly."

Charlie stared into the fire again and felt the heat of it against his face. "I...don't know how to act around women anymore."

"Oh."

Charlie stole a glance at his ex's husband to find out if he was being judged. Sawyer's brow wrinkled, but his crossed arms and wide stance still somehow made him seem open, easy to open up to.

"What do you mean by that?" Sawyer asked. "Because I know you're not shy."

Charlie chuckled ruefully. "No, not shy. But I also don't know how to be comfortable without being..."

"Too comfortable," Sawyer finished, and Charlie nodded, relieved. "I don't know that I'm the right man to talk to. Before Starla, I just didn't talk to women at all unless it was necessary."

Charlie rubbed at his chin. "Yeah, I don't know why I'm asking the forest hermit."

Sawyer glanced toward the back door. "Not feeling much like a hermit these days."

"I imagine not." He kicked at a knot in the deck.

"Now, hold on here. First of all, it's arrogant as anything to assume every woman's into you, so maybe adjust your thinking in that vein. But beyond that...maybe you can talk to them like a sister?"

"Just brothers at the Miller house."

"Well, what about your sister-in-law? How do you talk to her?"

He hadn't considered that. He did joke around with Lacey, but it wasn't flirting. He looked around for an answer, and his gaze fell to a familiar blue cooler.

"Safe to assume there's booze in there?"

Sawyer grinned as he sat down in an Adirondack chair. "Yup."

Charlie considered Sawyer's question as he helped himself to a lager.

"It's just different with her. I know I can't go too far, because one, she's my brother's wife, and two, she's hard to offend. Probably why she's my brother's wife, now that I think about it."

"So you're worried about offending women?"

Charlie tipped his head back and forth, then took another sip. "Sort of. With Ruth, I just feel..." It was hard to describe. She *wasn't* his type, truthfully, but she was beautiful and she pushed all his buttons sometimes in a different way than he was used to. "I don't know. I just don't want to get too comfortable." He felt bad that she'd thought him unfriendly.

"Even at the risk of her discomfort?"

Now that was something he hadn't thought of. "Is she thinking of quitting?"

"No, she seems content with the work."

"That's good." Still. He didn't want her to be unhappy. He remembered the way she'd raced off after she invaded his privacy with his laundry. Maybe it wasn't a big deal, but a man was allowed to have boundaries.

Jason burst out onto the back deck. "They're out here!" he announced loudly, then enveloped Charlie in a huge hug. "There he is, that's my guy." Sawyer got an ardent handshake, and the discussion turned to work. Before he knew it, those two were taking off to see the Ducati that Sawyer had just finished working on. Charlie was alone on the deck when Starla came out with the burgers.

"Is he..."

Charlie gestured toward the garage. "Got sucked into the motorcycle vortex. I can do it for you."

"Are you sure you don't mind?"

"Nah. It gives me a reason to stay out here where it's quiet."

Starla smiled as he took the plate. "Thank you."

"You're welcome." Maybe it was just because they didn't live together anymore, but she looked older. More gray in her hair, more lines around her eyes, a general heaviness to her walk and her demeanor.

"Tired?"

She brushed her hair back. "Dahlia's sleep schedule is killing my energy. And I'm pumping. And working. Plus two other kids and a..." She stopped before she said "husband," but Charlie knew.

"Plus throwing birthday parties for twelve people."

"Yeah," she said with a sigh. "That too."

"You want me to take Easter?" He didn't know what possessed him to offer, except a feeling that he was still trying to make up for what he'd done to her.

She lifted one eyebrow. "Well, that's a very generous offer, but you can't cook."

"Don't worry about that. I've got Easter. You can just come and enjoy."

"And you'll host? At your house?"

"Yeah, I can host." Dang, now he had to clean, too. Still, it wasn't fair that she had to carry all the family gatherings. Maybe his mom would help. *Maybe Ruth would help.* By all accounts, the woman loved an event with a theme.

That alone seemed to put a little energy back in Starla's demeanor. "Well, that'd be great, Charlie. Thank you."

"What's happening, what did I miss?" Jason bounded back onto the deck.

"Your brother's going to host Easter."

"Oh *yes*, that means I'm getting ribs for Easter."

Charlie scowled. "I know how to do more than grill."

"Since when?" Jason shot over his shoulder as he went to hug Starla.

"I already got a hug." She giggled into his chest.

"Here's another one. Free of charge." He leaned back. "Unless you don't want it."

"No, I want it," she said, snuggling back into Jason, and the burgers gave Charlie a reason to turn away so he didn't have to watch. He'd be happy just to be friends with her like that again.

CHAPTER THIRTEEN

Ruth

It was the kind of gray, quiet afternoon where even the woods seemed stiller than usual. Ruth had been doing projects all day, most of them at the kitchen table, just to look out the window. Dahlia was asleep in the sling on her chest, sucking on her fist adorably, kicking her thin leg in her sleep. Ruth put a lid on the spaghetti sauce so it wouldn't spatter and burn her.

Emily looked down at her phone, then gasped. "They're saying it might snow tomorrow!"

"Who does?" Aiden asked, rushing over.

"The weather people," Emily shrieked, and Ruth smiled as she chopped parsley for the sauce.

"You know what we have to do, don't you?"

"Pray?" Emily asked, her voice still shrill, both of them looking at her with enormous eyes.

"I'm sure that wouldn't hurt," Ruth agreed. "But no, I meant tricks you do at bedtime to ensure snow tomorrow."

"That's not a real thing," Aiden sneered, peering at the phone again.

Ruth, being accustomed to fourth grade skepticism, simply shrugged.

"I mean, if you want to risk it, that's your call. But you're braver than I would be."

"What kind of tricks?" Emily asked, rushing over to her.

"Well, I've heard quite a few over the years. Flushing ice down the toilet. Wearing your pj's inside out. Those are the easy ones."

"But there's more?"

"Oh, yes." Ruth smiled. "Lots more."

The girl whirled to her brother. "Come on, Aid. We gotta try."

Aiden looked pensive. "I'm not wearing my pajamas inside out, but maybe I'll try the other stuff once I hear what it is."

When Charlie got home a few hours later, he paused.

"Should I ask why there are cotton balls littering the entryway?"

Ruth put down her book. "If that bothers you, maybe don't look under their pillows tonight. We were trying to entice the snow."

"Entice it?" he said, bending to scoop up a handful. "It's either going to come or it's not."

"That's probably true. But you should've heard the raucous laughter as we flushed ice cubes down the toilet and dug through the art drawers for white crayons." She watched him for a moment. He was so strange sometimes. It was like he couldn't let himself indulge in a fantasy of any kind. She didn't understand him. And by the way he was watching her, he didn't understand her, either.

"Thank you," he blurted out, and Ruth felt her eyebrows lift in surprise.

"For what?"

Charlie sighed. "For reminding them that they're kids. For making life magical when it's not."

"Who says it's not?" she replied softly. When Charlie didn't answer, she rose from the couch. "I'll clean up the mess tomorrow. Sorry."

"Don't be, I shouldn't have...it's fine. I'll cross my fingers and toes for their snow tonight."

"There's no need. We already put spoons under their pillows." She hurried past him toward the laundry room, but he called after her.

"Were they at least clean spoons?"

"Mostly," she called back.

As she gathered up her purse and coat, Charlie came to the doorway. "There's no need to hurry in tomorrow if we do get snow. Nobody buys cars in that kind of weather."

"All the same, I'd like to share it with them. If you don't mind."

"No. Of course. If you want to, you should. I just wouldn't want to see you damage that pristine ride of yours." Was Charlie...smiling? Ruth's heart fluttered a little; Charlie was really handsome when he smiled.

"What's wrong with my ride?" she asked, crossing her arms over her chest.

"Nothing if you're a farmer from the 1980s. Does it even have air bags?"

"I don't need air bags. I'm a very careful driver."

"Deer don't care."

"Oh, I have a deer whistle."

Charlie cocked his head. "A what?"

"You know," she said, gesturing with her hands. "The...a deer whistle." When her employer continued to stare blankly at her, she felt a blush creeping over her chest. "You call your-self a car guy and you don't have one?"

"I don't even know what it is!"

"Here, I'll..." She gestured with her head for him to fol-low her out the front door. To her surprise, he did. Maybe it was because that's where he'd left his shoes, or maybe it was just because he thought he could upsell people on them at the dealership. But either way, he followed her down the steps to her truck. She pointed at the small plastic tubing at-tached to the front of her grill.

"And this is supposed to do what, exactly?"

"It makes a high-pitched noise, I assume. I don't know. My dad put it on."

"And this works?"

Ruth shrugged. "All I know is we've never hit a deer, not one of us."

"Huh." He was still staring down at the car, so she did, too. "Interesting." Charlie looked up. "Well, at any rate, drive safe tomorrow. I don't want to go through the nanny-hiring process again."

"Ah, it's all about you, is it?" It was a joke, but the words tasted acidic, like tea steeped too long.

"It was a terrible process, Ruth. Also, the kids love you."

"I love them, too."

Charlie snorted. "Even when Em won't clean her room? Even when Aiden throws shade about everything?"

"Of course. They're just being kids, Charlie. They're just trying to figure out who they want to be. Aren't we all?"

"No." The word was as cold as the surrounding air, and it lingered in the dark. "I know who I am."

Ruth stared at him for a long moment. He was clearly in pain. But she didn't understand why he insisted on hiding it; she wasn't going to tell anyone. She wasn't going to mock him or belittle him.

"Well, I guess you're lucky, then." Ruth opened her door and climbed up into her truck with no intention of looking back. But when Charlie waved to her, she waved goodbye, too.

CHAPTER FOURTEEN

Charlie

Well, I screwed that up royally, Charlie thought as he went inside. This was one of the reasons that he'd hired her. One of the reasons she was a perfect nanny for his kids. All the reference letters had talked about her imagination, and yet...this wasn't what he'd expected. He didn't know what he'd expected from her. Hiring your family's nemesis wasn't an everyday occurrence. But he'd thought maybe forts or something. Not this blatant optimism, not encouraging his kids toward nonsense. They should be grounded in reality. That was a life skill, wasn't it? Not that he was an expert in reality. For a fleeting moment when she was showing him that odd deer whistle, he'd wanted to kiss her. Then, as he panicked inside, he'd deflected with that stupid joke about replacing her, and it'd gone downhill from there. Imagining kissing Ruth Zane was definitely not living in the real world.

Charlie pulled his dinner out of the fridge and sat down. But no sooner had he speared one bite than Em appeared in the hallway.

"Didi's crying."

"Okay, sunshine. I'll come get her. You go back to sleep, okay?"

Em nodded, but then she shuffled over to him and put her head on his shoulder.

"Do you think it'll snow?"

They technically forecast it with a ten percent chance. But it wasn't likely. Still, he didn't want to crush her dreams, especially when they'd gone to all that effort with the cotton balls...

"I don't know." And it felt true on more levels than he cared to admit. "But I hope so."

The next morning, there was indeed snow on the ground. Charlie knew this because he woke in a panic: it was unbelievable how close the word "snow" when howled by a child with glee sounded like "no" howled by a child in distress. He put a hand to his chest to slow his racing heart, but it still took a minute for his brain to stand down from its red alert when he heard Emily's bouncing feet and repeated cries of delight from the top of the stairs next to his door. He flopped back onto the bed, even though he knew there would be no more sleep. It felt unfair since he couldn't go to work, either.

"Oh, there will be work," he assured himself aloud, and Dahlia kicked her feet and fussed as if to confirm the opinion. "Are you awake early because of the snow, too, sweet pea?" Downstairs, he heard the front door open and close and the security alarm beeped.

"Ruthie!" Emily cried. "Did you see? Did you see?" Was it really that late? Charlie looked at his phone: it was only 6:45. He heard Ruth's soft voice assuring Emily that she did see and asking her not to wake the others. "Oh, Daddy's up. I heard him complaining."

Charlie grumbled as he went into his closet to find pants. He'd already taken off his pajamas when Aiden appeared in the doorway. "Remember knocking?"

"Oh, yeah," Aiden said dismissively. "Your door was open."

"Try again."

Aiden rolled his eyes as he turned and went back to the bedroom door. "Knock. Knock. Knock."

"Just a minute," Charlie called. He looked at his T-shirts...normally, on a day at home, he wouldn't care what he wore. So why he pulled out his nicest polo shirt, he couldn't say. The kids were waiting. There was no time to analyze it. "What's up?" he asked Aiden as he pulled a fleece on and zipped it up. He was going to work from home, anyway. This was work appropriate. That's what it was; he was just dressing for success. *Success doing what?* his brain snarked, but he ignored it.

"There's no school today." Aiden held up the phone so he could see; it appeared, based on the school district website, that they had canceled school. "Can I go play on my tablet?"

"Why are you asking me when Ruth's here?"

"Because Ruth's not my mom."

"Ruth said no, didn't she?" Charlie smirked as he found some wool socks.

"Can I play on my tablet or not?"

"I think you've got your answer..."

Aiden sighed and dramatically turned to leave the room. But Charlie couldn't let him get away with that. He engulfed the boy in a hug from behind.

"Do you need to be tickled?"

"No." He squirmed to get away.

"Are you sure? That attitude is pretty strong. I've heard tickling helps."

"No, I'm good. Lemme go."

Charlie released him and watched him trundle off toward the bonus room. "Just so we're clear, you don't need TV, either."

"I wasn't going to. I'm looking for *City of Ember*." It was the one book he seemed to want to read. Charlie had replaced his copy more than once, much to Starla's chagrin. She and Sawyer were forever trying to entice him with graphic novels and comic books, but no. It was *City of Ember* or nothing. Charlie thought it was a strange choice, but he respected the energy. He jogged downstairs; that rumbling, nervous feeling in his stomach was probably just hunger. The fact that he didn't eat breakfast was irrelevant.

"Good morning," Ruth chirped. "Didn't expect to see you so early." He made straight for the coffeemaker, which happened to be right next to where she was working, making oatmeal. "I thought you might need extra time to get to work in case you changed your mind."

"I'm not going in today."

"Oh! Great, well, we're going to try to build a snow fort if you'd like to join—"

"I'll be working from home."

"Oh." That "oh" had a very different pitch to it; it reminded him of a car that was having transmission trouble. It was strained in a way that he didn't like. "Well, your loss." The oatmeal smelled good; it smelled more like pie than gruel. Ruth noticed him looking into the pot. "Would you like some?"

"No." His stomach growled, and he stared at the coffee dripping into the mug.

Ruth snickered. "You are just too stubborn for words, aren't you?" Charlie felt his face flush at her casual observation.

"What does that mean, Ms. Zane?"

"Just that I can see in your eyes that you want this oatmeal. And I can hear from your belly that it's empty. But you're depriving yourself for some unknown reason."

"I can't eat that many grains."

Ruth cocked her head. "Oatmeal is a good source of fiber. Also, it's prebiotic."

"I don't know what that means," he grumped, snatching his coffee out from under the spout before it was full.

"It means it gives the good bacteria in your gut something to munch on."

"Ew," Aiden said as he took his bowl. "This has bacteria in it?"

"I'm not eating it," Emily announced from the window seat where she was curled up with her feet on a heat vent, watching the snow pile up.

"No, it doesn't—never mind. Suit yourself, Chuck. And Em, you're going to want something hot inside you when we go out to play. It'll fuel us up good." Charlie took one more look over his shoulder as he went into his office; Ruth and Em were both tasting their bowls, adding a little brown sugar to the top, and the big smile on Emily's face said it all. He was starting to get used to Ruth's odd nickname for him...and secretly, he even liked it a little. Then he heard Dahlia squawk, discontented at being left alone upstairs, and he internally face-palmed; he'd forgotten all about her up there. Ruth was off toward the stairs before he could say a word. Charlie left the door open a crack; he really should monitor what was going on with all of them in case Ruth needed backup. It wasn't because her laugh made his stomach feel weird, full of popcorn still popping. It wasn't that at all. Charlie answered emails and talked to Jase, who had managed to make it into the garage.

"All's quiet here."

"Wish I could say the same." Charlie spun his desk chair to look out the window, where Emily and Aiden were arguing about the best way to build the front wall of their snow fort, while Ruth calmly made snowballs with Dahlia strapped to her chest. The baby was so bundled, he couldn't even see her.

Jason chuckled. "Kids driving you wild?"

"Something like that. What's your plan today?"

"Thought I'd use the time to rebuild that Stingray's engine."

Charlie snorted. "Who do you think is going to buy that thing?"

"I don't know. The internet's a thing. I could...send it somewhere."

He shook his head. "All right. But Mr. Carr is expecting his truck back tonight."

"Oh, right. I'll do that first. Shouldn't take me long."

"Might be more business tomorrow if people are sliding off the road."

"They think four-wheel drive means four-wheel stop," Jason said with a laugh.

"Yeah. Well, have a good day. I'll check in with you at lunchtime."

"Thanks, man. Love you."

"Love you, too."

"And hey—" Charlie almost missed it; he was already putting his phone away.

"Yeah?"

"Go outside and play with your kids. They're only little once." His brother hung up before Charlie could reply. Movement outside drew his gaze to the window again; the kids had chosen different activities (Emily making a snowman and Aiden continuing the fort), and Ruth was walking in that bouncy way that parents do when they're trying to get a baby to sleep. She caught his eye through the window and smiled. Charlie turned back to his desk, feeling annoyed. He wanted these two to leave him alone and let him work; he had child support to pay. People depended on him—Jason depended on him. He was carrying on their father's legacy. Why couldn't they all understand that?

His phone dinged.

Kellan: You coming to Divorce Support this week?

He'd meant to talk to Ruth about it, but kept forgetting.

Charlie: no childcare
Kellan: okay, maybe next week?
Charlie: yeah, I'll try.

He dove into his email inbox, and an hour later, he heard the back door open to complaints about cold fingers and the need for cocoa. Ruth and the kids were in the laundry room, stripping off soggy coats and hats, when he found them. He leaned in the doorway.

"I have an appointment next week in the evening. Would you be able to stay on Wednesday?"

"Probably. How long does it go?" She was turning Emily's coat right side out, frowning at it.

"Not sure." He swallowed hard, his throat unaccountably dry. "It's a new thing."

"I see." Ruth looked skeptical, and Charlie scrambled for a better answer, but it came out prickly.

"It's a church group, okay? It's Divorce Support."

Ruth continued picking up the damp clothes and hanging them on a drying rack, but her movements slowed like she was considering his words. "That sounds like an important thing. I can make time for that."

"Good. Thanks." Charlie turned and hurried back into his office, and this time, he closed the door.

CHAPTER FIFTEEN

Ruth

On Friday, her Audubon friends decided they were feeling cooped up inside and wanted to get out and bird. That sounded fine to Ruth, so she got up early Saturday and did whatever dusting and tidying she could before 10:00. She left pancakes and bacon for her brothers, none of whom she had yet seen. She could hear her parents talking through their bedroom door, but decided not to bother them.

Ruth: Headed out to hike.
Dad: With the Bird Brains?

There was a book group called the Mind Readers, so her dad had taken to calling the Audubon group the Bird Brains. Ruth didn't share that with the rest of the group.

Ruth: Yep. Be back this afternoon. Probably around 2:00.
Mom: Be safe. Love you.

Ruth didn't see what kind of trouble she could really get into hiking Timber Falls with a group of people in their sixties, but the actual circumstances of what she was doing never seemed to factor into her mom's admonitions.

Ruth: I'm always safe. Love you, too.

The snow had melted except for random parking-lot piles and a few places in the landscaping around the library, which she passed by on her way to the falls. Jenny had told them that the trails weren't too slick. There were some advantages to having a friend who worked for the Forest Service.

Jean and Hattie were already standing around the parking lot, chatting, when she pulled up. There was a large open field where they did Fourth of July next to it, and two deer were grazing on the far side of it where the forest loomed. When she opened her door, the sound of chickadees and a woodpecker greeted her, and so did the other women. The sound of the falls was soothing, and she watched the spray drift toward the hills.

"No Perry today?"

Jean shook her head. "Some sporting event he wanted to watch on TV. I forget what it was. I think he just didn't want to get wet."

It was misting a little, but Ruth didn't think they'd get soaked.

"How's your mom, Ruth?" Hattie asked, offering a hug. Ruth accepted with a smile before she answered.

"She's good. She's working on a new quilt."

"Ooh, her work is so beautiful. I can't wait to see it," Jean said. "We miss her at our guild meetings."

"She misses you, too. We're going to see if she can video call in again; that seemed to work okay."

"We'd love that. Truly." Jean gave her a hug, too.

"Are we waiting for Frank?"

Hattie nodded. "And Jennie."

Ruth looked longingly toward the woods. It was like another world: the smell of moisture hung in the air. Most of the animals in the area seemed to steer clear of the area around the falls, knowing that there were often many people in it, though the parking lot was fairly empty today. But there were plenty of days when they'd see deer and chipmunks, in addition to many species of birds. Her favorite were the migrating birds: the ones you didn't expect to see, peering through the branches to get an exact picture of them in your mind, in case you never saw them again. She loved the common yellowthroats and fox sparrows and juncos and wrens, too. But even the idea of seeing a bird who'd been so many places despite such great odds—predators, people, cars—just thrilled her socks off.

When the other two showed up, there were more hugs all around, started by Hattie again, and then they were off. The path to the top of the falls was paved, which was a positive when birding with this group, some of whom were prone to unsteadiness.

"Hey," Jennie greeted, elbowing her as they took up the rear. "What's new?" She spoke softly, as they always did while birding.

"Not much. Just settling into my new job."

"Oh yeah, how's that going?"

Ruth shrugged. Her sense was that Charlie was actually quite a private person, so she resolved to be careful about what she said. "It's good. Great kids. And Starla's great, of course. And Charlie's..."

"Handsome?" Jennie teased, then fell quiet as the others stopped to stare up into a maple tree near the path. Ruth was still thinking about her boss even as she gazed up into the naked tree to see the nuthatch bouncing from limb to limb. She probably read too many gothic novels, but his broody, secretive thing kind of made her imagination go wild. And she already knew he didn't have a wife in the attic. Their house had a very small attic which was not easily accessible; she'd checked. It was good to know where kids might hide or get stuck.

The group started moving again as the nuthatch flitted away for greater shelter, and Ruth whispered back, "Yes, but he's kind of...cold?"

"Cold?" Jennie's voice was too loud, and the others turned to glance at her in mild condemnation. "You mean he's not flirting with you?"

"No, not at all. Not that I want him to," she amended quickly. "He's my boss. But...I guess I listen to too many rumors, because that wasn't his reputation at all."

"Starla leaving really broke him, I think. Maybe he's still broken. Ooh, what's that?" Jennie pointed up into a towering pine, and they all stopped to use their binoculars.

"Too big to be a downy," Hattie muttered. "Hairy woodpecker?"

"No, but look at the yellow on his head. That's not the same, is it?"

There was great (muted) discussion over whether this fellow was indeed a hairy woodpecker (common) or a black-backed woodpecker (rare) based on the exact color of that patch on his cute head. When his mate appeared, they could hardly contain their nearly silent excitement. The female's greenish appearance confirmed it: black-backed. She was far too dark to be a hairy. Jennie marked the spot on her app so they could come back later and see if they'd indeed nested here; it could bring some Big Year birders if they did, and that meant money for the town.

They continued to walk quietly, and the mist became heavier around them as they climbed. Ruth's thoughts were drawn to Jennie's comments about Charlie being a flirt; she had to assume it was worse than that if Starla had left him. How did one reform a cheater? Maybe he didn't know, either. Not that it was her job to fix him: her brothers had informed her that she had a bad habit of trying to change other people...but she was fairly sure they felt that way because she asked them to pick up their own laundry.

"You're making that noise again," Hattie whispered.

"Brother trouble," she explained, and Hattie nodded sympathetically.

"I've had a touch of that myself as of late."

"Have you?" She didn't know Hattie had any siblings.

"My husband's brother, actually. You remember him."

"I do, yes," Ruth said with a grin. Stuart Bagsby had crashed their meeting once, looking for Hattie; he had a tendency to drop in on her, which was mostly odd because he lived in Florida.

"Apologies, but if I don't sneak up on her, she takes a rather coincidental trip when I'm supposed to call on her," he'd explained with a grimace. "And I promised my brother I'd check on her. I keep my word."

Ruth knew Hattie's husband had died a long time ago, and based on Hattie's annoyance, she felt that debt had been long paid.

"Is he here now?"

"No, but he's coming. I can feel it. There's a scent in the air when he's on the way, I swear. The man really knows how to push my buttons."

Ruth tried not to giggle and failed, prompting more stern looks from the others. She got the sense that she knew how to push Charlie's buttons, too...and strangely, she enjoyed it. Too much, really. He was so *serious*. She just wanted him to lighten the heck up. She knew he had it in him...maybe he just needed more encouragement.

As the rest of the group watched a northern flicker, she decided she'd provide that encouragement...and hope not to get fired. "Button pushing can be fun, Hattie. You should try it."

"What, just push his buttons right back?"

Ruth nodded slowly. "I bet you know where a few of them are."

Hattie's gaze remained skeptical, but she didn't deny it. "I'm too old for it. That's a young woman's game."

"Oh, nonsense. Play is important at any age. Some of the oldest people I know are young at heart because they play. You should give it a whirl." Ruth paused to remove a branch from the path. "What could it hurt?"

"Nothing, I suppose," Hattie said, musing, and Ruth grinned at her.

"You're going to have the best visit ever."

CHAPTER SIXTEEN

Charlie

Almost a week later, on Thursday night, Charlie sat in his car in the church parking lot, watching men file into the building. There were more people here than he'd expected; Kellan had made it sound like this was an intimate group. There were at least fifteen people, by his count. And he'd been in the parking lot for a while in his warm car, wiping his sweaty hands on his pants. It was so dark he could barely see the ferns and rhododendrons that made up its sorry excuse for landscaping.

He should go inside the squat brick building; it was friendly and familiar despite its 70s architecture. He even wanted to. But when he tried to reach inside for the energy, he felt cold. Colder than the winter weather; he felt icy and strange. It was the way he felt sometimes when he needed to put aside whatever personal thing was happening and go sell someone a car they didn't need. But this would be personal—intensely personal. If it wasn't personal, there was no point in doing it. He'd never had a problem with little white lies, but it felt entirely different to look people in the eye and tell the untwisted truth.

Kellan came out the front door, searching the large gravel parking lot with his gaze until it landed on Charlie's SUV. Then he pulled out his phone.

Kellan: Someone said you were having a bit of trouble coming inside. Thought I'd check on you.

Charlie: I don't think I can do this.

Kellan: Okay.

Charlie: That's it? "Okay"?

Kellan: What do you want me to say? If you're not ready to come inside, I'm not going to try to convince you.

Kellan: Not my style.

Charlie had thought he'd fight a little harder to get him to try it, but maybe he was just too used to fighting.

Charlie: I'll come inside for a few minutes, but I have an appointment tonight.

Kellan: What appointment?

Rude of him to see right through a lie. Kellan was a weird pastor; pastors were supposed to be gentle and generous and gracious when you lied to their face. At least, Pastor Vern had been.

Charlie: An appointment with myself. To drink and watch reality television alone.

Oops. It was widely known that Kellan was in recovery; it was probably insensitive to say things like that. But it was the truth. The wine and TV was a ritual he'd started after Starla left. People were always talking about self-care, weren't they? This was as close as he could get.

> **Kellan**: I see. How's that helping you heal?
> **Charlie**: it's not. but it's easy.
> **Kellan**: Okay. We'll be here next week if you change your mind.
> **Kellan**: Unless you want to start healing. Right now.

Charlie watched as Kellan turned and went back into the building, feeling unsure. He wanted too many things, unattainable things. He couldn't go back in time and undo his mistakes, but he could stop making mistakes if he could gather the courage.

This was going to be uncomfortable. Charlie pushed the button to turn off his car and got out, zipping up his coat. He went inside with his head held high. He was Charlie Miller; no one who wasn't attending the group had to know why he was there. He could be dropping off donations or teaching a class. It was reasonable.

And as it turned out, a lot of the men he'd seen going into the building were there for a Boy Scouts leader training; he saw the sign for it as he made his way down the long, carpeted hallway. He peeked into the Sunday School room; there were only four other men there, and thankfully, enough adult size chairs for all of them. He used to pick up

Aiden from this room; there was still a spot on the carpet where he'd spilled grape juice once during snack, but it looked like they'd just put the plastic table with the loaner Bibles and the cookies over it and moved on.

He knew all of these men: Burt Graham, who drove the truck for a local dairy. Brian Singer, who'd played football with him in high school. Chris Tanner, whose family sat near his in church—their old spot, anyway. He gave them all a nod and a grimace; it felt more appropriate than a big smile. But they smiled at him, anyway; Chris stood up to shake his hand, and then he felt obligated to go around the whole room. Kellan just smiled smugly at him when he sat down, and it was annoying. Again, this was not pastoral behavior, and now he saw why his dad had been against Kellan when he was on the search committee.

He handed Charlie a book; he hadn't read it, of course, but maybe he could follow along. Interesting that it was a marriage book. He supposed that there weren't very many divorce books out there.

"I'm gonna do my standard spiel for Charlie's benefit, but it doesn't hurt all of us to remember. What's said here stays here. Build up, don't tear down. Remember that we're all here for different reasons, but ultimately the same reason—a relationship we cared about ended. So cut each other some slack if things don't come out right or we've got some anger piled up, which is usually just sadness in disguise." Kellan gestured to Burt. "Let's talk about our weeks first."

Charlie silenced his phone and tried to focus on what the others were saying. Burt's ex-wife had a new boyfriend, and he'd run into them at Riverside on Saturday morning. Charlie knew what that felt like, and he nodded along.

Chris's spouse had also been his bookkeeper, so his office was now a mess, and he was struggling to find someone new. Charlie nodded along with that, too. Chris had also found their wedding video on a bookshelf when he was looking for something to read, and he got a little misty. Charlie shifted in the hard metal folding chair. This was the part he'd been dreading. This was what he didn't want. He didn't want to sit here and cry. If he didn't let the hurt surface, it was easier to stomach. But that wasn't how change happened. He looked up and realized everyone was waiting for him to talk.

"Sorry." He cleared his throat. "Well, my business is thriving. We're on track to do 12% better than last..."

Kellan was giving him the eyebrow.

No. Right. This wasn't why he was here. It wasn't about impressing anyone. Unfortunately, that was still his default mode.

"I'm sure you all know Starla and some of the stuff that went down between us..." He winced as he thought back to her impassioned speech from the front rock of this very church about how over they were. He'd still thought he could win her back then. They were watching him patiently, and Charlie wrestled back his memories enough to find some words. "I'm...lonely," he blurted out, and the others nodded. "I just miss being touched. I miss having someone to debrief the day with, you know?" He stared down at the industrial carpet, and a thought dawned on him. "Yeah, you know. I guess that's the point of this." He paused. "Does anyone else have little kids?"

Just Chris raised his hand.

"So I love having them. It's this minuscule taste of what we had before, this little window into what was. And then they leave again, and the house is like a tomb. Only I'm still there, now with a mess to clean up." Lots of fervent nodding made him a little better. "I got a nanny. That's going well. And she's someone I'd never touch, so there's no...temptation."

"If I can add something," Burt started, and Charlie nodded. *Yes, please. Anyone else talk before I embarrass myself further.*

"I used to think that way, too. I cheated on her. But it's not a sin to want to love again."

"Love the way you put that, Burt," Kellan said. "Sometimes when we've made a truckload of mistakes, it's easier to just shut the door on something instead of trying to learn how to do it in a healthy way. I'd like to encourage you to stay open, stay..." Kellan stopped abruptly, his gaze out the window. The rest of them turned. A slender redhead was coming up the front sidewalk with a little boy in tow, and the pastor was frowning. "I...I'll be right back. Brian, would you share your week while I'm gone?" Kellan was up and out of his seat before Brian could even nod.

Brian obediently launched into a retelling of his week—he was seeing someone new and really liked her—then, as if by an unspoken agreement, they all went back to staring at the woman out the window. Kellan had met her on the sidewalk; his shoulders looked locked up with tension, and he was staring down at the child intently, even as he spoke to the woman.

"Is it just me, or does that kid look exactly like him?" Brian asked, and they all nodded.

"Did you know he had a kid?" Chris asked, and Charlie shook his head. Just a minute ago, he hadn't raised his hand when he'd polled them about little kids.

Abruptly, Kellan turned and went back inside the building. Brian added a bit to more to his dating story, so they were all laughing when Kellan walked back into the room.

"I hate to do this, guys, but something's come up. I really need to take care of this. Would someone else be willing to lead tonight? I'm sorry."

A flustered Brian took the leader book Kellan held out, and he was gone again before anyone could say anything.

"Well, this is a first," Burt said, sitting back in his chair. Charlie couldn't help but agree. He'd finally made it to the group, and the leader bailed on him. At least he'd be able to look Ruth in the eye next week and tell her he'd done it. Not that it mattered what she thought...

Yeah. Right.

CHAPTER SEVENTEEN

Ruth

A few days later, Ruth was just drying the last dinner plate when her phone rang. *Charlie?*

"Who's calling you at this time of night?" her dad asked, peering up at her from the kitchen table where his paperwork was spread out. The clock on the oven said 9:15.

"Hello?"

"I apologize for calling so late," Charlie said, and his voice had a falling-down tired quality to it. "But do you happen to know where Em's koala is? We cannot find it anywhere and she can't sleep without it."

Interesting that there was no blame attached there, thought Ruth. That was a bit of personal growth.

"Did you check under the kitchen table? I often find him there."

"We did. Under the kitchen table, under the bed, in the closet, in the playroom...he's not in any of his usual places."

"Hmm," said Ruth, moving toward the window to look toward their house, as if she could find it from there. "That's really odd. What about in your office? Or the gym?"

"We looked there, too." Through the phone, she could hear Emily in the background, making those big gushy sniffles after someone's been crying hard. And the decision was made.

"I'll be right there."

"No, Ruth, it's okay. We'll figure something out...Ruth?"

She hung up. There was no reason to let the little girl suffer. She toed into her shoes and grabbed her coat.

Ranger's voice had an edge to it. "Where are you going?"

"To work. I'll be back in a few minutes."

"Why does he need you over there now?"

"Lost animal. Em can't sleep without Coleman."

"So that's their problem. You can't work every minute of the day."

Ruth stared at him. Someday, the moment might be laughable, but not today. He couldn't even hear the irony of his words. These brothers were never going to change. If someone was going to change things, it would have to be her.

"You're absolutely correct. So I'm gonna need you to toss that laundry into the dryer for me. And when you say you're going to cook dinner, you should actually do it instead of letting everyone fend for themselves with sandwiches and Apple Jacks. Because I might not be around forever."

Ranger and her dad were both staring at her like they didn't know her. *Maybe because they really don't.*

"What does that mean?" her brother asked quietly.

"Just what it sounds like." She shoved her arms into her coat. "I'm thinking about moving out. I'd still send what I can for Mom. But I can't take care of all of you by myself." *Uh oh.* Tears were threatening to fall now. Time to fly this nest. She was out the door and power walking toward the cut-through when she heard Ranger call after her. Crunching steps behind her told her he was running, and she paused. He was holding something out to her.

"Flashlight."

"Thanks," she mumbled, and when she took it from him, she realized she wasn't wearing gloves, either. Then Ruth looked down. "Ranger, you're not wearing shoes!"

"You took off too fast," he complained. "This is on you."

She couldn't stand there for another minute. Ruth turned and walked into the woods without another word. The kind gesture of not wanting her to walk in the dark could not possibly be offset by blaming her for his own impulsivity. That was it. She could not stay in this house any longer.

Ruth turned and strode down across the yard in the dark, not bothering to turn on the light out of stubbornness more than lack of need. When she tripped over a root and fell, only her pride was truly hurt. But she arrived at Charlie's with muddy knees and palms and she hurriedly wiped them on her jeans as she climbed the steps. She didn't bother knocking.

"Hello?"

"We're up here," Charlie called.

Emily's face, tear-stained and puffy, appeared at the top of the stairs. "Ruth? Do you know where Coleman is?"

"No, sweetheart, but let's look together."

Emily's despair was immediate, and she gestured dramatically on each sentence for emphasis. "We *did* look, we *have* looked, he's *nowhere*."

She hurried up the stairs to comfort her, and a memory smacked into Ruth like a golden retriever—Emily, running back upstairs that morning to grab... "Wait. Didn't you take him to school for show and tell?"

Emily stopped sniffling. "Oh."

Charlie's chin dropped to his chest, and he pinched the bridge of his nose, as if it were the center of his patience and he was trying to hold it together.

"Go get him, please, and let's get to bed," Ruth prompted quietly, mindful that Aiden and Dahlia were both probably asleep nearby, and Emily clamped her arms around Ruth's waist.

"Will you tuck me in?"

Ruth glanced up at Charlie, not sure what he was thinking, but he gave her a stiff nod.

"Sure. But be quick. I gotta go home."

The girl skipped off, and Ruth went into her room and straightened the covers and turned off the overhead light. She could feel Charlie hovering in the doorway, watching her, and she almost felt bad that she'd found it so quickly. Almost. But this was why families were willing to pay her such a good rate; she'd go above and beyond for any of them. An accusing voice in the back of her mind whispered that she'd never come running quite like this before, but she parried back that she'd never worked for her neighbor before. It wasn't an inconvenience if it was him. Before she could correct the thought, Emily came bouncing into the room.

"Okay, let's try to settle down now, all right?"

"Will you sing to me?"

It was always a question she dreaded. She didn't mind so much when it was just the kids, but Charlie was still standing there. She paused for a moment and glared at him out of the corner of her eye, hoping he would take the hint and go do something else. But the man didn't move a muscle.

Quietly, she started into her favorite lullaby.

Tell me why the stars do shine,
Tell me why the ivy twines,
Tell me why the sky's so blue,
And I will tell you just why I love you.
Because God made the stars to shine,
Because God made the ivy twine,
Because God made the sky so blue
Because God made you, that's why I love you.

It was probably too intimate for children that weren't hers, but she did love them. She wanted them to drift off to dreams knowing that someone did. Most of the families she worked for, she didn't worry about that...but a few she had. Not this one. But it was a pleasant song, and it didn't have too many r's in it. It was her best chance at sounding good; she'd sung it to her younger brothers so many times. Emily's eyes were already heavy, and she snuggled down deeper under the pink down comforter as Ruth finished. Ruth gave her hand a squeeze as she stood up and wished her sweet dreams.

"Door open," Em mumbled as the adults moved out into the hall.

"You make that look so easy," Charlie said, his voice low, his eyes on his bare feet. What was it with the men in her life not covering their darn feet?

"I'm glad you called me. I don't know if she would've remembered it was in her backpack."

"I shouldn't have to," he muttered, and the frustration bled into the words like a drop of food coloring into a glass of water. She could practically see it spreading.

"Why shouldn't you?" She started down the stairs slowly, hoping he would follow. "You're not allowed to need help?"

Charlie fell into step behind her as they descended. "You wouldn't have needed help."

"I haven't been here long enough to prove it, but I absolutely need help sometimes. Everyone does."

"Well, I'll pay you for your time." Irritation burned like the time she rubbed her eyes after cutting up jalapenos.

"I didn't come because I work here. I came because I care. About all of you."

It was too close, she knew. Too close to the truth she hadn't dared to say out loud...and knew he could never reciprocate. But the pain in his eyes was too much. He felt like a failure; she could see it. She knew that look in the eyes of her dad when her mom was hurting.

"Thank you," he whispered, and it was so broken, so thick with emotion, she couldn't help it. Ruth opened her arms and just stood there, waiting. His guarded look came back, just for a second, before a tear rolled down his cheek.

"You don't have to," he said even as he shuffled toward her.

"I know I don't," she said, shaking her outstretched arms insistently.

As he leaned into her embrace, she felt silly for still wearing her winter coat. But it would make it weird if she paused the hug to take it off, wouldn't it? It was already plenty weird, standing in her boss's entryway, holding him while his kids were asleep upstairs.

His warmth bled through his gray T-shirt onto her hands, and she realized for the first time that he might be in his pajamas, too. It was even weirder than she'd feared.

"Ruth."

"Yes?"

"Why are you shaking?"

"Would you believe I'm cold?"

He scoffed a little, but he leaned in harder, and she felt the moment his laugh broke into a sob in the hard puff of breath against her neck.

"Oh, Charlie," she whispered, and when she rubbed his back, he just cried harder. He wasn't a child, so she didn't make any of the soothing shushing noises that she normally would. And frankly, she didn't want to discourage his tears, because he clearly needed a good cry.

"I'm sorry, Ruth," he choked out, but he pulled her closer.

"Sorry for being human?" she murmured into his soft dark hair. "Apology not accepted."

His body shook with a laugh again, even though she could hear from the way he was sniffling that he was still crying.

"I should let you go."

Don't you dare.

"That would be fine."

"Or I could keep holding you."

"That'd be fine, too." She paused. "Wait, who says you're holding me? I thought I was holding you."

"No, I'm definitely holding you."

"But I initiated the hug. I held my arms out. I think I have obvious hug ownership here."

He laughed again, and her head started swimming a little. *I'm holding Charlie Miller, who isn't at all the person I thought he was.* He squeezed her tighter for a long moment, then relented...but he still didn't let go.

"You're terrible at this," she informed him. "The squeeze is a clear sign the hug is over."

"So let go then."

"We could be here all night at this rate," she deadpanned, and that broke the moment. He stepped back hastily, but his gaze searched her face, so she smiled at him. "My family's probably worried about me."

"I think you could say that any hour of the day."

She chuckled. "Probably. But I think I'm moving out soon."

His eyebrows went high. "Oh, really? Well, please don't give them any sense that I was involved in that decision. I have no desire to be punched."

She stuck her hands in her pockets. "I don't think they'd punch you..."

"Don't you?" When she said nothing, he crossed his arms. "Well, for what it's worth, I support that decision. And if you want to stay in the guest room until you find a place, you can."

"*That* would get you punched." Ruth opened the front door; she'd worn her shoes in the house, but Charlie didn't say anything. "See you tomorrow?"

"Gosh, I hope so. I think we've proven I can't do this on my own."

Ruth just shook her head. "Night, Chuck."

"Good night, Zane."

She smiled all the way back to her house.

CHAPTER EIGHTEEN

Charlie

From his bedroom window, Charlie watched Ruth walk as far as he could, just to make sure she was okay. Who was he kidding? He was the one who wasn't okay; she wasn't the one who'd broken down in his arms. It *had* been her hug; he was just receiving it. But holding her had done something strange to his heart. It was an innocent physical connection, entirely appropriate among friends. And yet, it hadn't been. Having her in his arms had given rise to all sorts of other thoughts that he had no business entertaining about her...not that she probably thought about him that way. Hearing her sing to Em had started the thoughts, though, which wasn't how it usually went for him. *See a beautiful woman, flirt with a beautiful woman...* He usually never knew a thing about them before he went for it.

Not that he was going to go for it with Ruth. He didn't date anymore. There was no point in thinking about it. But he still didn't leave the window until she'd disappeared completely into the dark.

Charlie pulled out his phone.

Charlie: You sold that Streetfighter yet?

Sawyer: Nope. Haven't had time to list it anywhere. Why, you know someone who's interested?

Charlie: Yeah.

Charlie: Me.

Charlie couldn't focus at all the next day. It was the kind of day where he would normally roll up his sleeves and wash cars, but it was already raining. He still talked to a few customers under his giant red golf umbrella and answered a lot of emails and online inquiries...but no sales. Finally, it was time to go see the motorcycle.

As usual, the drive seemed to take forever. Traffic was heavy coming back into Timber Falls, meaning that he saw seven other cars. Starla and Sawyer had the kids, so he went straight up the mountain, following the winding forest service road. The trees were still dripping, but the rain had stopped, and Aiden and Sawyer were out in the garage. His kid seemed to spend a lot of time out there, and it made him wonder if he missed coming to work with him. Maybe Aiden was more like his Uncle Jason than Charlie had realized.

He wanted to go into the house to see Ruth, but he couldn't think of a good excuse as to why, which made him grouchy. Aiden and Sawyer turned when he came to the door of the garage.

"Hey, man," Sawyer greeted. He no longer looked at Charlie as though he'd like to punch him, so Charlie considered that progress. "You here to see the bike?"

"Yeah."

Sawyer gestured to the motorcycle closest to the door. "There she is."

Charlie glanced at it; he cared more about how fast it went than how it looked. He needed to *fly*.

"What's its top speed?"

Sawyer frowned a little. "Uh, I'm not sure. I can look at the specs, but I haven't tried it out myself..."

"No, that's okay. I'm capable of..." Charlie's voice drifted off as he looked around the garage. It felt strangely homey; strings of outdoor globe lights crisscrossed above him from the rafters, and it smelled of fresh pine and motor oil. The place was organized with surgical precision, which made sense given Sawyer's other line of work.

"Aiden, can you give your papas a minute to talk?" Sawyer asked, setting down his lug wrench.

The boy scowled, but he hopped off the stool and dragged his feet toward the door. Charlie offered him a high five on his way by, and Aiden smashed into his palm without hesitation. As soon as the boy reached the porch, Sawyer turned to him.

"Look, I ain't about to tell you what to do with your money, and Lord knows I'd be glad to make a sale, but why are you buying this machine? You're obviously not interested in it."

"Yes, I am. I'm here to see it, aren't I?"

"Quit being petulant and be real with me for a minute."

Petulant. That was a good word. He'd have to tuck that one away for his conversations with Ruth.

"Are you going to let me buy it or not?"

"Have you taken a class?"

Charlie rolled his eyes. "I know how to ride a motorcycle."

"I'll take that as a no. Do you have insurance?"

"I will once I own it, but I can't do that until I own it, now can I?"

"Petulant," Sawyer grumbled, tossing his rag aside. "Well, if you're dead set on it, I guess you'd better take it for a ride." Sawyer wheeled it outside; Aiden was watching from the front porch, but bounded down when he saw them come out.

"Can I go, too?"

"Uh, let me get used to it a little, then you can." At Sawyer's frown, he amended the statement. "If you go get on your helmet and jacket and stuff."

"I'm going," he said over his shoulder as he ran into the house.

"Take it easy on the forest service road until you get to the pavement. The gravel's real slick when it's wet—"

"Devereaux. I know how to ride a motorcycle."

Sawyer sighed. "Are you having a midlife crisis? Can't you just buy a Camaro like the rest of the middle-aged men?"

Charlie cocked his head as he swung his leg over the seat. "That's a thought. They *are* made by Chevrolet."

"See? Very on brand for you and less likely to maim or kill you."

"I don't hear you fussing like this when Ken wants to try something out."

"Because he knows what he's doing...whereas you—"

"Dude! Chill! If I wreck it, I'll pay for it."

Sawyer paced closer. "It's not the *bike* I'm worried about, you donkey."

"Aww, he's starting to like me." It came out sarcastic, but inside, it felt like letting go of a fist that has been clenched tightly too long, blood flowing back into extremities, relief setting free the deep fear he held that Sawyer permanently hated him.

"Barely. Maybe I just don't want your children to cry."

"Valid," Charlie said as he started the engine, "and as weird as it is, they're our children now." Smoothly, he opened the throttle to let the motorcycle roll forward. He did three laps around the large gravel area in front of the house before Aiden came back. Then Charlie paused so he could climb on the back and accept the helmet Sawyer offered him. When Aiden's arms came around his waist, it surprised him how big they seemed, and then they were off. The curves of the forest service road were fun, but Charlie really got what he wanted when they got to the highway.

"Woo hoo!" Aiden howled into the microphone, and Charlie grinned. They were only going forty-five, but it was exhilarating even without the wind on his face.

This was the feeling he'd been craving; that lack of responsibility, that feeling that he could do no wrong. He was being careful, knowing that Aiden was on the back. He'd always have to be a bit careful. Because he had done wrong, and it had cost him the most important person in his life.

But he needed to feel unhindered sometimes. Everyone did. The way he'd gone about it had been wrong, but maybe this could be an outlet for that need, that deep longing. And Ruth wasn't wrong that he wasn't good at letting go sometimes. Well, this would show her. He could let go with the best of them. Charlie took them down past Detroit Lake and turned around at the marina.

"Can't we go farther?" Aiden asked, but Charlie shook his head.

"No good place to turn around for a while." Civilization sort of dropped off the map out that way. This was definitely the direction he was going when he got his first opportunity for a solo ride. A few minutes later, they pulled back into Sawyer's driveway.

"I miss you, Dad."

The words surprised him. "Aren't you having fun with Mom and Papa?"

"Yes. But I still miss you. Maybe you could move into the cabin."

It was such a tenderly vulnerable thing to say, and Charlie's heart cracked a little.

"I miss you, too, bud. But I don't think the cabin's the place for me."

There was no chance to extend the conversation as Sawyer walked over.

"What'd you think?"

"It was great. I'll take it." He'd intended it as a toy for him, but if it gave him more meaningful time with Aiden, that wasn't a bad thing, either. "You wanna follow me down and I'll bring you back?"

"You're not gonna strand me?" Sawyer smirked.

"Not gonna lie, I considered it. But it's bad for business."

"Ah yes, everything goes back to that, doesn't it?"

Now he definitely wanted to leave him on the side of the road. But the person whose reaction he really wanted was coming down the stairs of the house with his baby draped over one arm, football-style.

"What do you think?"

Ruth walked around the machine, letting her fingertips trail over the leather and the chrome, and Charlie couldn't tell what she was thinking at all.

It doesn't matter. This was for me. She doesn't have to approve. It doesn't—

"I love it."

Sawyer chuckled as he took Dahlia from her and he nodded with his head for Aiden to come inside with him. Maybe the man was useful after all.

Charlie uncrossed his arms. "Well, that's not what I thought you were going to say."

"Why?"

He didn't know what to do with them now, his arms. They felt too long. And heavy? He recrossed them over his chest. This was a natural posture, right?

"Just thought I might get a lecture about being practical or how dads should be an example or something."

"I'm not your mom, sorry. You want practical, go ask someone else. I spend all day telling kids to be safe." She was still staring at it...was that longing in her gaze? Was sweet Ruth a secret motorcycle fan? A sudden image flashed into his mind of putting her on the back of it and driving out to the coast, whipping through the cool forest, the blue sky and waves beckoning them. Charlie shook his head; he wasn't putting his nanny on his motorcycle.

"Not that you're not boring."

"I beg your pardon?" Charlie huffed. "What does that mean?"

"You're still boring. This," she said, waving a hand toward his new toy, "this changes nothing."

"How am I boring?"

"All you do is work. You have no joy."

"My kids bring me joy."

She was watching him now, one hand still on the seat. "Do they? You don't play with them."

"Hey, I played Pretty Pretty Princess with Em just last week!" And he hadn't wanted to, either. At least it was short.

"You did that because she wanted to, not because you wanted to."

Charlie took a step closer to her. "Well, that's what it means to be a parent sometimes. Life can't be all fun and games."

Ruth nodded slowly. "True. But it can't be no fun and games, either. I bet you don't even play with your breath."

What? What does that even mean?

Charlie cocked his head. "You're a difficult person to talk to."

"Look," she said, tipping her head back. Ruth released a cloud into the cold air. "What is that?"

"What do you mean, what is it? It's carbon dioxide."

"No, it's steam from a train engine. It's cigarette smoke. It's the air that lingers over a lake just before sunrise. It's whatever you want it to be. But you have to have an imagination for that to work."

"Hey." Charlie paced closer, and the hands he hadn't known what to do with earlier were now balled at his sides. "I have an imagination."

"Not that I've observed."

That's because in the past twenty-four hours, I've mostly imagined kissing you, and I'm not going to do that.

"Well, you don't observe me all the time."

Ruth got a strange look on her face that he couldn't interpret—jealousy? embarrassment?—and her gaze fell to the machine again.

"I'm happy you got a new toy, Chuck. You deserve it."

"Are you headed home?"

She cocked her head. "No, I'm going to the Audubon Society meeting."

He didn't think he'd heard her right. "Say that again?"

"Audubon? You know. Audubon."

"You...attend a group that's interested in German motorways?"

Ruth stared at him for a moment, then doubled over laughing. "No," she howled. "Not 'autobahn,' AUDUBON, the bird guy."

Well, now he felt silly. But even though she was definitely laughing *at* him, he didn't actually care, and that seemed like a first.

Charlie crossed his arms in faux annoyance. "I think it's a simple mistake to make."

"No, it's not, Chuck. It's definitely not." Ruth wiped a tear from the corner of her eye.

"You're interested in the motorcycle, so you might be interested in—"

"Stop. Please stop. My abs can't take it." She was indeed holding her stomach, bracing herself against the bike as tears rolled down her face.

"You're making fun of me for being boring, and you like *birds*? Really, Zane?"

"Hey," she said, straightening, wiping her face, "birds are amazing. They're the best thing about this planet."

"Have you never drunk coffee?"

"The statement stands."

"Or eaten a cinnamon roll?"

"Birds are better."

"Wow. With icing, right? And melted butter on top?"

"Guess I know what I'm making you for your birthday." An image flashed through his mind of Ruth baking him his own pan of cinnamon rolls, putting candles in the top, forcing him to make a wish, wrapping her arms around him from behind, her vanilla scent enveloping him, and he felt a longing for that moment as deep as he ever had.

"I'm just saying that it's more accessible than watching birds fly around and tweet and whatever."

"Maybe to you. Birds fuel my soul. They give me a reason to get out of bed."

"My paycheck's not doing it for you, huh?"

"Sorry, no." Ruth looked at her phone. "I'd better get home."

It was nice to talk to you. You're the most interesting person I've ever met. Thank you for not judging me. Charlie didn't think he should say any of that, so he just said, "Drive safe," which seemed like an innocuous thing to say. For a split second, he wished she could drive his truck down, just so he could talk to her alone again when they arrived at his house. *Pointless. Stop torturing yourself. This is masochism.*

"I always do, Chuck. Enjoy your reality TV and glass of wine."

"I will, thank you. Wait, how do you know I drink wine?"

"Don't leave your glass upstairs if you don't want it known..." she said as she crossed the front porch, giving him a wave as she went inside.

CHAPTER NINETEEN

Ruth

A few days later, Ruth was halfway through a game of Portlandopoly when she heard the garage door go up. Her heart leapt in her chest, which was silly. *So silly. So pointless.* You weren't supposed to race to the door like a Labrador when your boss came home. She did like the sound of that motorcycle, though. It was the sound of freedom. She wouldn't mind more of that. She'd been thinking a lot about her decision to move out; it was going to put financial pressure on the family if she couldn't find somewhere cheap to stay. The idea of a roommate didn't appeal to her, but she might not have much of a choice. But she knew it would have that motorcycle feeling, that powerful "yeah, we're going to do this my way for once" feeling. She'd just have to get creative about her opportunities, but she was good at that. Maybe she could eat more meals here...

Charlie opened the door, and she didn't let herself look. He probably had helmet hair, anyway. *He'd better, or he'll suffer Deputy Painter's wrath **and** mine.*

"Hey," he said, "Anybody got a hug for old Dad?" Emily held out her arms, but was clearly still considering whether to buy Powell's Bookstore. (No-brainer—always buy Powell's.) Aiden waved at him without looking up from the tablet.

"Wow, tough crowd."

Emily seemed to register what his presence meant for the first time. "Why are you home so early?"

Charlie slid his hands in his pockets and shrugged. "Just wanted to see my kids."

"Can we still have pancakes for dinner? Ruth was going to make pancakes."

"No, I was going to make crepes. They're *like* pancakes." She heard Dahlia calling in her wordless exclamation of baby outrage upstairs. "I'll get her."

"No, that's okay," Charlie said, turning for the stairs. "I'm going that way, anyway."

She should get her bag together; in just a minute, he'd come down in soft cotton, holding that sweet girl on his shoulder, and watching him just seemed to cement her crush harder. She should prepare to flee.

"Can you stay and eat with us?" Emily asked, attaching herself to Ruth like she'd read her thoughts.

"No, I should get home. Your dad can take it from here. I'll make you crepes tomorrow."

"Tomorrow's pizza night," Aiden said from the couch.

"Monday, then. Just don't give him a hard time, please. He's doing his best." She gently extricated herself from Emily, giving her an affectionate hair ruffle as she stood. She was waiting by the front door when he reappeared at the top of the stairs. Oh, the gray University of Oregon shirt. That one was her favorite. It fit him just right across his shoulders...

"Anything I should know?" he asked, cradling Dahlia in the crook of his arm.

"Besides 'always hold a baby with two hands on the stairs'?"

Ruth nearly slapped a hand over her mouth. She didn't know why these sassy comments flew out of her mouth around Charlie, but it was so inconvenient. Thankfully, he grinned as he transferred his daughter to his shoulder.

"I defer to the expert. Anything *about my kids' behavior* I should know?"

"Nope." She edged toward the door and bent to put on her shoes. "Quiet afternoon. Homework is done. Laundry's folded, except yours, of course."

"Sounds good." When he didn't say goodbye, Ruth glanced up at him. He looked like he wanted to say something else, just gazing at her with subtle amusement and maybe something else. Something like want.

"I have to go," she muttered.

"You could stay, if you want. I like crepes. They're mostly protein."

Was he inviting her to dinner? Or did he just feel bad that she wouldn't earn as much money tonight?

"No, I should go. See you tomorrow, barring disaster."

"In case of disaster, please text," he called as she closed the door behind her. *He shouldn't care. I want him to, but he shouldn't.* She thought about Charlie as she took the cut-through home along the river. It laughed at her, bumping over rocks and pouring over fallen logs, laughed at her for getting her poor heart all tangled up like the long stringy sea-weed that flowed off the smooth, sunken stones. It was very silly. She knew that. But she didn't care. Everyone was al-lowed a fantasy now and again. Everyone wanted things they couldn't have; hers just happened to be her boss's heart.

She kicked at rocks and felt the sting of them through her thin shoe. She resented the wind's gentle caress on her face, its winter kiss so much less than she wanted. Ruth was almost done feeling sorry for herself by the time she got home. But she'd gotten so muddy, she thought she'd better go in through the laundry room, rather than track through the living room. She was still coming through the door when she heard deep voices in the kitchen.

"She was serious. She's going to leave." Ranger's voice was loud, like he was afraid they weren't listening to him.

"Never going to happen," Levi said, and Ruth shut the door as quietly as she could, even though she felt the words like a slap. "She's not going to abandon Mom like that."

"It's got nothing to do with Mom," Wyatt argued. "It's about us. We have to pitch in and help more."

"She works less than we do," Ryan said, but the statement lacked conviction.

"Really?" Ranger snapped. "I must be rooming with someone else, then. Because I feel like I barely see her, and when I do, she's working *for us*. How can you not see that?"

"This is her way of helping out," Levi said. "We bring in more money, so it's fair."

"Fair!" Wyatt cried. "She stayed here and kept everything running while you went off to culinary school; how is that fair? She's the only reason Ryan and I didn't drop out of high school. She's had to be an adult since she was a kid. And it's absolutely not fair."

Tears sprang to Ruth's eyes as she listened from the laundry room, and she wiped them on her mittens.

"Did you ever even consider that she might've had a dream? Something *she* wanted to do with her life besides wash your clothes and vacuum?"

"Look, Ruth's an adult," Levi growled. "She's free to make her own choices. But she knows how much we need her. She's not going to take off on us like that."

"So it's okay to just take advantage of her kindness?" Wyatt asked. "Of her sense of responsibility?"

"Hey." Four bearded faces whipped toward her. She went to the sink and washed her hands as they stood there in awkward silence.

"How much of that did you hear?" Levi asked, and if she wasn't mistaken, he actually sounded a tiny bit chagrined for once.

"Oh, I heard just enough." She dried her hands, then she pulled out the white rice and measured out two cups, letting it plink into the pot in a waterfall.

"So?" It was Levi again.

"So what?" she asked, grabbing the liquid measuring cup.

He grunted impatiently. "Are you leaving?"

"I thought you already knew I wasn't." It was petty, but he deserved it. Mom and Dad weren't here to put him in his place.

"Ruthie..." Ryan started.

"I don't need to hear any more. I'll keep you apprised of my plans."

"Apprised?" Wyatt snorted.

"Yes," she said, her face hot. "Just because I didn't go to college doesn't mean I can't expand my vocabulary." She'd heard the word on an episode of *Meet the Press* that Charlie was watching in the morning. *PBS for the win.*

Wyatt groaned. "Ruthie, I didn't mean—"

She whirled. "Enough. I have had *enough* of being the butt of the jokes and the one who suffers in silence. You all act like I'm the stupidest person in this family. Well, guess what? You're right." A sob tried to come out and caught in her throat. "And I'm just proving it by staying here. It's time for you all to grow up. And you're never going to do it if I'm here to take care of you."

"Ruthie, we don't think you're stupid." Ryan's voice was too sweet, too concerned for her to bear. "And no one's making jokes about you behind your back. We all love you. We really appreciate all you do for us."

She turned back to the counter and prayed she wouldn't cut herself as the broccoli and green onions blurred in front of her through her tears. "Dinner will be at 5:30. Now please leave."

She heard them shuffle off as a group. *Right.* Because as much as they argued and teased, they were a group: they were the kids. And she was just their big sister who really hadn't been a kid for a long, long time.

She was ready to be something else. The question was whether they were, too.

CHAPTER TWENTY

Charlie

At 6:51 a.m., Charlie got a text.

Ruth: I'm so sorry, but I woke up with a terrible cold. I can't come today.

Well, that was a bummer, but it wasn't her fault. She probably got it from his kids, after all.

Charlie: Okay, thanks for letting me know.

He'd only had front-desk employees before; he paid Jason the same whether or not he came to work, mostly because Jason loved being at work and rarely got sick. Technically, Charlie owned the garage, but he felt his brother was more of a partner. But if this was an actual employee, she should get paid sick days too, shouldn't she? He tried to remember back to how his jobs had been in high school, but he couldn't. They'd all been short summer stints, barely long enough to learn the ropes of something, let alone accrue sick time.

A quick internet search told him that most people got five to nine days, depending on how long they'd been at the job. She hadn't been here long, obviously, but he still felt it was important. And it had nothing to do with his conscience stinging as he pictured Ruth lying in bed, worrying about money.

Charlie: You'll be paid your normal rate for to-day.

Ruth: Well, that's very kind of you, but also...why?

Charlie: You deserve paid sick leave, too.

Ruth: It's not in my contract. I'm hourly.

Charlie: I'll fax you an amendment and you can bring it when you're better.

Ruth: Wow. Okay. Thank you.

Charlie: I'm just following the law.

Ruth: Go eat a donut, Chuck, you've got the grumps again.

Charlie: Just once, could we have a professional conversation without it devolving into childishness?

Ruth: I'm sick, what's your excuse?

Charlie: Get some rest.

Ruth: Thanks again for the sick leave.

Charlie: I'll see you tomorrow if you're feeling better.

Ruth: "You're welcome" is spelled like this: Y-O-U...

Charlie: GOODBYE, RUTH.

Ruth: You're a worse speller than I thought.

Fuming, Charlie punched the call button next to her name. *You shouldn't let her get the better of you like this...* But now it was ringing, so what was he supposed to do?

"People don't usually call once they've said goodbye." Fudge, she sounded terrible. Dahlia fussed at him from the floor where he'd set her down under a toy with dangling things, and he picked her up.

"I'm a fantastic speller."

Her laugh quickly devolved into a hacking cough, and his concern deepened. "Sure you are, Chuck."

"Have you taken medicine?"

"I have a mom, Chuck."

"Yeah, but it's not like she's taking care of you today, is she?"

There was a long pause. It was the kind of pause that let you know you'd said something wrong without saying a word.

"Sorry, that was..."

"Insensitive. Yeah. Even though it's accurate."

"I didn't mean to sound like I was blaming her; I'm sure she'd help you if she could. I just know you," he blundered on. "And you're great at taking care of other people. But I bet you're terrible at letting others care for you."

"If anyone offers to take care of me, I promise to let them."

Charlie felt her invitation hanging in the quiet on the line, and he fumbled for something to say. "Well, good." But then it occurred to him that maybe no one had offered, and that had his stomach sinking like his profits last year. "I'll check on you later."

Ruth chuckled again, and her subsequent wet sniffle made him want to hold the phone farther away from his ear, lest he be infected. "Whatever you say, Chuckles."

"No. I draw the line at Chuckles. It will not stand."

"Bye, boss." Charlie listened until the line went dead. He turned to find Aiden staring at him, arms crossed.

"Where's Ruth?"

Charlie turned to grab a box of cereal out of the pantry. "She's sick today. You're stuck with me." Being in the kitchen reminded him that Ruth was supposed to come tomorrow to help him cook for Easter on Sunday, and that had his heart and his stomach sinking. He'd so wanted to show the family that he could do this...maybe he'd have to get takeout after all.

"Yay, a Daddy day!" Emily cheered, hugging him from behind, and Charlie smiled begrudgingly.

He hurried them toward food and backpacks and shoes and gathered up everything his mom would need to keep Dahlia until after work.

Charlie: Would be willing to spend the day with your favorite granddaughter today?

Mom: Oh Charles, really? I was supposed to have ladies auxiliary today.

Mom: Also, it's rude to only message someone when you want a favor.

Charlie: Sorry, Mom. Ruth's sick. I'll see if Starla can do it…

Mom: No, I'll take her, of course. No reason why our time should go to her.

Due to his "rudeness," he couldn't avoid a longer-than-necessary conversation with his mom and barely dropped the other two off at school on time. He punched it the minute he was out of the parking lot; he wouldn't have as much time to work this afternoon as he normally would, so every second counted. But he knew he'd miscalculated when he saw the deputy's flashing lights in his rearview mirror. Charlie cursed as he pulled over. Not only was he going to be even later and now needed to pay a ticket, he had to endure the humiliation of sitting here while all the other parents went by. *Great.*

A redheaded officer dressed in a tan uniform approached the window, and he rolled it down.

"Good morning, Mr. Miller."

"Morning, Deputy."

"The school zone ends…" She pointed up the road. "Down there."

"Yeah, I…see that. Now."

"License and registration, please."

Charlie sat uncomfortably in the driver's seat while she did the paperwork. His impulse to charm his way out of this felt wrong now, but no new impulse had replaced it. Except maybe sulking, but he didn't want to do that, either. So he just sat there and tried not to make eye contact with any of the other drivers. Unfortunately, he failed just as Ruth's dad and brother Ranger passed him in a Toyota Rav4, unmistakably smirking. Ugh, their taste in cars was as terrible as they were.

He made it to work with no more delays, but Jason took one look at him and laughed.

"You look like someone spit in your cornflakes."

"You know I don't eat breakfast."

"Something bad happen this morning?" Jason asked, diving back under the hood to loosen something with a ratchet.

"Ruth's sick, so I had to take the kids to school. And I got a ticket."

"Ouch. No mercy from Elizabeth, huh?"

"Not today." He swallowed. "But I deserved it."

His brother smiled. "You said it, not me."

"I'm gonna get to work. Is Henry here?"

"Yeah, *he* was here at 8:00…"

Charlie picked up a rag that sat on the edge of an open Oldsmobile and winged it at his back. Jason just laughed.

"You take your meds today?"

"Yes, Dad," he called back.

Thankfully, Henry had kept things running for him this morning, and there was a list of things that needed seeing to, but nothing urgent. It was a strange feeling; Charlie wasn't sure he liked it. He sent out a bunch of invoices and ordered some new parts they were low on and talked to three customers about the same gray Blazer. He got a few phone calls, but people seemed to have figured out that Henry could answer their questions quicker than he could. And Henry had a good way with people; he often heard them laughing as they left. It was like his dad always said, "sale or no sale, send them home happy."

In the afternoon, he sold a Bolt to a pair of delighted environmentalists and a used fifteen-passenger van to someone who ran a daycare. He wondered if they knew Ruth, but didn't ask. But it made him wonder how she was doing and whether she might be able to come tomorrow.

Charlie: Just for planning purposes, how are you feeling?

When there was no answer immediately, he made himself finish his tuna salad before he checked it again. Still nothing. She was probably sleeping. It was good to not hear anything, he told himself. He had to tell himself several times before he started to believe it, though.

He had to leave early to pick up the kids, but everyone seemed fine with it, which was annoying. He waited in the pickup line; well, he led the pickup line. First was always a good place to be. He got a text from Starla around 2:30.

Starla: I heard Ruth is sick. You need any back-up?

Charlie: No.

Starla: Okay, well, I'd be happy to have Ainsley walk them over to the library.

Charlie: No, thank you. I'm good.

Starla: Don't text and drive, Lizzie really hates that. She gave her own husband a ticket the other day.

Charlie: I'm parked at the school. Also, I love her.

Starla: She's taken.

The back door opened, and Aiden and Emily climbed in, chucking their backpacks onto the floor.

"I don't have any homework, so can I go over to Cord's?" Aiden said as he buckled his seat belt.

"I'll have to talk to his parent..." Charlie was no fan of Cord, who'd once asked him what it meant when his mom called Charlie a "tomcat," even though he was human.

Charlie pulled into the parking lot, sent Starla a quick text to get Cord's mom's number, then arranged the details. He'd get more done with Aiden out of the house, not antagonizing Emily.

By the time he dropped off Aiden (who he would have to come back for later) and picked up Dahlia (who was, of course, asleep and very unhappy to be awakened), Charlie was exhausted. He held Dahlia with one arm as he contemplated dinner.

"Daddy?"

"Hmm?" he asked as he scrolled recipes on his phone. He was hoping for something healthier than their usual takeout or frozen pizza, if only for his own sake.

"Will you play with me?"

He gestured toward the phone with his head. "I kind of need to make dinner."

"It's only 4:00. You still have an hour." She stared up at him, grinning maniacally, as if she knew she'd trapped him.

"I'm not as good at cooking as Mommy and Ruth are. I take longer."

"Maybe you should practice. I'll help you."

There they were, Charlie's least favorite words out of a child's mouth.

"What do you know about cooking?"

"I know how to make mac and cheese. I'll show you. Then we can play Dance Your Socks Off when Dahlia goes to bed."

Charlie stared at her, impressed. It was a solid plan, and he didn't really get that much time one-on-one with Em. And more than that, she reminded him so much of himself as a child, always angling for something. His plans had been much more selfish than "cooking and playing with my dad."

"You know what," he said, putting down his phone, and he saw her brace herself for a "no," a stressed look in her eyes. "That's a brilliant plan." He held up one hand for a high five, and Emily beamed as she whacked his open palm.

As Charlie had expected, it was a messy choice.

"Are we supposed to add that now?" Charlie asked as Emily dumped the butter in with the water and pasta in the pot.

"Oh yeah," she said, opening the white cheese powder packet. "Definitely."

"Hold on there, sister, let's read the directions." He helped her sound out her way through the instructions, and by then, the water was boiling. "Should we make a salad to go with it?" Charlie asked, rooting around in the fridge.

"Do *you* want a salad?" she asked diplomatically, and he pivoted to look at her. Then he laughed.

"No, I don't want a salad." It felt freeing to say it out loud. "I want mac and cheese, straight from the pot."

"That sounds like a poem," Emily said, needlessly stirring the boiling water.

"What should the next line be, then?"

"I want it good, and I want it hot!" she shouted, and Charlie laughed again. Sleepy Dahlia stirred in his arms, and he instinctively shifted his weight from right to left. He had to set her down to drain the pasta, but she snuggled into the car seat. All it took was a little rocking with his foot as they ate to get her to drop off, which was perfect for going to pick up Aiden. Emily kicked his butt by a mile at the dance video game, but it felt good to move just because he wanted to. Just because he was playing with his kid and trying and making her laugh. Even Aiden seemed happy when he picked him up; he smiled at Emily, already bathed and in her jammies.

"How's Ruth?" Aiden asked, and Charlie pivoted to see him.

"How should I know?"

"Weren't you texting with her?"

"Yeah, a little." Charlie turned to face forward and shifted into gear. "Are you worried about her?"

"No. Just..." Aiden sighed. "Never mind. You don't get it."

"I guess not. But I'd like to, if you want to explain it to me."

"I just want to know if she's coming tomorrow. That's all." It was a hollow lie, and they both knew it; but more than that, it echoed what Charlie had told her earlier, and he wondered now if it had hurt her feelings. If he'd hurt them.

"I'll text her again when we get home."

"Here, give me your phone. I'll text her."

"I don't think so." For some reason, the idea of Aiden sending her a message she thought was from him made him prickle inside. He already felt like he had to choose his words carefully around her. He didn't need the kid saying something insensitive. "When we get home."

But it wasn't until the kids were all in bed that he remembered to do it.

Charlie: You okay over there?

Charlie: It's gonna be awkward if I have to drag three sleepy kids down the road to check on you.

Charlie: You could send up a flare.

Charlie: Or smoke signals. But I'll need a way to decode them.

Ruth: Take it easy, Chuck. I'm fine.

Ruth: I took a thing to knock out this cough and help me sleep a while ago and I think it's kicking in so I should be there tomorrow unless I'm not better, I guess

He felt a strange relief just hearing from her, even though it sounded like she was half asleep already. *It's just a cold. Relax, Miller. Someone's taking care of her.* What troubled him more than her illness was how much *he* wanted to be the one to do it. Brushing back her dark hair from her forehead, bringing her more medicine or a ginger ale, making her lie down. He'd make sure she got good rest.

Charlie: Okay, that's great to hear. If you need to take another day, it will be paid, so take the time you need to feel better.

Ruth: Did you play with them today

Charlie: I did, actually. Em and I played Dance Your Socks Off and made dinner together.

Ruth: you have three kids though did you play with the other two

Charlie: Go easy on me, I'm new at fun.

Ruth: Ha ha you are, you're new at fun. It's funny

Ruth: you really tried with the motorcycle, though. I love it

Charlie: Get some rest. We'll see you tomorrow hopefully.

Ruth: LOL I dropped my phone

Charlie: Get into bed, Zane.

Ruth: Okay good night love you

It was a good thing he was already sitting down. Charlie sat bolt upright on his sectional, completely ignoring the latest episode of *Insurance Island* he'd put on. *She doesn't mean that. She's drugged up. It's just a thing people say at the end of conversations, and so her brain prompted it, and she's on cough medicine, so she typed it. Simple explanation.*

But his brain wasn't content with that. *You only say that with family, though. You're not family. You're not even dating.*

And they wouldn't be. It wasn't possible. But the longer he stared at the words, the more he wanted to say...*something* back. Not that, of course. But he did like her. He did...feel things. Charlie tossed the phone to the other side of the couch, as if that would keep him from writing back. From saying something stupid that a boss should absolutely not say to his employee. Then it buzzed again.

Ruth: Did you hear me, Chuck? Is that weird. That's probably weird.

Ruth: I just don't like to say your name with an R
in it, that's all.
Ruth: oh, this bed does feel nice, good call on
that one, captain

He tried to think of a way to explain this, something that
didn't mean what it seemed like it meant. Something that
made it an accident. But he was being impeded by logic and
the fact that she kept saying his name.

Ruth: I want your name to sound great when I
say it. Because you're great. You're running your
own business and you work so hard. You take care
of your customers and I know you gave me some
kind of discount which you didn't have to. You're
nice but you try to keep it secret and I don't know
why, but your secret is out mister. You don't even
bring home random women anymore I don't
think. You're a good dad, even if you're boring.
You could be exciting if you tried. I'd love to see
you try.

Ruth: also you know what's a funny word?
Bushtit.

Ruth: gets me laughing every time.

Ruth: Are you sleeping

Ruth: probably sleeping

CHAPTER TWENTY-ONE

Ruth

Ruth woke to her alarm the next morning; she felt more like she was rising from the dead than an average night's sleep. That cough medicine must have been stronger than she'd thought; it affected her strangely sometimes. Her brothers had reported her sleepwalking and even sleep eating when she'd taken it in the past, but she'd been desperate to get some good rest last night. And she had slept really well.

"Ruth. Alarm." Ranger's muffled voice sounded from the other side of the room, and she reached for the phone.

"Sorry."

"You feeling better?"

But her brain couldn't keep track of the question given what was still on her screen from last night. As she scrolled through the bubbled conversation, one hand flew to her mouth in horror.

"No," she breathed, and Ranger pulled his head out from under his pillow.

"No? You're still sick?"

"What? No, I'm fine," she said, still scanning over the mortifying things she'd written to her boss the night before. "Go back to sleep."

Ruth launched herself out of bed and hurried for the bathroom, the only place she had any privacy in this house.

She slammed and locked the door and lowered herself onto the closed toilet with shaking legs.

What have I done? She just kept reading over the texts, but every time she did, her stomach sank closer and closer to her toes. She didn't know what was worse: saying she loved him or taking it back. And of course, she'd admitted her true feelings...for him *and* his motorcycle. And now she had to go work with him all morning alone, prepping food for tomorrow, or he was going to let his whole family down. She couldn't just bag on him like that, no matter how rampantly she'd just embarrassed herself. *Bushtit? Honestly.*

The door handle rattled, and she startled at the noise, hastily hiding the phone.

"Ruthie! I need to pee," Ryan called through the door.

"How did you know it was me?"

"No one else locks the door. C'mon, I don't want to wake up Mom and Dad to use theirs."

"I have as much right to bathroom time as anyone else. Go find a tree."

"I'm not dressed. Please?"

Grumbling, Ruth unlocked the door and stepped out for her grinning brother.

"Thanks, Ruthie. You're the best." His big, sloppy, beardy kiss on her cheek did nothing to assuage her. "You gonna make pancakes?"

"No, I'm working today."

"Aw, darn." He closed the bathroom door before she could clarify whether the "darn" was for her sake or his. Ruth gathered up her clothes, so she could duck back into the bathroom the moment her brother was done. She took a long shower. Unfortunately, it still wasn't long enough to figure out what she was going to say to Charlie when she saw him later. She spent too much time drying and curling her hair, so she threw on a hoodie and grabbed a piece of bread with peanut butter folded over and a banana. She sent a text on her way out.

> **Ruth:** Headed to the Millers for the morning.
> **Mom**: Have fun, sweetie.
> **Ranger:** No pancakes? Darn.
> **Ryan:** That's what I said! Levi, will you make pancakes?
> **Levi:** No. I do that enough at the restaurant.
> **Dad:** Boys, it's a mix. You just add water.
> **Wyatt:** Too much work.

Ruth muted the thread and started walking faster. A few months ago, she would've made them pancakes before she left. But if she kept doing that, they were always going to depend on her. It was time to start letting go, for all their sakes. She was moving out. Her conscience nagged at her that she hadn't so much as browsed the internet for another place, but she pushed the thought away. She had other things to think about now: what the heck was she going to tell Charlie?

I'm sorry, I was drugged out of my gourd so I could sleep and come help you today?

Please forget everything I said last night?

That made it sound like she didn't like him, but really, she meant what she'd told him. Yes, he was prickly, but he'd been through a lot. And from what she could tell, he was changing. She couldn't imagine a younger Charlie ever going to Divorce Support...he'd been so cocky. Obnoxious. Smarmy. But the man whose house she'd worked in and whose kids she'd watched for three months told a different story...he seemed deeply insecure when it came right down to it, which kind of shocked her socks off. But he was reading those books he brought home. The bookmarks moved. And he was really ambitious—perhaps it was to a fault at times, but he obviously cared if he'd fixed her car so cheaply.

*Okay, so not **forget everything** because I do like him. What then?*

A car behind her on the driveway brought her back to the present, and she moved off to the side, and Starla waved from the driver's seat.

Oh, hello, buffer. This is perfect.

"You're not here for the kids, are you?" Starla called with a smile.

"No, no," Ruth called back. "I'm just helping Chuck with a project."

"Oh, how nice. Well, thanks for taking good care of him." Starla seemed perfectly genuine, and yet there was something under the words...amusement? snark? She didn't have time to figure it out before the front door opened and Emily and Aiden came shuffling out, yawning, pillows under their arms. Charlie was right behind them, hauling Dahlia's car seat.

"Let's go, guys. Don't keep Mom waiting." He looked up and noticed Ruth, and his smile was nothing less than dazzling. Oh yeah, she had a serious razzing coming about those text messages, but she let her shoulders fall with relief that he wasn't upset. She'd take teasing over awkwardness any day of the week.

"Good morning, Ruth. How did you sleep?"

"Very well, thank you."

"Oh," he said through a laugh, "I'm *so* glad to hear that."

Starla was bouncing an openly curious look between the two of them now, but Ruth tried to ignore her.

"How about you?"

"Oh, me? I slept *great*. Fantastic. I'd say 'like a baby,' but I think Dahlia's mission in life is to thoroughly debunk that idea."

Ruth tipped her chin up. "Glad to hear it."

Charlie stepped closer to Ruth as Starla bent to buckle Emily's seat belt, and his voice dropped so only she could hear.

"Do you remember what you sent me?"

There was only one way to play this, and it amazed her a little that she hadn't thought of it earlier: total denial.

"No idea what you're talking about. Shall we get started?"

Charlie cackled, his hand coming to his flat stomach, throwing his head back.

"You are deriving far too much joy from this," Ruth chided, but she felt a smile steal across her own face just from watching his delight.

"Oh, I'm sorry," he said through more laughter. "How much joy am I allowed to derive when my nanny drunk texts me?"

Starla's face sobered at that, and Ruth rushed to explain.

"I wasn't drunk—I took cough medicine as we were working out details for today. That's not the same at all."

Starla nodded understandingly, but Charlie just laughed harder.

"If you say so," he choked out.

"I do say so," Ruth replied, and it wasn't just her breath that was frosty. She wanted to push him, to tickle him, to wipe that smile off his handsome, smug face with a...*uh oh. No kissing allowed, Zane.*

At least Starla was smiling again, albeit possibly at her expense. They both paused their conversation to wave good-bye to the kids as Starla drove off. Charlie clapped his hands.

"Did you want to take a motorcycle ride first, or should we get cooking?"

Ruth whacked him gently with the back of her hand as she went inside.

"Did you get shallots?" Ruth was digging around in the pantry while Charlie checked the boiling potatoes with a fork. They'd been navigating the small space between the island and the counters all morning, and the pantry felt like an oasis of space.

"Wait, shallots or scallions?"

She poked her head out. "Scallions are long and green with white, tiny-rooted ends. Shallots are round and purple-ish. Which did you get?"

Charlie grimaced, and even that was annoyingly handsome. "I don't remember. I bought so many things."

"I'll check the fridge."

"I definitely would have put them in the fridge," he said, nodding. "All produce went into the fridge."

"Onion-types like that don't need to, but it does keep you from..." She managed to slide past him, but she was too close to the fridge to get it open. Ruth bumped into Charlie with her backside as she tried to open the door and felt her skin prickle with awareness. "Sorry."

"It's a small space." But when he turned and gave her a look over her shoulder, she wished she'd tried harder not to touch him. It was a soft look, an invitation without words, and Ruth quickly ducked her burning face into the cool air of the fridge. *You cannot date your boss. Especially this boss. He wouldn't even want that.* She wished it was that easy to convince herself. No, she wished he'd convince his face, because she knew she wasn't misreading that.

"Here they are," she said, forcing cheerfulness into her voice. "Good work, Mr. Miller." That last name was another excellent reminder: he wasn't for her. Their family history dictated it. But she couldn't ignore the fact that she'd just used a bunch of r's without even thinking about it. She usually only did that with her family...

"Thank you, Ms. Zane."

She bumped him—on purpose this time—with her elbow as she joined him at the island. "I don't think I'm old enough to be a 'mizz,' am I?"

"Is there a standard?" He bumped her back with his hip, and she couldn't tell if it was intentional.

"I think I'm firmly in 'miss' territory, sir. I am a youngin.'"

"Oh, I see."

"Unlike you."

Charlie laughed. "I'm only four years older than you."

"And yet, I spy a bit of gray," she said, fluffing the top of his hair. Rather than gazing into her eyes or commenting on her closeness, Charlie immediately spun to examine himself in the doors of the double ovens.

"Where?"

Ruth exploded into laughter, and Charlie turned back with a flat look.

"Your face," she gasped, wiping an errant tear. "Oh Lord. You're *so* vain."

Charlie crossed his arms. "You're too young to understand."

"To understand vanity? I don't think so. My brother Levi is the same way. The amount of money that man spends on beard oil."

"*Ms.* Zane, don't judge the man for caring about his appearance. He's an example to us all."

"Vanity," she reiterated, leaning closer. "A waste of money."

He lifted a hand and caught one of her large curls on his finger. "And I suppose this happens naturally?"

Ruth resisted the urge to toss her hair. She didn't want to lose that contact. "Not entirely, no."

"So why are women allowed to coif and curl and I'm not?"

He was still touching her hair, just that little bit, tugging on her curl gently. Ruth just stared at his face, unwilling to move, unwilling to breathe. It was such a nice face: high cheekbones, deep brown eyes, full lips, a slightly crooked nose that only enhanced his beauty. And that was the word for it: beauty.

"If you want to get a perm, I won't stop you."

"What if I wanted..." Charlie blinked. Hastily, he dropped his hand and turned back to the counter, bracing himself against it. "So what are we doing here?"

Trying to hide her disappointment, Ruth gestured to the recipe halfheartedly.

"You need to trim the sugar snap peas."

"Like, with scissors? I cut them in half?"

"No. Watch." It was a relief to have something else to focus on in one way and crushing in another. She pulled out a paring knife and showed him how to break off the ends, pulling the strings. She showed him how to tie the chickens, placing them breast up in the shiny new roasting pan he'd bought. She helped him shape the crescent rolls he popped from the can and mix the lemon cake he'd bought, stealing a taste of both. They weren't homemade, but they were good enough. He was working at his skill level, and it was definitely growing. And it would've been too overwhelming for him to cook for ten people from scratch.

They worked until lunchtime, then Ruth made them each a salad. He didn't notice until she was already done.

"You didn't have to make me lunch."

"It's true. I'm nice. Hey, that one's mine. You don't deserve pepperoni."

"What if I like pepperoni?" he asked, wrinkling his nose at the canned chicken she'd put on his. "Didn't I do good work this morning? Why don't I deserve it?"

"Pepperoni is for people who don't tease me about my late-night texting habits."

Charlie laughed. "That's fair. You want to sit outside?"

They could listen to the river and sit on those nice benches around the edge of the large deck, flanked by those nice expensive planters with bulbs popping up. The sun would probably catch in his chestnut hair. He'd probably wear those aviators that she liked, his skin warmed by the spring sun.

"Yeah."

It was still a little cold, being only April, but the weather was clear. They talked as they ate: about the kids, particularly Aiden; about Charlie's silly reality shows; about Ruth's brothers and how annoying they could be, but also how incredibly proud she was of them—Levi had gotten another offer from a restaurant in Salem (but turned it down). Ryan was doing very well in college. And all the while, Ruth felt her courage growing, her need to speak the truth about how she felt about Charlie rising, intensifying. She was just about to blurt it out when something overhead caught her eye. Charlie noticed her looking.

"What kind of bird is that?"

"It's a hawk." And it put into her mind a metaphor too beautiful to pass up. "Did you know that red-tailed hawks circle each other when they're attracted?" Ruth kept her gaze on the sky, but out of the corner of her eye, she saw Charlie's head snap toward her.

"No, I didn't." His voice cautious, a tiptoe into the conversation.

"It's elaborate," she went on. "High-speed tumbles and dives. Sometimes they even lock talons or beaks." She definitely wanted to lock beaks with Charlie. Like, a lot.

His answer was quiet. "What if they crash? What if gravity proves too much for them or their bird parents hate each other?"

Okay, so we're on the same page here.

"But what if they soar together? What if they lift each other up?" She tipped her head back down then, but it didn't help much. Those trendy sunglasses shaded his gaze, and she couldn't tell what he was thinking at all.

"I know I've been circling you a little." He swallowed so hard she could see his throat move. "But I'm not a good bird. I'm the wrong kind of bird for you."

Ruth felt the shaking coming; it always did in tense situations. "And why's that, exactly?"

His jaw tightened. "You know why."

"I really don't." She wished he wasn't so far away; why hadn't she sat next to him on the bench bordering the deck? *Oh, right, so I could look at him.* That same vulnerability that he'd had the night she found Coleman was back, and she wanted to squeeze his hand. Rest her head on his shoulder. Offer some sort of comfort.

"You know why," he repeated, lowering his voice. "I shouldn't have flirted with you. I won't anymore. I'll be more professional."

Ruth set aside her plate. "I don't want you to be professional. I want you to tell me what you want."

"I can't have what I want." Charlie got out of his seat and started toward the French doors.

"I doubt that. I bet it's the same as what I want."

Pausing, Charlie shook his head slowly, but it was less "no" and more sadness. It didn't help her own shaking, but her heart stopped sinking a bit. He was stubborn, but she was worse.

"We shouldn't," he whispered. "I can't. I'm a crappy partner. I'll just let you down."

She raised one eyebrow, but didn't argue with him. You didn't win a war in the first skirmish, after all. And now she'd established that he wanted her: he was just scared.

"I guess if that's how you really feel." Ruth got to her feet, and Charlie took a step toward her.

"You're shaking." He held her at arm's length, both hands rubbing her shoulders.

"Yeah, stressful situations do that to me."

His head dropped, and he broke contact, shuffling backward. "I'm sorry."

"Don't be. You're the one missing out." Ruth smiled at him as she gathered up both their lunch dishes. "Let me know how it goes tomorrow?"

"Yes, I will. Thank you for all your help." He was back to Boss Charlie now, arms crossed...but he was still watching her as she turned to go inside.

"Ruth."

Her heart leaped, and she spun back to face him.

"I like hearing my name from your mouth, however you want to say it."

It was as close to the confession she wanted as he was going to get.

"Good to know, Chuck," she said softly, and when she winked at him, she thought he was going to chase after her. But by the time she gathered up her stuff and found the front door, he was still out on the deck, staring at the river. Ruth sauntered home, but with new determination. She would accept his no, of course; being a fool didn't remove his right to consent. But she had a feeling those words would stick in his mind. In the meantime, she meant to show him just what a suitable partner he really could be.

CHAPTER TWENTY-TWO

Charlie

Ruth had set him up perfectly: all he had to do that morning was stick the chickens in the oven, warm up the side dishes, and bake the rolls. It was almost too easy. So he went the extra mile. Predictably, his parents arrived first.

"Oh, Charlie. It looks lovely in here." He had to admit that the daffodils looked really nice with the white tablecloth. His kids would probably mess it up, but bleach was a thing for a reason, right? Surely linen was bleachable.

"Thanks, Mom."

"You do all this yourself?" his father asked as he hung up his coat in the closet.

"No, Ruth helped." There was no point in lying; they all knew he was crap in the kitchen. "But I did all the actual cooking. She just pointed me in the right direction." Adding this didn't help their dour, pinched expressions whatsoever.

"Don't depend on that woman any more than you need to, Charles," his mother said, her voice as grave and serious as if she was giving her last bit of wisdom before dying. "It will only end in disappointment."

My only disappointment is when she goes home, thought Charlie, but he was smart enough not to say it.

Talk from there shifted into his decorations ("Are those from your yard? They're just lovely.") and he was just getting out the shrimp platter when Starla and Sawyer and their side of the family showed up. Jason, of course, was late enough that he missed out on shrimp entirely. "I can't believe you let the kids take it all," he complained as they watched the kids hunt for plastic eggs out in Charlie's giant backyard. "You know I love shrimp."

"Be on time, then."

Jason scoffed. "Time. What is time, anyway?"

"The age-old ADHD question..." Charlie murmured, still watching the kids, and Jason grinned.

"Did you have fun with Ruth yesterday?"

It was a complicated question. The first part? Absolutely. Teasing each other, touching innocently, chatting with her in the sun. It had been heaven. And then those confounded birds had ruined everything. No, *he'd* ruined everything...because he didn't reach out and catch her arm as she walked away. He didn't spin her back toward him and cup her soft face and admit how much he wanted to see what kind of relationship they could make together. He'd only blurted out a pathetic attempt to fix things when it was obvious she was actually going to leave.

"Yes," he said simply, and Jason grinned harder.

You're the one missing out. Man, didn't he know it. He couldn't blame her for taking off so quickly when he'd embarrassed her like that.

"So, are you going for a second date?"

Charlie massaged his temple. "This wasn't a date! She was just helping me cook."

"Oh, wait. Really?" Jason's surprise was genuine. "I thought that was some kind of ruse."

"No, it wasn't a ruse!" The other adults were turning to look at him now. Starla sauntered over.

"I have to get Ruth's recipe for these bruschetta. They are to die for."

"It's my recipe," Charlie replied, "and I'd be happy to share it with you."

"Oh!" Starla appeared to be letting that sink in as she stuffed another one in her mouth. "It's fantastic."

"Thank you."

The timer went off in the kitchen, and Charlie opened the French doors to go take his chickens out of the oven. But he had a shadow.

"Charlie," Starla said, and he didn't like her tone. It wasn't chiding or condemnatory. No, worse than that. It was musing. "Why did you ask Ruth to help you?"

"Because she's a great cook. She cooks for us almost every night, and the kids gobble it down."

"Hmm. But why not your mom?"

"My mom hates to cook, and you know it."

"But she'd be glad to come over if it meant spending time with you. Or Lacey would've helped you."

Charlie paused the conversations as he took out the heavy roasting pan and shut the oven door with his elbow. "So you're a mind reader now?"

"Hardly. I just think maybe..."

He turned to look at her. "What?"

"Do you have a crush on Ruth?"

"What?" he snapped. "Of course not. And if I did, I certainly wouldn't discuss it with *you*."

"Okay, fair enough." Her voice was small, and he kicked himself mentally. He didn't want to ruin their holiday, but he also...didn't want to talk about this. "But the way you were flirting with her yesterday just...surprised me."

Charlie could feel a headache coming on as he put the cold casserole dish of mashed potatoes into the warm oven.

"Is there a point to this, Star?"

"I'm just saying. If you're holding back because you think I wouldn't approve since she works for us, don't do that. We love Ruth. And if you have a shot at being happy with someone, you should take it."

He crossed his arms. "And make me the biggest cliché in Timber Falls? I don't think so."

Starla smirked, her fingers toying with the fringe on the dish towel by the sink. "There are worse things in the world."

Charlie got out the peas, just to have something to do. *We're alone. We should talk about Aiden.* And changing the subject was a welcome idea as well.

"Do you think Aiden needs counseling?"

Starla frowned. "Is this about being a cliché still?"

"No, I just...worry about him. He seems so angry. Haven't you noticed it?" When she said nothing, he swallowed hard and dove into the truth. "I've been meeting with Kellan in the Divorce Support group, and it's been good. I think it would be good for him, too."

But before Starla could reply, the French doors flew open, and Emily came running in, her braids flying behind her.

"Dad, look what I found!" She crowed, waving a $20 bill like a flag.

"Wow, looks like the Easter Bunny was extra flush this year," he said, shooting a glare at his dad, who ignored him.

"Sorry," he mouthed to Starla, who just shrugged.

"Not your fault," she silently replied.

"Smells good in here," Sawyer said, patting Dahlia's bum as she fussed in his arms.

"You want me to put her down upstairs?" Charlie asked, and Sawyer shook his head.

"I think she's just hungry." Starla put out her hands greedily, and Sawyer passed Dahlia over.

"Come on, Didi, let's go see what's happening here…Charlie, can I use your study?"

"As long as you stay away from the paperwork. I don't want her barfing on anything."

"She does barf a lot, doesn't she?" Sawyer asked as he watched them go. "Is that normal?"

"Why are we talking about barf right before dinner?" Aiden asked, snagging a black olive off the charcuterie tray.

"Because it's something babies do, and Dahlia is part of this family."

Aiden mumbled something under his breath, but took his place at the table. It wasn't long before Starla was hollering for Sawyer, and Charlie winced when he took her a towel.

What was her deal? This had been going on for a while now. Well, there was no time to think about it while he was pouring wine and sparkling cider and trying to get everyone to sit down. It felt good to have them all here; he just wished Ruth was here to share the fruit of their labor with them. It was a strange feeling to miss someone who wasn't technically attached to him at all. She was an employee. He'd never missed his dentist at Thanksgiving or his barber at Christmas. Why should he miss Ruth today?

And yet he did. He just wanted to bump into her. He wanted another one of those hugs she'd given him or to make her eyes twinkle like they had a secret. He pulled out his phone.

> **Charlie:** You didn't have to cook two meals, did you?
>
> **Ruth:** No, Levi does a big thing; he doesn't like my peasant food.
>
> **Ruth:** Why? Were you concerned about me?
>
> **Charlie:** Of course not.
>
> **Ruth:** Because that would be an interesting sentiment from my boss...
>
> **Charlie:** I SAID NO.
>
> **Ruth:** Mmm. How'd your food turn out?
>
> **Charlie:** Excellent. They were all very impressed. With you.
>
> **Ruth:** LOL. I didn't do that much. You did most of the actual cooking.
>
> **Charlie:** Don't think they believe that, but they're eating happily.
>
> **Ruth:** I'll swear an affidavit.
>
> **Charlie:** Not necessary.
>
> **Charlie:** Thanks again for your help.
>
> **Ruth:** Any time. I enjoy cooking with you.

Charlie shoved the phone deep in his pocket and turned his attention back to his guests. Then he pulled it out one more time.

> **Charlie:** And your cooking is not peasant food, you take that back.
> **Charlie:** I love your pumpkin pasta.
> **Ruth:** I knew bacon would be the way to your heart.

CHAPTER TWENTY-THREE

Ruth

The fourth time Aiden bit Emily's head off for an innocent comment and the third time Em retaliated with violence, Ruth couldn't take it anymore.

"Please get on your coats and get in the car."

Emily's eyes were wide. "Where are we going?"

"You'll see." It had been one of those dreary Oregon spring weeks where the gray just never seems to end, and it showed in everyone's attitude. Even Dahlia seemed grumpy as she strapped her into her car seat. Aiden and Em dragged their feet, claiming lost shoes and missing coats. But when Ruth found both, they put them on.

"Can I take my tablet in the car?" Aiden held it under one arm as if permission had already been given.

"I suppose. But don't let it get wet." Ruth drove them out to the highway.

"Why's it going to get wet? I'm not going hiking. I don't like it."

Emily piped up. "Last time Mom took us hiking, she met a husband. Maybe Ruth will meet one."

"Oh, is that so?" Ruth chuckled. "Papa saved you from a bear?"

"Noooo," Emily said, laughing.

"He was cutting down a tree?" In the rearview mirror, she saw Aiden crack a smile.

"No," Emily crowed, "we were caught in the rain and Papa let us inside."

"But we already knew him before that. Mom did, too," Aiden added.

"Well, maybe I need a husband," Ruth mused. "I didn't know this was such an effective strategy."

"You don't," Aiden said firmly. "No one does."

"Oh?" She turned into her driveway.

"I don't, anyway. I'm never getting married."

"Why's that?" Em was popping her lips at Dahlia and Aiden just silently unbuckled his seat belt as she put it in park. "Here we are."

"Ugh, why'd you bring us to a dirty little house?"

"This is *my* house," Ruth said, though she wasn't surprised Emily felt that way. "I have something to show you. Come on." Ruth unzipped her coat and put Dahlia in the sling; her eyes looked heavy, but she seemed to perk up in the cold air. Aiden tucked the tablet under his arm as they walked, but stalled when she passed the front door. "Ruth?"

"It's this way," she called over her shoulder without slowing down. Squelching footsteps behind her told her they were following behind. She ducked under a branch just starting to bud. There would be cherry blossoms littering the driveway soon. Dahlia's eyes looked heavy again, and she tucked the blanket in tighter around her.

"How far are we going?" Emily asked.

"Not too far."

"Are we going to the river? I can see the river from my house," Aiden added, "in my warm living room." Ruth ignored him. It was only about half a mile through the orchard and the stand of birch trees, but she always felt like she was stepping back in time. Dahlia was asleep before they even got near the river, curving away from the house she lived in now, which wasn't anywhere near it for flood reasons. It didn't happen much, but they weren't taking chances.

"Here we are," she said as they rounded the corner. The cabin stood just as she remembered it, moss covering the thatch roof, the firewood stacked neatly under the overhang. "Whoa," Emily breathed. "Who lives here?"

"My great-great-grandfather did," Ruth said, leading them to the doorway. "He built this house when he first got the land, a very long time ago." She touched the place where he'd carved "Zane 1881" onto a piece of cedar and hung it above the door. Inside was musty; they'd put glass in the windows sometime later, and it kept most things out. She brushed a hand over the table and brought it up coated with dust, which she wiped on her pants. "Sometimes my parents come out here and hang around when our house feels too small." And it didn't hurt that the short drive didn't leave her mom exhausted.

"I'd come here all the time," Aiden said, and when Ruth turned to look at him, he was touching the antlers on the wall.

"You know there's no internet, right?" Ruth teased, but Aiden didn't laugh.

"But you can fish, right? And hunt?"

"Sure, as long as it's the right season and you've got licenses and whatnot."

"That's so cool." His eyes were still on the mantel where carved wooden animals sat. "Who made these? Your grandpa?"

"I think so. I'm not sure." She found the matches and lit a lamp, then turned them over to look for initials. "Yep, my grandpa. That's him, ZZ. Zechariah Zane."

"Is that a real tea set?" Emily asked, going up on her toes to see into the French-paned kitchen cabinets.

Ruth nodded. "Yes, that's real china. The same one they found at Fort Vancouver."

"Can we use it?"

"Probably too dirty. Plus, there's no tea out here..." She opened a cabinet. The sound of wings startled her, and she ducked, putting a hand on the back of Dahlia's head. A bird came darting out and circled the room, chirping and diving at them. Ruth recognized the behavior: she must have babies somewhere nearby. The kids were hollering, covering their heads, scrambling for the door, and Ruth followed suit. She left the door open so the bird could leave, but she was guessing it didn't want to.

"Whew!" Aiden exclaimed, red-cheeked and grinning. "That was close."

"We almost died!" Emily shrieked, and Dahlia stirred in the sling. Through all the noise and hubbub, she was still asleep. Babies were enviable that way. Ruth gave Emily a hug, winking at Aiden over her head, and he rolled his eyes good-naturedly.

"Can we come back here and go fishing?"

"Sure." What made it better than the Millers' land? Ruth had no idea. But there was a nice sandy spot down the embankment that he seemed to be eyeing, and anything that got them outside was good.

"I'm *never* coming back here," Emily announced. "I almost died."

"Okay," Ruth soothed. "All right. Shall we head back to the car?"

"Or we could walk home," Aiden said.

Ruth beamed. "Are you sure? It's kind of a long way."

"But your land touches ours, doesn't it? Isn't there a path along the river?"

"Yes, there is."

"I am *not* up for that," Emily said, but they both ignored her.

"Let's do it," Ruth said. "We'll have an adventure!" Charlie was home when they arrived back at the house, and the kids were still talking about the chipmunks and chickadees they'd seen, though interestingly, they left the cabin out of the story. She hoped it wasn't because the feud had infected their generation, too.

CHAPTER TWENTY-FOUR

Charlie

Charlie checked his phone for the third time. This was quite a switch; Ruth was late, and he needed to get to Divorce Support if he was going to be on time. He chuckled a little to himself. His own anticipation was a surprise, but it was nice having friends who understood. And they were actually friends: some of these guys now knew him better than his own family. He looked out the front window again. And even more than being late, he was worried about Ruth; it wasn't like her to be late. She'd said she just needed to run home for a few minutes to check on her mom, because the rest of her family was out tonight. It shouldn't have taken this long. Out of the dark, a figure materialized, running from the woods. She was faster than he'd thought. Then his heart seized—what if something was wrong with her mom? Or she'd been robbed? He took two long strides and threw the door open.

"I'm sorry," Ruth panted. "I'm so sorry, my truck wouldn't start."

Charlie put a hand to his chest to slow his rocketing heart rate. "So you just ran? Why didn't you call me for a ride?"

He was fairly sure she didn't answer because she couldn't; she was bent over with her hands on her knees, her chest heaving.

"Go," she said, waving toward the garage. "Don't be late."

"Are you sure you're all right?"

She nodded, righting herself, wiping the sweat off her forehead. Then she took him by the shoulders and began steering him toward the garage.

"There's no need to push," he grumbled, but he dug in his heels so she'd have to push harder. He wasn't sure if it was really wise to play with her like that, but they were almost to the door, anyway. And it felt too good to stop. He should get his fill of touch tonight at group; they always hugged him. Then maybe it would be easier to resist her flirting. Not that it was the same kind of touching...

Wait, was Ruth flirting with him? After their conversation about the hawks a few weeks ago, he'd assumed that was all done. He thought about their interaction all the way to the church. And he was still thinking about it when he sat down in the small room.

"Well, I might as well start this week," Kellan said slowly. "I found out I have a five-year-old son."

They all stared at him. Then Brian, the bravest of them, took a breath to ask a question.

"How'd that happen?"

Charlie couldn't resist. "Well, when a man and a woman love each other very much..."

Everyone chuckled, and the tension broke. It hadn't occurred to Charlie, but Kellan probably felt pretty weird confessing something like that to his congregants.

"His mother is someone I knew back when I was using. I knew we'd slept together once, but I didn't know...I didn't know about Arrow. We weren't even really friends."

"Is his mother still using?" Chris asked.

"No, she's been clean since she found out she was pregnant. Which is pretty amazing."

"Wow." Burt was a man of few words, but this time, he'd summed things up well, Charlie thought.

"Tess—that's his mom—didn't know how to find me, and then I guess she found my blog on the church website, and she wanted to see if I was interested in getting to know him."

"And are you?" Charlie asked, his curiosity getting the better of him.

"I think so?" Kellan was normally so darn comfortable; even from the pulpit, he just looked relaxed. But now? He looked like he'd just been handed a test for a subject he hadn't studied in his life. He rubbed at the stubble on his face, which was also uncharacteristic. "I don't know. I feel like I should. But I've never been a kid person."

Suddenly, Charlie felt like *his* counselor instead of the other way around. "I never was until I had Aiden. It's different when they're yours."

The other men nodded, and Kellan seemed to consider that.

"Take him to the park or something," Chris said. "If he gets cold or falls down, just buy him a cocoa at Riverside. That's what I do."

That had been his dad's strategy, too, thinking back. There was no problem money couldn't solve. That was probably why he hated the Zanes so much. They wouldn't even entertain the idea of selling James their land, and on a fundamental level, that challenged his dad's worldview. He was still musing when Kellan answered.

"I could probably do that."

"Bring a towel for the swings," Burt put in. "Nobody likes a wet caboose." They all nodded like this was some sort of ancient proverb, a bit of timeless wisdom.

"Yeah." Kellan was writing it down, and Charlie snickered a little inside. He was so out of his depth. "How was everyone else's week?" The pastor seemed more than ready to move on from his own personal troubles. Brian had broken up with his girlfriend. Chris found a new accountant, but now his ex wanted partial custody of the kids. Burt had hurt his back again. Then it was Charlie's turn.

"No, I'm good. Everything's good." Charlie gave them a winning smile, but somehow, he wasn't sure they were buying it. He looked at Kellan to move on, but he just watched him, amused. The silence was intolerable.

"Well, there is one thing. I have kind of a crush on my kids' nanny." Before anyone could judge him, he rushed on. "But I'm not going to do anything about it. There's nothing to be done. She's a Zane and I'm a Miller and that's the end of that."

"Sounds like the Meyers and the Bagsbys all over again." Burt chuckled.

Charlie blinked. "Hattie's family?"

"Oh yeah. You're all too young to remember, but they had quite a feud brewing back in the day. Something about stolen chickens. Turned out to be a coyote, but by then, accusations had been made and the damage had been done."

"There are coyotes here?!" Kellan obviously felt Burt had buried the lede on that one.

"I didn't know Hattie had that kind of history."

"Oh yeah," Burt chuckled. "Maybe you two can help your clans bury the hatchet."

"I don't see that happening."

"What would it take, do you think?" Kellan wasn't from around here. He couldn't be expected to understand.

"A miracle." And he wasn't exaggerating.

"This is a great segue into our topic tonight: restitution. In Narcotics Anonymous," Kellan said, "one of our steps is to make amends to people we've wronged. Sometimes it takes a long time; years, even. But the point is to consider what a difference it would've made in these two people's lives if the conflict had been resolved to both families' satisfaction all those years ago. Charlie could see Ruth without fear. When we let things fester and let bitterness take root, it affects more than just us. I want you each to take some time and think about who you've hurt in the process of getting divorced. There's paper and pens if you want to make a list. You won't have to share it unless you want to."

Charlie pulled out his phone. That wasn't the kind of thing he could just leave lying around. He opened up his notes app. It was easiest to start with Starla...he wrote down times he'd lied to her and manipulated her into doing what he wanted. Then he went on to Emily: she had to live in two houses now, and he knew she missed Starla when she was with him. And Aiden...

That last one was a tough one. The day Starla caught him, Aiden had been there, too. The shame of that burned him like a brand; he should never have had to see that. And it wasn't what he wanted Aiden to believe about love and relationships. His sweet, funny kid seemed to carry around skepticism like a shield now. And it was his fault.

But there was a way he could make it right...maybe several. And he'd never tried, now that he thought about it. No, he had tried—tried the way *his* dad did. Bought him new video games and football jerseys and ice cream instead of just saying he was sorry. But there was no easy way out of this. Money couldn't solve it. And that deep anger the kid carried around, it wouldn't be wished away or paid off. It demanded justice. Charlie sighed.

"How long is your list?" Chris asked quietly.

"Long," Charlie replied. And he hadn't even named all the women he'd cheated with and dumped.

"Yeah. Mine too."

CHAPTER TWENTY-FIVE

Ruth

"This is a trash pit, Ruthie." Ranger stood in the middle of the empty studio apartment, wrinkling his nose in distaste.

"I think the previous owner had a cat. Possibly an incontinent cat."

"You can't seriously want to live here," he said, walking over to a window to look out at the driveway below.

"It's not ideal," she admitted, "but it doesn't have a ferret."

"Hey," he said, spinning to face her, "you love Duchess."

"I don't love the way she smells."

"That's getting better. I got that new tea tree shampoo. It'll get better."

But the rest of it won't. She'd been asking her brothers to do more around the house for ages, and nothing ever changed for more than a day or two. They were adults; she couldn't discipline them anymore. Here, she'd have time to read. She could cook whatever she wanted without complaints. She wanted that. The word *deserved* felt like a sin to say out loud, and yet, she was an adult. She'd helped raise her brothers. She didn't owe them anything but her love.

Below them, loud music poured through the floor, and Ranger gave her a meaningful look.

"Maybe we'll look at one more," she called, and he started for the door so fast, she was surprised he didn't leave tread marks on the stained carpet.

The next one was a tiny house on Mr. Oberst's property.

"Ruthie Zane, what a pleasant surprise," he greeted her, his hand out. "You used to sit for my granddaughters."

"Yes, I remember Angeline and Aurora," she said, smiling warmly as she shook his thin hand. They were in high school now, which just made her feel old. "How are they?"

"Oh, about to graduate. Rory's off to U of I, and Angeline's in teacher school at Western Oregon."

"How wonderful. I'm so glad to hear it." Her gaze fell to the house. The outside was natural wood, and it seemed to fit in with the forest, sitting cozily under the trees.

"Here, let me open it up for you." He mumbled something as he worked the keys out of his fleece vest pocket. "You're the one that got fired, aren't you?" For a stunned moment, Ruth thought he was directing the question to her, but then Ranger's jaw tightened.

"Yes, sir."

"Did you find more work?"

"My dad hired me back after my racial reconciliation training." That had been a painful chapter in the Zane family history, for sure.

"Good man, your dad," Mr. Oberst said, his gaze still somewhat overly stern as far as Ruth was concerned. "Taken good care of your mom all this time. Raised you boys. Kept his business going. He helped me insure the paintball business so I won't get sued."

Ruth blinked. "The what?"

"Oh, didn't you know? I run a paintball business now, let the kids play in the woods. It's called Wild."

"Great name," Ruth said with a smile.

"Oh," he said, opening the door and turning on the lights, "Maggie Durand thought of that one. She stops by to help me with projects from time to time."

"I bet it accurately characterizes the clientele, too," Ranger said, shooting Ruth a meaningful look.

"Yeah, but they don't come up near the houses. That's out of bounds." The house, of course, was tiny—there really wasn't room for the three of them to stand in it, let alone socialize. "I'll meet you outside."

As soon as the door shut, Ranger started in again.

"There's barely room to boil water in this kitchen, let alone cook for all of us."

Ruth laughed. "What makes you think I'll be cooking for anyone but myself?"

Ranger looked hurt. "You're not even going to invite us over?"

"I mean...no? I'll stop by the house sometimes. You'll still see me when I take care of Mom."

She'd never seen her brother look so baffled.

Ruth lowered her voice. "Bud, this place is cheap. It's the cheapest I've seen. And it's in beautiful shape, unlike Cat Pee Central. The cheaper it is, the more money I can send home to take care of Mom."

"The cheapest thing would be to stay at home."

"Well, I'm not doing that. I can't anymore. And I know you understand why."

"I'll make them change. I'll do it all myself. You don't have to do this."

Ruth watched his face: his expression was hard around the eyes, but she knew it was a front. She pulled him into a hug.

"It'll be okay, bud. It really will." Truthfully, she wasn't sure of it, not with any discernible reason in her head. But her heart felt calm. And she wasn't shaking. They all needed this.

Ranger hugged her back, then cleared his throat.

"You're sure? This is the one? Because you can't even have a proper date in here."

Ruth snorted. "Yes, because I have sooooo many dates. I have amaaaazing prospects. Men are liiiining up to take me out." Her thoughts flitted to Charlie, but she didn't let the sting of that rejection sink in. Against all odds, she had faith in the man.

Ranger stepped back, shaking his head. "We might be to blame for that. Because they should be. You're great."

"Don't tease."

"I'm not!" He spoke loudly enough that it bounced off the walls. Then again, it was a very small space.

"Okay, goodness, hush."

There was a long pause as they both looked around the room.

"Duchess is going to miss you."

She wrapped her arm around her younger brother's broad shoulders and squeezed. "I'm going to miss her, too."

CHAPTER TWENTY-SIX

Charlie

When he turned Ruth down, he had not been prepared for her tenacity in breaking down his argument. For the next few weeks, she pointed out its flaws relentlessly. When he started taking his own wine glass downstairs, she texted him a thank you. He left her a note when he thought Emily might need to come home from school early, since she'd had a cough that morning, and Ruth acted like it was above and beyond.

Charlie: That's normal.

Ruth: Oh man, I wish that was normal. Do you know how many times employers just leave me hanging in the evening? Showing up way after we agreed?

Charlie: Well, they shouldn't.

Ruth: Not the point, Chuck. You're considerate. You're kind. Those are the marks of a good partner. Just saying.

And the worst part was that it was working. Every time she pointed out another thing he hadn't screwed up, he doubted his decision harder. He kept finding little reasons for her to stay: "We'll never be able to eat all this." "Can you show me how you did Emily's hair like that?" "Wow, I never would've found the wood polish there..." He felt a little bad about that one, because he'd hidden it first, just so he could chat with her while they looked. They'd both laughed a lot.

But by far, the most pathetic one was when he asked Ruth to help him with Aiden's sleepover. His son had been begging for one for weeks, but he just didn't think he could handle ten kids in the house by himself...he was not interested in a Kindergarten Cop situation. And he only said yes because he knew she loved a theme.

"We'll do it all video games," she said, clapping her hands. "A cake like an Xbox! Ooh, and they can all design their own avatars for their cups!" When her eyes lit up like that, it was so hard not to love her. Nearly impossible. So when she arrived around lunchtime on Saturday, her arms full of supplies, her eyes sparkling, he nearly told her then. But like a chicken, he lost his nerve, and then the whole thing ramped up once the kids started arriving. This was not the time, he knew, to ask her what he wanted to know. There were preteens running around and the dishwasher was going and the TV was on even though nobody was watching it.

He should wait for candlelight or moonlight or some kind of romantic *something*, but it never seemed like the right time, and if he kept waiting for it, it might never come. He felt like he was sitting in the church parking lot before Divorce Support all over again.

"Ruth."

"Hmm?"

"I changed my mind."

She didn't look up. "About the meal plan? It's a bit late for that, boss..."

"No. About the...circling." That got her attention. Her head snapped up, and her dark gaze bore into his.

"Oh?" Dang, when she looked at him like that, it was hard to think, let alone put on some kind of winning persona. He was wearing a ten-year-old T-shirt with Dahlia spit-up on it; he probably wasn't helping his cause. Her dark eyes were so trusting and guileless, and she was just watching him so patiently, waiting for him to go on. Only he hadn't gotten that far in his head.

"Yeah." He swallowed. "I want to circle you. Mash beaks and stuff." *Wow.* If this worked, it would be a freaking miracle. She still wasn't saying anything, but a slow smile broke across her face, and he felt like he was watching the sun come up on a cloudless morning at Foster's Point. "Not saying I'm ready to build a nest or anything, but...yeah. Maybe some of that other stuff."

"Well, we should talk about that."

"Yes," he heard himself saying as he nodded. "Good. Let's do that. Tonight?"

"I was supposed to have Audubon tonight, and then tomorrow I'm moving..."

"Okay. That's fine. We don't have to—"

"Charlie." He'd already started backing away without realizing it, so he stopped. "I want to," she said quietly. "I just can't tonight. How's Sunday?"

"Sunday's good. They'll be with their mom, so you and I can...talk." Based on the way the tiny muscles at the corners of her mouth were moving, Charlie guessed she was trying rather hard to hold back a smirk and very nearly succeeding.

"Yes, I look forward to our...talk." He was shuffling closer now, his feet carrying him toward that gorgeous smile. "I mean, we will talk. That wasn't a bluff."

"Okay." She was still smiling, but the way she tipped her head back was an obvious invitation. An invitation he desperately wanted to RSVP to.

"But there might also be some beak-mashing..." he murmured, leaning down toward her lovely face.

"Sounds good to me..."

"Dad, can we—" Aiden stopped short, in body and in thought. He looked between the two of them quizzically.

"Did you need something, bud?" Charlie asked, turning toward him to shield Ruth from his son's judgmental gaze.

"We want to sleep in the backyard in tents."

"Actually in the backyard where I can see you or out on the property somewhere?" It just wasn't fenced off well enough for anything else. Maybe when they were older...

"Where you can see us."

"Yeah, that's fine." He turned back to Ruth, but he saw Aiden's gaze go stormy as he did.

"And when's Ruth going home?" His son's unabashed rudeness shocked him.

"Aiden! You don't ask that about someone we invited."

But she seemed unruffled by the question. "I can go home whenever you'd like. I'm just available as a bonus adult for your dad."

"Well, you're not getting paid, are you?"

She leveled a cool *where are you going with this* look at him. "No, I'm not. I'm just being a good friend."

"Right," Aiden pressed, and Charlie finally knew what he was getting at. "Because that's all you are, right? Friends? With my dad?" There was a long pause. The question was directed at Ruth, and they'd just had an extensive discussion at Divorce Support about why it was important not to talk over other people, especially women. But he was also Aiden's dad, and Ruth wasn't his parent. She didn't deserve to be put on the spot like this.

"Aiden, let's talk about this later. When you don't have friends over."

"I knew it," the boy whispered, then turned and ran from the room.

"It'll be okay," Ruth said, and he felt her reach for his hand. "We'll talk to him together." If it wouldn't have made things worse, he'd have kissed her. But the thoughts Kellan had planted about restitution had taken root in his mind, growing into a thorny plant that grabbed at his mental pant leg whenever he brushed by it.

"Do you think he needs to see a counselor?" he asked quietly.

Ruth stared at him still, but the way her gaze went far away told him she was mulling over the question. "I don't know. I don't see how it could hurt, and he did say something the other day about how marriage was a terrible idea. But it is another battle to fight. Another thing he probably doesn't want to do. One parent can only fight so many of those. It may mean that you let some other things go." Charlie rocked back onto his heels as he thought about that.

"I don't know what Starla and Sawyer think, either. I tried to talk to her about it when they were here for Easter, but we got interrupted. I could probably convince them."

"You're rather convincing when you want to be." Now that he'd let her know he wanted Flirty Ruth back, she didn't seem to be able to stop.

"This is serious!"

She smiled. "I know. I'm sorry, I'm being serious. But it is difficult to take you seriously with spit-up on your shirt like that." *Oh. Right.* Charlie turned and went upstairs. At the top, he could hear Aiden and his friends in the bonus room. He wandered down the hall. His son sat on the couch, arms crossed, scowling at the screen.

"Michael died. Your turn, Aiden."

"I don't want a turn." Cord shrugged, and Michael gleefully retained ownership of the controller. From that distance, Charlie couldn't tell if his son's eyes were glassy, but when he subtly wiped a tear away, he knew. He had to get his kid some help. Even if it cost him more than money.

CHAPTER TWENTY-SEVEN

Ruth

Levi was staring at her again. He stood in the hallway just outside the bathroom, coffee in hand, looking tousled and annoyed. "Did you need the bathroom?" she asked, as she pulled out her Epsom salts from under the sink and put them in an old peach box. The grocery store in Salem had had more than enough fruit boxes for her meager belongings.

"No."

"Did you need something from me?"

"No."

She pulled back the curtain to the shower and grabbed her shampoo, conditioner and razor. "So you're just going to stand there?"

"Yeah."

Ruth shrugged. "Okay." She started to close the door when he reached out a hand to stop her.

"Levi, go away." But her brother just shoved his way inside the bathroom and closed the door behind him. "Hey!"

"Are you doing this because of *him*?" The way Levi spit the last word out made it clear he was talking about Charlie.

"No."

"Then why?"

"Because I'm a grown woman," she snapped, "and you don't own me!"

"Neither does he, Ruth. He cannot have you."

"Oh, seriously, Levi? I didn't realize you were this foolish. My love life is absolutely none of your business, and if you disagree, then we've got a bigger problem than I thought."

"You do not want to be associated with those people, trust me."

"I'm already associated with them! And they're nice! You don't even know them!"

"I know enough! I can't abide the thought of you dating that...that..."

Both their phones buzzed simultaneously.

Mom: Both of you come here, please.

Ruth felt guilt wash over her; they must've been louder than she realized if her mother could hear them through the wall.

They looked at each other, then turned to obey. But Levi did not seem chagrined as he led the way into her parents' room.

"Good morning," Deborah said, and they echoed her greeting together. "Is it moving day?"

Ruth nodded, and Levi just glowered harder in her direction. "I'm sorry, I thought I'd mentioned it."

"You probably did. All my days run together sometimes." She turned to Levi. "I think you should help Ruth pack. It's your fault she's leaving, after all."

"My fault?" He pointed indignantly at Ruth. "She's the one abandoning us."

"When you have children someday, you'll understand that growing up is not abandonment; it's what children are supposed to do. And Ruth is not a child. Neither are you. Which doesn't explain why I've been awakened this early on a Saturday to such squabbling." Mom folded her hands in her lap. "If you had no sister, you'd have learned to do things for yourself, and maybe that would've been better. But God, in His grace, gave you one to do the things I couldn't do. But she has filled that role long enough, and it's time for her to have a life. Her *own* life." She turned to Ruth. "And she's not going to feel guilty about it for a minute, are you?"

Hot tears pressed at her eyes. "Well..."

"No," Deborah said sternly. "You're not. You have done enough, Ruth. I don't know that your dad and I have thanked you enough for all you do for our family."

"You have," Ruth said quickly. "You definitely have."

"We're going to love you no matter where you live, no matter what you do or don't do, because that's what families do." Deborah held out her arms, and Ruth gladly bent to give her a hug. But she wasn't done.

"Levi, I know this affects you negatively, but I encourage you to see what a good thing this is *for Ruth* and be happy for her."

"It's not just the move, Mom. She's dating Charlie Miller; did you know that? She's dating her *boss*." He must have heard her on the phone, planning their date. *Curse these thin walls.*

Her mom let her go, then patted Ruth's arm.

"Ruthie, would you excuse us, please?" She didn't think she could look at Levi without gloating, so she avoided his gaze as she left. As she shut the door quietly, she heard her mom ask Levi to sit down...and him refuse.

Going back to her packing, she could hear their muffled voices through the wall of the bathroom, but not what was being said. It wasn't her business, anyway. "Hey, Ruthie," her dad said, appearing in the bathroom doorway with a grin. "Moving day, right? My truck's all gassed up."

And why was his enthusiastic support harder to take than Levi's disdain?

"Thank you, Dad," she whispered, and when he opened his arms, she yielded her strong facade. A dad hug was the one thing in the world that could always make her cry; he held her too tight and the tears she'd held back got squeezed out.

"I'm proud of you," he whispered, and she nodded. "Ignore your brothers. This is a good thing. This is great. We'll be fine."

"Well, you won't be rid of me. I'll come around to help sometimes."

He pulled back. "Don't take this the wrong way, but...maybe don't? For a while? Let them get some things figured out when they don't like living with unwashed clothes and dirty dishes."

"Okay," she said, wiping the tears with one finger. "It's a plan."

She'd already hit the thrift store and picked up some dishes and serviceable pans, but other than that, she didn't have much she'd need to buy. A lot of the furniture was built in so it could be folded up into the wall to make space. She was just sorting out in her head whether she could fit it all into two trucks or whether she'd just make more than one trip when there was a quiet knock at the front door.

Wyatt opened it, and she heard him say, "What are you doing here?" It was more surprised than malicious, but Ruth's heart beat harder when she heard Charlie's voice.

"Just wanted to drop off a housewarming gift for Ruth." He was doing that slick, posturing thing that she hated. She wanted to shake him by the shoulders.

"I'll give it to her," Wyatt said, reaching out, but Charlie pulled back.

"I'd rather give it to her myself."

"Hi," she sang, hurrying toward the front door before this devolved any further. "You're here!"

"Yeah, I just walked over. I don't know exactly where your new place is."

"That's fine, thank you," she said, giving Charlie a bright smile, and she could practically feel the annoyance in the house surge to flood-like levels. "And you brought me a present?"

"Yeah." Her brothers were congregating behind her, based on the muttering and shuffling feet, so she stepped outside and closed the door. The large cardboard box he was holding was closed with two flaps.

"It's not alive, is it?"

"Well, yes." He chuckled ruefully. "I know you don't need more things to keep alive, but the internet said it helps to make a small space more homey."

She peeked inside, and a riot of green in every shade greeted her. "Oh, plants!"

"You don't have to take them."

"I want them!"

He pulled them back. "I just realized it might be adding work to your life in an unhelpful way."

"No, I want them! Gimme." She tried to snatch the box out of his hands, but he held on.

"It's really heavy."

She pulled on it again. "I'm really strong."

"I could come with you and deliver them to your new house."

"Ah," she said, grinning. "So this was a ploy."

"A nice ploy, though," he grumped, and she couldn't resist kissing him again. "A gifty ploy."

"Don't sulk. You can come. I was just about to take the first load over."

Charlie grinned. "And I'm muscle now, is that it? Now who's scheming?" He walked over to her truck and she opened the back door so he could put the plants inside.

"Oh, I've got muscle aplenty. I just like you around. I'll grab my coat." They walked back to the front door, only to find a wall of brothers blocking their way.

"Yes?"

"He can't come inside," said Levi firmly. Ruth's insides went nuclear with anger.

"Excuse you?" She was totally using her mom voice now. "What did you just say to me?"

Charlie touched her arm. "It's not a big deal."

"Like hell it's not!"

A large hand clamped down on Levi's shoulder, and her dad came through. "What's going on out here, I—" He stopped short when he saw Charlie. Ruth saw the moment he figured out what his sons were doing and his gaze sharpened. "Come to help with the move?" he said, sticking out his right hand, and Charlie shook it with a smile.

"Yes, sir. If you don't mind."

"No, no, come on in," he exclaimed. "In my house, anyone who wants to help is welcome." *Subtle, Dad,* thought Ruth, but she mostly kept the smirk off her face. "Any friend of Ruth's is a friend of mine. My back will be thankful for the reprieve."

Charlie picked up a box of books near the front door, then edged his way out, like he wasn't sure he should turn his back to this group. "Which truck?"

"Either one," Ruth called. "Thanks, babe!"

That prompted a host of new grumbles, which she ignored. Her brothers stood like a gauntlet on either side of the door as she, her dad, and Charlie packed the trucks. She didn't know if they'd explicitly made a pact not to help, but Ranger and Ryan looked unhappy. Finally, they were done. She gave each of her brothers a hug. She didn't feel sad to say goodbye to Ranger—she was going to see him next week, as they'd already made plans for him to come over to dinner. And Levi had made goodbye easy by being a jerk. But it felt too real to say goodbye to Wyatt, who squeezed her so tight and cleared his throat like he felt like crying, and Ryan...Ryan had always been her baby. It sounded silly, she knew, calling this giant hulk of a guy her baby, but he was. He'd been just six when Mom got sick, and she'd been the one packing his lunchbox and helping with homework and teaching him right from wrong all this time. And leaving with no plans to see him felt...final? Too final.

"Movie night?" he choked out, and despite her dad's advice, she nodded.

"I'll bring pizza," Ruth said.

"No, *I'll* bring pizza."

"All right," she said, patting his back, and when he let go, she didn't bother to wipe the tears away. "You all know I'm only moving across town, right?"

"It's normal to have big feelings when things change," Charlie said quietly, and Ruth just nodded. When they piled into the trucks, all four of her brothers stood in the driveway and watched as they drove away.

CHAPTER TWENTY-EIGHT

Charlie

Sunday finally arrived. Charlie paced in his bedroom, peeking out the front window. When he stubbed his toe for the second time on Dahlia's crib, he decided he should go downstairs. But he couldn't see as well out the window downstairs. She wasn't late; their date wasn't for another fifteen minutes. He hadn't even put the pizza in the oven yet. It was preheated, though. He paced into the kitchen; yes, it was preheated. He straightened the silverware on the kitchen table and picked off a piece of cereal that was still stuck to it. (How had they both missed that?) Did they need silverware for pizza? Was that weird?

Headlights flashed against the wall, and he heard the crunch of wheels on the driveway. He made himself walk to the front door and wait until she rang the bell to throw open the front door.

"Hi."

Ruth smiled up at him. "Hi." And all the questions he'd had for her about what movie she wanted to watch and if pepperoni was okay died on his lips. Because Ruth was wearing heels. Shiny red heels that complimented her little black dress perfectly.

"Is this okay?" She smoothed down the skirt that flared perfectly at her waist. "I wasn't sure what we were going to do."

"Yes! No, it's good. Come in, come in." He offered his hand...to do what exactly he didn't know; his threshold wasn't treacherous. He just really wanted to touch her. Charlie inwardly facepalmed at his fumbling. *Get it together, man.*

"You look great, baby."

Ruth took his hand, but scowled. "Don't do that."

"Do what?" He tried to drop her hand, but she didn't let go, and then they were just standing in his entryway holding hands like two teenagers going to prom.

"That slick Charlie thing. I used to watch you in the gym, flirting with all the women. Well, all of them except me. Not that I cared."

He shook her hand out of his like she'd burned him. "What?"

"You really don't know what I'm talking about?" Was that...pity? This date was off to a great start. "Here, I'll show you. You be a lady on a treadmill..."

"No," he said, annoyed. "I know what you're talking about. But I don't do that anymore."

"You just did. I watched you. You called me *baby*."

Charlie grimaced. "It just slipped out. I..." What had he been thinking, trying his old moves on a woman as savvy as Ruth? As grounded and practical and lovely as her? She wasn't going to find that kind of treatment charming whatsoever.

"Here," she said, turning back to the front door. When she opened it and stepped through it, his heart did a free fall into his stomach. Had he really just managed to screw up their first date only thirty seconds in? Was she *leaving*? The door closed, and he stood there, speechless. Then the doorbell rang.

Befuddled, Charlie opened the door and peeked out. Ruth was grinning at him.

"Hi."

"Hi?" So...she wasn't leaving? His heart slowly started to climb its way back into his chest, especially when she stepped close enough to kiss him, even though she didn't.

"Can I come in?"

"Oh. Yeah. Um..." Charlie stepped back, opening the door wider and smashed the same toe he'd stubbed earlier on Dahlia's crib. He bit back a swear word and Ruth giggled.

"The kids aren't here; you can say it."

But he didn't. He just held out both his hands, palms up, and when she took his hands, he said what he'd meant to say the first time.

"Ruth, you look beautiful. Truly."

"Better," she whispered. "You look very nice yourself. Is that your new cologne?" She leaned close to him, and he smiled.

"How do you know it's new? Ruth, are you sniffing my colognes?"

She shrugged, unrepentant. "Maybe." She began backing toward the kitchen.

"Maybe?" he echoed, following her, and his heart kicked up as she stayed out of kissing range. "It wasn't the Closet Fairy again?"

"Organization Fairy. And no, she wouldn't invade your privacy like that..."

Charlie lunged forward and caught her around the waist, and she squealed.

"Quit poking your nose in my stuff, Ruth Zane."

"Make me." Her defiant gaze just made the words inflame him all the more.

"Why are you so bold? Weren't you afraid I'd fire you?"

She laughed. "Maybe a little. But you need me."

"I could've hired Henry." She smelled good, too; she was wearing a light perfume that smelled like sunshine.

"Henry Kellogg? He's no good for the long haul. You needed a professional."

"Well, you are that...except for ignoring my instructions about staying out of my stuff."

She reached up and brushed the hair near his temple with her fingers. "Except for that."

"I like holding you," he murmured. "You feel good. This feels right."

"You feel quite good, too. And I really do like this new cologne." He was about to tease her again for sniffing things in his bathroom when she leaned closer, taking a long inhale near his neck that had him feeling a little emptyheaded, his heart beating faster. He wanted to kiss her hard. He wanted to take her upstairs. He wanted to...

"Keep your shoes on. We're going out."

Ruth's eyes brightened. "On the motorcycle?"

"You're not dressed for the motorcycle."

She grimaced. "I knew this was a mistake. I'll go home and change."

He held her tight as she tried to step toward the door. "Not so fast, Zane. We can take a ride another night, when you're not so..." He searched for the right word as he gently stroked her cheek. "Glamorous. I like you like this." Charlie glanced down at her heels. "Even if your height is unnerving."

Truth be told, that wasn't the only thing that was unnerving. Holding Ruth in his arms in an empty house was just too tempting.

"How is my height unnerving?" she murmured, throwing her arms around his neck.

"Your face is very close to my face. I'm used to you more..." He put a flat hand about nose height. "Here."

"That's because I don't wear shoes in the house, as my boss requested. Besides," she added, her gaze latching onto his, mischief sparkling in her depths, "when our faces are closer together, it makes some things easier."

"I thought we were going to talk first," he murmured, and she tipped her head to the side, assessing. Their lips were exactly a heartbeat apart, and he wanted so badly to lean forward and taste her, tempt her, show her how much he'd been thinking about her, how much he wanted her...

"Cool," she said brightly, breaking the spell. "Do you wanna grab food first?"

Food. Yes. If he ate food, his mouth would be too busy to kiss Ruth and maybe not stop kissing her when he should. But she was all dressed up and it seemed wrong to foist his run-of-the-mill take-and-bake pizza on her.

"Yeah, let me just..." Charlie dashed into the kitchen and shut off the oven, grabbing his keys off the island. Thankfully, she didn't follow him. "Let's go."

"We can take my truck," she offered as he set the alarm.

"My SUV is much nicer than your truck."

"Well, if that's the standard, everything you own is nicer than what I own. Does that mean I don't get to contribute to our dates?"

"Ruth…" he groaned as he shut off the lights.

"Yes?" she answered sweetly, batting her eyelashes at him.

"I don't want to take your truck. Can we take my car? Please? I planned this date. When you plan it, we can take yours."

"Deal." She was grinning bigger than he'd ever seen her, and he couldn't help brushing up against her as he opened her door on the passenger side. "Why does that smile terrify me?"

"Because you know how great I am at planning things."

He nodded solemnly as she buckled her seat belt. "I do know that. You're wonderful at it."

"I am, yes."

Why was it so hard to just shut the door and take them to dinner? Why did it feel like her red lips were calling to him?

"Chuck."

"Hmm?"

"You're staring again."

"Am I?" It registered in his brain that she'd used an r, and that was just the thing about Ruth: she seemed to trust him, and he didn't think he deserved it. She was open and loving and free and he felt bound by his mistakes, bound by his nature to make more of them. He so desperately didn't want to mess this up, not just because he'd have to find a new nanny, but because he'd have to find a new woman that he felt this comfortable with, who made him laugh like this, who called him on all his BS and added sparkle to his life.

"Why did you say yes?" he murmured, lifting a hand to stroke her soft cheek. "To me. To this. There must be better options for you."

Ruth snorted. "Better options than a devastatingly handsome, successful man who runs his own business, loves his kids, and looks at me like I'm Snow White?"

"I'm not convinced you aren't; let's examine the facts. You often wander in the woods—"

"On my own property," she said, laughter choking her words.

"You have a way with small, surly people."

"They're not miners."

"You're excellent at housework."

"That can't be denied," she said, pretending to buff her nails on her dress.

"All you're missing is the wicked stepmother, so stay away from apples, just in case."

"Oh my goodness, you *do* have an imagination!"

Just one kiss couldn't hurt, could it? Charlie leaned toward her, his arms braced on the door frame, but she put a finger over his lips before he reached hers.

"You said talking first."

"I did?"

"Mm-hmm. And you said food first. A lady has needs."

"Well, I can't let my lady down, then." Charlie smiled as he leaned back and shut her door carefully. He felt a little better, even though he was still fairly sure he was going to screw it up somehow...but there was a certain sense of safety in having tried twice already and being thwarted both times by her making him stick to what he's said. Maybe this would be okay. It wasn't fair to put that burden on her, though...

"How fancy do you want to go?" he asked, backing out of the garage.

"It's your wallet, Chuck."

"What are you in the mood for, though?"

"Time with you when I don't have to stir anything, wipe anything, or discipline anyone."

Charlie bit back a snarky comment about how she obviously didn't know how naughty he could be. "Seriously, though. Italian? French? Sushi?"

"I've never had sushi..."

"Ooh, I smell an adventure."

She laughed. "Don't you get sick?"

"Heck no. And it's delicious. You know you want to try it. I can tell you're intrigued."

He glanced at her just long enough to have his opinion confirmed by the quirking of her lips.

"I admit to being curious; I just don't know if I'm brave enough."

"If you're audacious enough to reorganize my clothes without my permission..."

"Hey. I told you, that was the Organization Fairy! And there was no chance of me throwing up all night from *that*."

Without looking, he held his hand out, palm up, and felt her place hers in it. "I'll hold your hair back if you are. Come on. Let's live a little."

"I live often, thank you."

"I know you do, that's why I l-l-like you." Oof, that was close. It was not love, it was far too early for love; if he loved her, it was in the friend way, the way he loved a new personal record in his running or a record-breaking month in sales.

"I thought I had the speech issues," she teased, and when she squeezed his hand playfully, he squeezed hers back. Charlie was forced to let go of her hand when they got out of the car at the fancy sushi place she'd found on her phone, after convincing her to forego the one-dollar-sign places she'd suggested first. She was worth it.

But he picked it back up again as they waited to be seated, and then accepted seats at the bar.

"Are you left-handed?" she asked, as she slung her purse over the back of the barstool.

"No, why do you ask?"

She gestured toward their joined hands with her head. "Just trying to figure out how you're going to eat."

"Don't worry about me, gorgeous. I can take care of myself."

"I do, though," she said, and it was so soft, he almost didn't hear her over the clink and shuffle of the restaurant. "I worry that you're lonely."

Letting a little of his old charm through, Charlie lifted the back of her hand to his lips, holding her gaze. "I'm not tonight."

CHAPTER TWENTY-NINE

Ruth

Charlie was quiet as they got back into the car, and Ruth glanced over at him.

"Everything okay?"

"Of course." His smile looked easy, but she knew better by now; the fingers of his right hand were tapping the drive shaft, and it wasn't remotely in time to the music.

"Chuck, if you want to say something to me, you should. We said we were going to talk, so let's talk."

He moved both hands to the steering wheel, and he looked like he was trying to throttle it. "I've...made mistakes. In the past. Even tonight, I was slipping back into that old skin, the way I used to try to...sell people on me. And I'm mad at myself, because I know better. You shouldn't have to police me or correct me like that. I made you uncomfortable, and I didn't even think about it. You had me convinced that I could do this, but now..." He was drumming on the steering wheel now with his thumbs.

"You're not sure?"

He nodded, still wholly focused on the dark road. Ruth pondered his words for a minute, then turned off the radio.

"So you didn't have fun tonight?"

Charlie rolled his eyes. "That's not what I said."

"I know it's not." Ruth tipped her body toward his, trying to pivot in her seat to see him better, but it didn't help. "But that's what matters, right?"

"No," he said forcefully. "Because I hurt people that way, being that guy. I don't want to hurt you, Ruth. That's the last thing I want to do." He scoffed, shaking his head. "And now I'm making your comfort about me. See? Hopeless."

"It seems to me that you're putting an awful lot of pressure on yourself." She paused, her own fingers drumming on the SUV's leather door handle. "But then again, you always did."

"And what's that supposed to mean, Zane? Are you really comparing this to a high school geography essay?"

Ruth grinned. "How'd you know?"

"Because I still think about that conversation, too," he said quietly. "I wasn't even supposed to talk to you, and there I was, spilling my guts over a silly paper."

"You have that effect on me, too—I hadn't told anyone about my mom's illness. And your dad was being too hard on you. From what I can tell, that's often the case. And now you've decided to do it for him, which is very convenient. For him, I mean. Not for you."

He scowled, his eyebrows pulling into a deep V. "Expecting respect isn't too much; that's the basics, Ruth."

"But it's not just respect," she said slowly. "You're expecting perfection. Yes, you made a mistake by calling me baby, but I corrected you and you responded immediately. I can't ask for more than that."

"You deserve better," Charlie muttered, running a hand through his soft, floppy hair. "You don't deserve a dumpster fire like me."

"Don't talk about my boyfriend that way, please." She didn't want to distract him from driving, but she thought it would help to touch him, so she hesitantly stretched out and put a light hand on his leg. Charlie swerved a little, but he reached down and covered her hand with his, gripping her fingers tightly. "He's going through a hard time. You should cut him some slack."

"It's his own damn fault if he is." Charlie turned into the long driveway and pulled slowly straight into the garage. She didn't want to leave like this; they'd had such a good time, she didn't want him going inside alone to stew. But it seemed like he was worried about taking things too far.

"You're so hard on yourself," she whispered. "I hate it."

"Pretending didn't get me anywhere, Ruth. It just lost me my wife."

She squeezed his hand. "I think there's a balance between ignoring your faults and focusing on them exclusively. We can acknowledge that you've got some work to do in your personal life without letting it steal our chance to be together, can't we?"

"We?" He shifted to hold her hand with both of his, and a warm, tender feeling sunk into her chest, like a cat settling down to nap.

"Yes, Chuck. *We*. I want to be a *we* with you. And you don't have to sell me on anything. I like you already."

"Even if I say the wrong thing a lot?"

"Imperfect people deserve to be loved. Everyone does."

Charlie was staring out the windshield at the ski gear mounted to the wall, and she wasn't sure what he was thinking.

"Sorry, I was just…" He paused. "My dad does pick on me a lot, doesn't he?"

Ruth nodded. "From what I can tell. I'm not there, obviously, but he seems to have a lot of criticism. Not much of it seems constructive."

He was quiet again for a long time, so long that the light went off in the garage, plunging them into the dark. When he still didn't move, she brushed her thumb over his palm.

"You can't come inside." His voice was serious, almost sad.

Ruth shrugged. "Okay."

"It's not about you, I just don't trust myself. And I don't want to mess this up before it's even really started, not when things are so…fragile."

"You're that bad of a kisser, huh?"

After a stunned pause, Charlie chuckled, and there was a rumbly quality to his voice when he spoke again. "No, Ms. Zane."

"You don't need to be embarrassed, Chuck. A lot of people are bad kissers."

"You're not going to goad me this time. I mean it." He was trying so hard to be stern, she could tell. It was so adorable. When she opened her door, he let go of her hand, dragging his fingers over her skin like he didn't want to. She hopped out of the tall car, jumping down to the concrete in her tall heels. She still felt a little wobbly in them, but she looked great and she knew it.

Charlie got out, too, and trailed her over to her truck. "Can I kiss you goodnight?"

"I don't know if I want one after our earlier discussion. I don't have time to teach you how to improve..." It was total BS, of course. She'd only made out with previous boyfriends a handful of times, and it had been years. If anyone's kissing technique sucked, it was hers. Still, her jokes seemed to be getting to him. She opened the driver's side door, but Charlie gripped the top of it before she could open it and get inside.

"Please. I've been thinking about it. A lot." The heat in his gaze confirmed the fact, and Ruth thought it best not to try to guess what he was thinking about right now.

She crossed her arms over her chest. "Why should I let you kiss me if this isn't working out?"

Charlie frowned. "I didn't say it wasn't working out, I said I'm afraid of messing it up. There's a difference."

"Because of your awful kissing technique. Right."

"You are impossible," he said, pure exasperation tinging his words, and Ruth couldn't suppress her grin. She put her back against the truck and placed her hands between her nice dress and the dirty vehicle, lifting her chin in invitation, but didn't give him the words he wanted yet.

"I know you think your charms are irresistible," Ruth said sincerely, "but I think we've proven tonight that your old moves won't work on me. I've got exceptional self-control."

"Until it comes to staying away from my colognes..." He tucked a lock of hair behind her ear carefully, and the gentle contact made her skin tingle.

"Insatiable curiosity is not a bad thing, dude. In fact, someday, it may work to your advantage..."

Charlie groaned. "You're trying to tease me into an early grave, aren't you?"

"Is it working?"

"Yes," he said emphatically, and Ruth cackled, throwing her head back. The stars twinkled at her like they were just as amused at their interactions as she was. When she met his gaze again, he was grinning at her, all his hesitancy and vulnerability gone.

"Well, we can't have that," she said, caressing his smooth cheek, and he leaned into her touch like a man starved for it. She gave up trying to protect her dress—that's what washing machines were for, right?—and took his face in both her hands, and the deep sound that rumbled out of his chest made it completely worth it. He bounced his gaze between hers and her lips, practically begging her to close the distance between them. But he'd jammed his hands in his pockets, and he wasn't pressuring her.

"See how controlled you're being right now?" she murmured, tracing his cheekbone with a light touch. "You've changed, and you'll keep changing. I know it."

"Kinda hanging by a thread here," he panted, his breath warming her face, and she snickered. "But I guess you're right."

"I am. And since consent goes both ways, can I kiss you, Charlie?"

He surged forward in answer, cupping her neck and pulling her against him, their lips meeting firmly—if a bit chastely—for her taste. She closed her eyes and parted her lips, and he followed her lead, his grip on her tightening, as if he was afraid she'd stop. The faint taste of wasabi still on his tongue made her smile, but his kiss was languid in contrast to its sharpness. What started with barely bridled urgency melded into something somehow more devastating, his warm lips and the scent of his cologne lulling her into a kind of stupor, like she was existing just for the next sweep of his talented tongue against hers. Then he pulled away suddenly.

"Okay, that's enough. Drive safe."

Ruth opened her eyes. "But...I...Chuck?"

She reached out a hand to stabilize herself against him, a little dizzy from the abrupt stop, but he was gone, striding away from her, almost back inside the garage already.

"Hey!"

He waved over his shoulder. "Great date. Let's do it again. See you later." The door into the house slammed behind him, and he was gone. Ruth burst out laughing and pulled out her phone.

Ruth: Thread broke, huh?

Charlie: No comment.

Ruth: Close your garage door. You don't want animals getting in there.

Charlie: Leave first. And text me when you get home.

Ruth: You're weird, Chuck. See you tomorrow.

CHAPTER THIRTY

Ruth

Monday was a rude crash back to Earth: Dahlia wouldn't stop crying. Ruth had cared for colicky babies before, but this was next level. She walked the long upstairs hallway with her, bouncing and rocking Dahlia on her belly across Ruth's arm. Every once in a while, she'd let out a belch, which seemed to startle her enough that she'd stop crying, just for a second. But she always started up again.

After ninety minutes, which felt like nine hundred, Ruth put her down on Charlie's bed and lay down next to her.

"It's okay, Dahlia," she soothed, but she didn't think Dahlia could even hear her over her wails. She probed her belly with her fingers, then frowned. She'd just fed her, but it seemed...empty. Had she really thrown up that much?

She'd been crying so much, she wasn't even passing tears anymore, and the spot on her head seemed much more sunken than it should. *Dehydration.* That wasn't good. Babies should not be dehydrated with all the milk they were getting.

Ruth picked up a still-screaming Dahlia and went into Charlie's bathroom. Her cries seemed worse bouncing off the subway tile. She stood on his fancy glass scale and noted the number. Then she went downstairs. If this didn't work, she was going to need a little break...she couldn't listen to screaming less than a foot from her ear for so long. She was only human.

Ruth warmed the milk, continuing to bounce and rock Dahlia as she did. She tried turning on soothing music. She tried the sling. None of it seemed to make a dent in Dahlia's frustration.

Finally, the bottle was ready. She'd learned not to feed this child on the couch, after having to invest in carpet cleaner. Ruth sat at the kitchen table, still strewn with a few breakfast dishes she'd missed, and tried to settle Dahlia in with the bottle. The baby sucked it down quickly, even putting her hand on the bottle as if to say, "Take this away at your own peril."

Ruth stroked her head tenderly, humming, trying to communicate that she was here, that she was going to take good care of her. It was a promise Dahlia seemed to appreciate as her eyes grew heavy; she struggled to keep them open as she drank and drank. When she finished, Ruth put her up on her shoulder to burp her, given how quickly she'd gulped it down, and she let out two massive burps. But as soon as Ruth stood up to put her back in her bed, Dahlia threw up again. Most of it went on the floor, which was good news, not only for Ruth's clothing but for her research. She raced up the stairs to Charlie's bathroom again, Dahlia wailing in her arms. Shaking a little, she pressed her foot onto the scale and weighed them again. It was exactly the same. And this wasn't like her mechanical scale in her bathroom at home; this thing was accurate down to the ounce. And according to this scale, she hadn't retained any of what she'd eaten. It read exactly the same. Ruth stared down at the numbers.

She'd only had an eight-ounce bottle...how many tenths of a pound was that? She pulled out her phone, trying to search for the information as Dahlia cried. *If a gallon of water is about eight pounds...* Her head hurt; it felt like it was splitting open between the stress and the noise. As best as she could figure, that eight-ounce bottle was about half a pound. So she should've seen *some* movement on the scale...shouldn't there? She wasn't a doctor. Then the thought was obvious: *Dahlia needs a doctor.* She put the baby down, apologizing to her, and stepped out of the bedroom to call Charlie.

Four rings. No answer.

She called Starla. Four rings. No answer.

She called them both again, because she knew if anyone in her family called twice, she'd stop whatever she was doing and pick up. But they didn't. Maybe they'd left their phones on their desks. Maybe they were in their cars. She tried the front desk at the library: Starla was out. She'd gone to Salem for copier paper, sticky notes and thumbtacks. Had this woman not heard of the internet, which would gladly deliver all of that to her door? She called reception at the dealership, wishing she had his brother's number, too; they were probably at lunch. Maybe he'd left it in the paperwork she'd had him fill out initially...she hurried downstairs for the binder...her heart sank when she opened it up. He'd left it blank. But he had signed the temporary guardianship, allowing for medical professionals to care for all the kids in his absence. Starla had signed, too.

She stared at it. Was it bad enough to use this? She stared at their signatures, Starla's swoopy one in such contrast to

Charlie's sharp lines. Then she did the only other thing she could think of: she called her mom.

"Ruthie?" her mom answered with a yawn.

"Did I wake you? I'm sorry." A surge of tears surprised her, and one slipped out before she could stop it.

"No, it's fine. What's up?"

She explained what was going on, rapid fire, adding bits she'd noticed over the last few weeks. And it was strange, but saying it out loud, she knew what she wanted to do. She wasn't imagining this; something was going on. But she ended with her question regardless.

"Would you take her to the doctor?"

"I think you've got more experience with babies than I do now," her mom said gently, "but yes, I would. Send a message to tell them what's happening, and then go. It's not going to hurt anything."

She could still hear Dahlia crying. She'd probably fall asleep if she put her in the car...

"Okay. I'm going."

"Keep us updated, hon. I think you're doing the right thing."

Ruth hung up without agreeing. She really didn't know, but her gut told her that she wanted Dahlia seen by a professional, and that wasn't her.

"All right, baby girl," Ruth said, gathering her up. "We're going for a ride."

CHAPTER THIRTY-ONE

Charlie

Charlie was in a virtual meeting when his phone rang. Unfortunately, it was in his pocket, and if he looked at it, this vendor was going to be offended. Charlie had already missed their meeting once because Henry hadn't reminded him. Sometimes he wondered if Jason wasn't the only one with ADHD. Or maybe he was just a single dad with a new assistant.

It was a tire company who'd just moved into the area, one of those chain stores owned by someone in a different state. He and Jason had gotten their tires from Rex for the last ten years; he wasn't as cheap as these guys, but he also came out on a Sunday if they really needed him. He couldn't see these guys showing up on Sunday. Or even after five. But he listened politely so that if people needed their cars fixed, this store would send their clients to Miller Motors. Relationships mattered, the old and the new.

He asked about the specific sizes they carried for trucks, just to seem like he was listening. The phone rang again. *This meeting is never going to end.* It was probably someone from Divorce Support, though they usually used the group chat if they had something to say.

It didn't occur to him that anything was wrong; he'd been getting a lot of calls from telemarketers lately. And lots of people called with questions to his cell phone, because they knew there'd been no one up front. Small-town news moved quickly that way. And he didn't mind. Usually, when people called, it was important. Like the school...*Ugh.* He hoped it wasn't them. He really didn't want to have to go pick up Aiden again. He thought his issues had been better since Ruth came into their lives...*Ruth.* Ruth made him want to blow off work, put her on his motorcycle, and drive to the beach. She made him want to lie in the grass and look at clouds. Go swimming in the dark under a sea of stars. He didn't know why; it was just something about her that was...alive. Not the way that he lived, slogging from one thing to the next. She carried a heavier load than he did, taking care of her mom and her lazy brothers, but she still kept a twinkle in her eye. She just made life *fun.* He hadn't entirely figured out how to incorporate that joy into his life, but he was making progress.

The guy on the screen had finished, and they were staring at him expectantly.

"Should we send a contract over?"

"Sure," Charlie replied with a fake smile, "send it on down and we'll look at it. I can't promise anything, but I'll read it over."

They did that awkward goodbye that is amplified so much more through a screen, and Charlie ended the meeting. Immediately, his phone pinged with a message, and he groaned. Charlie stood up to get it out of his pocket easier, but what he read made his knees shake.

Ruth: At the ER with Dahlia.

He could hear his father's voice in his head: *Shouldn't have left her with a Zane.* But he rejected it immediately. Whatever had happened, it was just an accident. He found her number in his recent calls with lightning efficiency.

"What happened?"

"She won't stop crying. She seems really dehydrated." That wasn't good for babies; he knew that much. More of him was shaking now, but he told himself that his girl was in good hands.

"I'm coming, I'm on my way right now." He hung up before Ruth could say anything more. "Henry," he called as he grabbed his coat off the back of his office chair. "My daughter's in the hospital. I'll be out all afternoon and maybe tomorrow."

Henry's eyes widened. "Oh. Okay. Is everything all right?"

"I don't know yet." He stuck his head into the shop. "Jace!"

His brother looked up from the Suburban he had his head poked into, loud music blaring from somewhere.

"Something's wrong with D, I gotta go," he called over the noise.

"With Ruthie?"

Now why did everybody call her that? Yes, she was adorable, but it made her sound too immature. And having kissed the woman at the end of their date, she definitely wasn't.

"No," he yelled, "with Dahlia."

His face pinched with concern. "What happened, an accident?" he shouted back. Of course his big-hearted brother would come to the same conclusion he had. That's why he wanted to be like Jase when he grew up.

"I don't know, I gotta go. I'll text you."

"Lemme know if you need us," he called as the door swung shut.

Charlie called Starla on the way to his SUV. There was no answer. Maybe she was driving, on her way there as well. It was Tuesday, so Sawyer would already be there, working. It gave him some comfort, but not much.

Was she throwing up? Did she have a virus? Had *he* done something wrong? Of course this would happen during his week...Charlie snapped on some music to keep from panicking. It was still on the classic rock Ruth had picked the last time they were together, and it helped a little.

Charlie made himself pick a regular parking spot instead of throwing it into park still running by the front doors. He made himself lock the car as he left. But he could not make his legs walk as he crossed the quiet parking lot, and he arrived at the front desk breathing hard.

"My daughter?"

The nurse stared at him. "Oh, the baby? Yeah, are you...?"

"Her dad." *One of them, anyway.*

"You're down this way." The woman was probably walking normally, but the conversation and journey down the hall seemed to take forever. He felt he'd aged years since he first saw Ruth's text.

The nurse knocked softly, and Kyle Durand called, "Come in."

A crying Dahlia lay on the examination table as Kyle probed her belly, while Ruth stroked her wispy hair and looked into her eyes, smiling.

"I'm here," Charlie said, still panting. "What's going on?"

"That's still being determined. You can have a seat."

Oddly enough, that sounded like a good idea to his legs, which were still feeling wobbly. "Is Starla on her way?"

Ruth nodded, never taking her eyes off the girl. "Sawyer's assisting with a surgery, so we couldn't tell him. But he should be done soon."

"Okay." Charlie dragged a hand through his wet hair. Wait, wet? Was it raining? He hadn't even noticed.

"Has she had many bowel movements?" Dr. Durand asked, putting the tips of his stethoscope into his ears.

"No," answered Ruth. "Not today, anyway."

"Not when she was with me, either," Charlie offered. "I just thought she was having them later."

"And I thought earlier."

Turned out, having four people take care of a sick baby was a bad idea.

"I'm here," Starla said, as out of breath and wet as he was. Ruth stepped aside for her, and Starla cooed to Dahlia, nuzzling her with her nose, holding her tiny hand. But it had no effect.

"Is she in pain?" Charlie asked, but Dr. Durand didn't answer; he may not have heard him over the screaming and his blocked ears.

"Let's get some fluids into her, then we'll talk about next steps."

Next steps? How did the man make that sound so ominous? Was Dahlia sick or not?

"Will you admit her?" Starla asked, and Kyle's expression stayed carefully blank.

"I haven't determined that yet." At the same time, Charlie noticed Ruth quietly gathering up her purse and coat.

"You're not leaving, are you?" The other adults turned to stare at her, and Ruth ducked her head.

"You're both here now. You don't need me."

Charlie stood and crossed the room in three steps. "Come on."

He took her gently by the elbow and led her out into the hallway, and the sudden quiet was a relief.

"I do need you."

Her gaze softened, and she touched their foreheads together for a moment. "No, you don't."

"Yes, I do. I need you here, not as her nanny, but as my...girlfriend. I'm barely holding it together, Ruth. Please. Please stay."

The way she tipped her head told him she was still going to resist.

"But Aiden and Emily—"

"Can hang out with Ainsley for a few hours."

"Have you asked her?"

"No," he admitted, "but she won't mind. She loves a crisis."

"Why don't you see if she's available, and if she isn't..."

"Then my mom can pick them up. Or Starla's mom. Seriously. Please, Ruth." Charlie tugged her closer, ignoring the curious look he got from a passing nurse.

Ruth pursed her lips, then blew out a long breath. "All right."

"Thank you. Seriously, Ruth."

"All right, settle down."

"Why? Am I embarrassing you?"

"A little," she said, inching backward, and he let her go with a smile. But there was no time to tease her, because Sawyer came barreling down the hallway at full speed.

"I came as soon as they told me, where is she?"

Charlie gestured toward the door, and Sawyer burst inside. "I'm here."

"Good." It was quieter inside now as Starla nursed Dahlia, her legs hanging off the exam table.

"Good, you're all here. I apologize. I'm not used to accommodating a family of your configuration," Kyle said, as they shuffled around, trying to find seats. Charlie ended up yielding his to Ruth as he crammed himself into the corner, but he didn't mind so much when she reached back and squeezed his fingers. He held on and didn't let go, resting their joined hands on her shoulder.

"Ruth was correct to bring her in; she's very dehydrated and somewhat malnourished. Her eyes show the start of jaundice."

"How did this happen?" Starla asked, still rocking her.

"It's likely it was no one's fault," he replied. "I'd like a pediatric specialist to confirm my diagnosis before I share it, and we'll do an ultrasound just to be sure. But if it's what I suspect, she has a genetic defect that's easily treatable with surgery."

Sawyer straightened at that. "What kind of surgery?"

"We will wait," Kyle said sternly, "to have my diagnosis confirmed." The adults all glanced at each other, and Charlie was pretty sure he wasn't the only one warring between amusement and dread inside. "I'm going to retrieve a nurse to start the IV."

"Will you admit Dahlia?" Ruth asked quietly.

"I don't think so," Kyle replied. "But my colleague and I will confer about that as well." He stood and shook hands with each of them, then sanitized.

The moment he left, Sawyer cursed softly. "I know what she's got."

All four of them crowded around the sleepy baby, who went wide-eyed for a moment to see all four adults pressed in around her.

"Hi, pumpkin," Sawyer rumbled, and she appeared to relax again. He pressed his fingers into her belly, moving them in a circular pattern.

"There." Sawyer grabbed Ruth's hand and put it on Dahlia's belly, and Charlie felt a ping of pointless jealousy. "Feel that?"

"What is that? It feels like a cyst or something."

"Can I feel?" Charlie tried to probe the same point, then recoiled. Something hard, as big as a marble, was in his girl's belly. Had she swallowed something she shouldn't? She was so little. How had she even gotten it? Aiden and Em would never knowingly harm her. "What is that?"

"That's her stomach. It's blocking food from entering her small intestine...the muscle gets overdeveloped for some reason. It's called hypertrophic pyloric stenosis."

"Could she have died?" Charlie asked.

"Not too likely, but not impossible if she got dehydrated enough. I can't believe I didn't catch it."

They all looked at Ruth, and Starla put a hand on her arm.

"Thank you, Ruth," she whispered, as the tears started to fall.

"Oh, I'm sure you all would've done the same. It's really not—"

"If you say 'not a big deal,'" Charlie said calmly, "you're fired."

Ruth glared at Charlie. "It's *not* a big deal."

"You're the worst."

"Right back at you, buster."

Starla and Sawyer chuckled, and they all quieted as they watched Dahlia sleep in Starla's arms.

"We're together, by the way," Charlie said, still staring at the baby. It made it easier to tell them the truth. "Ruth and I are dating."

"I thought maybe when you went into the hall. I'm happy for you," Starla said softly, and there wasn't a trace of sarcasm in her voice.

A loud knock and a cheerful, "Hi there!" startled the adults, but not Dahlia, who'd finally passed out from exhaustion.

"She didn't nap at all today," Ruth whispered as the nurse placed the IV. "She cried so much."

"You did great," Charlie told her, squeezing her hand. "You're the best."

Ruth whacked him in the chest with the back of her hand. "Next time, answer your phone. If your nanny is calling you, it's important."

"Yes, ma'am," he smirked. "What if my girlfriend is calling me?"

"Also important. Answer her also."

"How will I know which is which?"

"Answer *all the time*, Chuck."

He put a hand on her lower back without thinking. "Were you scared?"

"Yes, I was scared! Of course I was scared!"

"Would you like a hug?"

"I'll cry if you hug me."

"Is that a yes? I can't tell."

"I don't like crying in hospitals."

"Is there an ideal place to cry?"

"In the shower or in my old bedroom. Assuming my brother wasn't there."

"I'm sorry, you shared a room with your brother? Which one?"

"Ranger."

Charlie tipped his head from side to side in thought. "He's not so bad."

"He has a ferret."

"I'd like to revise my opinion..."

Ruth shrugged. "She's actually pretty cute. Her name is Duchess."

"Dear, you should not have to share a room with any wild creature."

His stomach dropped a little when she got a gleam in her eye. "But some wild creatures can be a lot of fun."

"My comfort must have worked. You're back to your old self."

"Not by half," she sighed. "Can I go home now?"

"No. But that reminds me, I need to text Ainsley." This would be interesting. She probably wouldn't answer if she was teaching, but hopefully, she'd see it at the end of the day.

Charlie: Can you do me a favor?

Ainsley: Explain.

Charlie: Dahlia's at the hospital and we're all here. Can the big kids hang out with you for a while?

Ainsley: OH MY GOODNESS YES OF COURSE WHAT HAPPENED

Ainsley: My poor angel

Ainsley: Is she all right?

Charlie: We think so. Kyle is working on it.

Ainsley: Oh good. I can't believe he didn't text me?!

Charlie: That's a HIPPA violation.

Ainsley: I'm sure that's how he'll justify his error as well.

Ainsley: They can hang with me as long as necessary. Take your time.

Charlie: Thank you.

He started to put his phone away, then paused.

Charlie: And I don't think I ever said it, but thank you for supporting Starla when she left. And before. You're a good friend.

Ainsley: I didn't do it for you.

Charlie: I know. But I can still appreciate it.

Ainsley: Okay.

It was probably the most civil conversation they'd had in years. Charlie thought Kellan and the guys would be proud when he told them. He wasn't sure when that had mattered more than what other people thought, but it did. They mattered. And if he texted them, they'd offer support. So he did that, too.

Brian: Are things weird with all the parents there? Plus Ruth?

Charlie: Not yet. But we haven't had to make any decisions yet.

Chris: Well, let me know if you need food or anything, I could drop something by.

Charlie: Thanks, I will.

Kellan: Okay to send a message to the prayer chain?

Charlie: Sure. Thanks.

This was why. This was why he didn't have to be alone, why he didn't have to punish himself for what he'd done. He could do it differently if he had help. He could hold himself accountable, not in the toxic way his father had tried to, but in a new way, one bound by shared flawed humanity and frailty. "Are you all right?" Ruth was at his elbow, staring at him. "You look peaky. If you pass out, I don't think I can catch you."

"I'm not going to pass out," he mumbled, but he pulled her closer and kissed her cheek, and when she smiled, he felt like everything might be okay after all.

CHAPTER THIRTY-TWO

Ruth

In the end, Kyle decided Dahlia could go home. That week, Ruth hung out at Charlie's every evening after work. He seemed relieved to have the extra help, and none of them wanted to be far from Dahlia. On Saturday night, they all ended up on the couch, snuggling, even Aiden. The big kids had both been very upset about Dahlia and seemed determined to shower extra love on her. Aiden was holding her, rocking her gently, while he waited for his turn on the Xbox. Ruth had somehow gotten separated from Charlie and was squished between Emily and the end of the couch. She was trying not to think about what it was going to be like for Charlie to be apart from Dahlia next week.

"Ruthie," Em asked, her voice thoughtful even through a mouthful of cheese puffs. All thoughts of good nutrition had gone out the window when she made blueberry pancakes that morning. Even Charlie had eaten one; that's how rough things were. "Are you going to stay the night again?"

Her gaze snapped to Charlie's over her head, and he was frowning.

"Ruth's never stayed the night."

"But I got up to go potty, and I heard you laughing." It had been pretty late when she went home last night...technically, it had been today. And with everything that had been going on, they hadn't quite gotten around to telling the kids yet.

"Your dad and I were having a little date," Ruth said, pausing the game. "We really like spending time together, so we want to do it more."

"Are you going to get married?" Emily asked.

She met Charlie's gaze over her head, and he gave her a little nod as if to say, "You're doing fine."

"We're not really thinking about that right now. We're just trying out having some dates and seeing how that goes."

"Night dates?" Emily's skepticism was obvious. "On the couch?"

Ruth wished Aiden would look up so that she knew what he was thinking. Instead, he just kept rocking Dahlia.

"Yep," Charlie chimed in. "Ruth and I like talking to each other."

Aiden snorted. "I bet that's not all you like doing with each other."

"Aiden," Charlie said as a warning, but it didn't matter. The boy silently passed Dahlia to his dad, then got up and started for the front of the house.

"Where are you going?" Ruth called.

"To bed," Aiden yelled back. "Is that a crime?"

"No."

"Then why am I being interrogated?"

Charlie sighed. "Hormones are the worst."

"You should go talk to him," Ruth said, reaching for Dahlia, but Charlie squeezed the baby tighter.

"He'll yell less if I take her with me."

"Strategy. I like it."

Emily snatched up Charlie's controller and unpaused the game, then took over as the elf that was currently destroying Ruth's princess character. It was hard to focus when she knew Aiden was upset like that. She wanted with all her heart to bound up the stairs and assure him that everything would be okay, that he would get used to her in this new role, that she wasn't going to try to replace his mom. But Charlie hadn't invited her up. She understood it, she really did. But it was still uncomfortable.

A soft click came from the entryway, and the alarm system beeped. Ruth leaped off the couch, feeling caught. Charlie's mom, Carol, stood stock still in the entryway, frozen in the act of toeing off her shoes.

"What are you doing here? Where's Charles?"

*Do not antagonize her, do not antagonize her...*it didn't take much with the Millers. There was fairly instant dislike whenever she encountered any of them.

"He's up with Aiden. Can I help with anything?" She made her voice receptionist-sweet, like she'd heard the gal at Shear Brilliance do.

"I'll just put this in his kitchen," she said, lifting the casserole dish in her hands. "I'm sure he could use some good food."

Okay, *ouch*. Ruth swallowed down the hurt of that jab. "Sounds good."

"What *are* you doing here?"

"Just hanging out."

Uh oh. Carol's face was too smooth to truly wrinkle, but Ruth could see that she was scowling as deeply as she could.

"He's paying you for the weekend? While he's here?"

"No, he's not paying me, we're—oh."

He hasn't told her.

"Hey, Mom," Charlie said. He scurried down the stairs so fast, Ruth was worried he might fall and hurt himself. *And he would kind of deserve that.* "I'll take that. Ooh, do I smell Italian wedding soup? You didn't have to do that. Thank you so much." Soup? That was appropriate, considering he was now in hot water with her. Mrs. Miller and Charlie were starting toward the kitchen, but Ruth planted her feet. She wasn't going to tolerate lies. Not with this man or any other.

"Charlie, can I speak to you, please?"

He was still holding the soup tureen when he turned. "Uh. Yeah. Just..." He shifted his grip. "Just let me put this down. Mom, would you like to visit with Emily for a minute?"

"No, thank you. I just came to drop this off." She was already sweeping by Ruth for the front door, obviously irate based on the glower Ruth received.

"Mom, could you just wait a minute? Hang on. Hang on," he said, running after her, and he caught her just before she stepped over the threshold.

"I'm clearly interrupting something," Carol said icily. "I'll connect with you later."

"I'd really like to talk to you now," Charlie said, still trying to do his charming thing. "Just for a minute?"

To Ruth's surprise, he turned and put an arm around her waist.

"Ruth and I have been seeing each other. I've been meaning to tell you, but I hadn't found a good time."

His mother's gaze was cold. "As if there is a good time to tell me you've gone back to your old ways."

His fingers dug into her hip a little harder. "It's not like that."

The other woman smiled unkindly. "Just don't tell your father. There's no reason to upset him over one of your flings." The way she cut her gaze to Ruth was meaningful, and she took a breath to try to excuse herself from the situation, but Charlie got his words out first.

"I'd like you to leave now." Both of the women stared at Charlie, who looked a little surprised himself.

"What did you just say to me?" his mother breathed out, glancing behind him toward Emily.

"I said I'd like you to leave. I don't like the way you're treating Ruth. She deserves better than that. And I will be telling Dad, by the way."

"His next heart attack will be on your head, then."

"No," Charlie said quietly, letting Ruth go, "Dad's in charge of himself. If he has a heart attack, it'll be because he worries too much, drinks too much, and still smokes cigars when you're out."

His mother gasped. "He does not!"

"I can smell them from here through my bedroom window. Would you like me to walk you home?"

She straightened. "That won't be necessary. Enjoy the soup. I'll come and collect the tureen while you're at work on Monday."

Charlie rolled his eyes.

"Don't you roll your eyes at me, Charles James Miller. And don't bother coming to dinner tomorrow night if this is how you're going to act."

"Fine. Shall I send the kids over?"

"I hardly think so." And with that, she turned and stomped down the front steps, even though the effect was lost due to her sensible shoes.

Ruth turned to him and took his face in her hands. "You deserve better than that, too." He put his hands over hers and said nothing, but she didn't think she was imagining mistiness in his dark eyes.

"If you say so."

"I do." She kissed him gently. "And thank you for standing up for me."

"I know you don't like conflict."

Ruth rocked back on her heels, but didn't let him go. "How do you know that?"

"I pay attention." He leaned forward and closed the distance between them. "And it's easy, because I'm fascinated by you."

There was a flash out of the corner of her eye, and Ruth turned her head just in time to see Aiden disappear from the landing upstairs.

Charlie sighed. "Do you think I should go talk to him again?"

"Depends. How did it go last time?"

"Not great." He lowered his voice. "We talked about how that's not an appropriate thing to say in front of his sister, and how if he's upset about something, we can talk about it.

Actually, you know what? Thinking back, I think maybe I did all the talking."

Ruth giggled a little. "He's tricky like that. But at least he knows you're there for him."

"I hope so." He was gazing at her again in that way that said, *Let's put Em to bed and make out.* But then Dahlia cried, and the look disappeared. He glanced toward the living room. "You take the big one, and I'll take the little one? I don't think Aiden wants to see either of us."

"Deal."

She started to turn, but he caught her and kissed her with surprising passion, so much so that all the blood rushing around made her scalp tingle.

"And then we meet back on the couch."

"Definitely deal."

"Don't go home. I know you have stuff to do. I just...need to be with you for a little while. Please."

It was funny how he sort of cascaded these requests, like he could hear how controlling he was being and tried to dial it back, softening his approach.

"I said 'definitely deal,' didn't I? I like a little Charlie time too without a kiddo between us. Even though I love them."

"You do, don't you?"

Ruth nodded. And yet an unasked question hung in the air...*Do you love me?*

She backed slowly toward the living room. "You. Me. Couch. Twenty."

"Twenty? You're ambitious," he laughed, and when it took her forty minutes (a chapter of *Stuart Little*, a song and a back rub), he laughed at her again.

CHAPTER THIRTY-THREE

Charlie

When Jason found out about what had happened with their mom, he boycotted Sunday night dinner in solidarity.

"This really wasn't necessary," Charlie said, sitting on a padded barstool, picking at a bowl of trail mix with one hand. Lacey had nabbed Dahlia when he first arrived and didn't look like she'd be putting her down any time soon. The adults were all sitting around the kitchen at Jason's house, which was squeezed between two other nearly identical houses in a newer subdivision.

"Yes, it was," his brother returned firmly. "They don't even know Ruth."

"Neither do you," Charlie smirked, and Jason tipped his head in acknowledgment.

"But I want to! She should've come for dinner tonight."

"Lacey invited her, but she had a family commitment."

"Bummer. I mean, not a bummer that she has a family that loves her, but a bummer that she couldn't come. I even vacuumed."

"No, you didn't," Lacey said, carefully frosting the sheet cake in front of her with one hand.

"I didn't?"

"No. It was on your list, though."

"Why didn't you remind me?" Jason complained, stomping through the living room toward the hall closet.

"Because I'm not Charlie!" she called after him, still focused on her work.

"You can put the baby down if you want."

Lacey glared at him. "My niece went to the emergency room this week. I'll hold her, thanks."

"It won't make a difference. She still needs surgery."

"It's entirely for my benefit."

"Babe, you ready?" Jason asked, and Lacey pulled out her phone.

"Go." Charlie wanted to continue the conversation, but the roar of the vacuum made it difficult.

"He makes you time his chores?"

She nodded. "He says it's motivating. He tries to break his record. We call it chaos chores," she called over the noise. Dahlia was looking around, wide-eyed, then reached for Lacey's long, black hair.

"Nice try, lady," Lacey cooed, flipping her hair over her shoulder, and Dahlia just smiled and kicked her feet. Lacey gestured with her head toward the other room, and they went into the playroom, where it was quieter; Aiden, Emily and Iris were outside on the trampoline. He peeked through the window to make sure his kids weren't being too rough with their little cousin, but they all seemed to be having fun: Emily and Iris sat in the middle while Aiden ran around the outside, giving them high fives as he went by. He could hear Iris's throaty giggles.

"He's a good kid," Lacey said, following his gaze.

"Yeah. Most of the time," Charlie said, running his fingers through his hair.

"He'll find his way. Kids almost always do."

"But this one is..." He paused. "I don't know. I think I'm screwing him up."

"Why?"

"He's just been so angry lately. Ever since..."

Lacey sat in the padded rocking chair and lay Dahlia on her thighs, taking her hands in hers.

"Since what?"

"Since he and Starla caught me. With Tracy."

"Oh. What did he say when you talked to him about it?"

"That's the thing," he said, instinctively picking up a stuffed monkey, a rag doll with yellow hair, and a fuzzy frog and putting them in the open toy box. "I never exactly...did. I think Starla did."

"But you're not sure?" Lacey was still looking at Dahlia, kissing her hands, one and then the other, and it made the admission easier.

"No. I'm not."

"What's stopping you?"

"I don't know what to say. I don't know how to bring it up without being weird, but he's obviously hung up on me and Ruth. He's acting super weird about us."

Lacey kissed Dahlia's belly, and she giggled.

"You should ask him about it. Ask him how he feels about Ruth."

Charlie snorted. "In case you haven't noticed, prepubescent boys are not crazy about sharing their feelings unless it's their idea."

"I had noticed. But I've also noticed that people do better with good modeling. Maybe if you share how you feel about her, he'll feel like he can, too."

"Or maybe he'll ask if he can go back to his show."

Lacey laughed, and Dahlia did, too, delighted. "You'll never know until you try. You're my parenting guinea pig, remember? Go forth and mistake."

"Time!" Jason yelled, breathless, and Lacey stopped her timer.

"Six seconds slower."

"Dang it," Jason said. "The kids slowed me down when I had to yield for them."

"You can have a do-over any time you want," Lacey said, still fawning over the content baby on her lap. Charlie wanted to tell her that single parenting felt more fraught with mistakes. Yes, most parents compared themselves to others, but it was tougher when you now compared yourself to your ex, who was parenting the same kids what felt like a million times better. Mistakes felt bigger now, more like he wasn't measuring up in a significant way. And not having someone to bounce ideas off of just made him feel that much less secure about his own decisions.

A timer beeped in the kitchen, and Jason spun and went in there.

"This chicken looks epic, babe!"

Lacey looked up at Charlie. "Don't you just love his enthusiasm?"

Charlie grinned. No one *got* his brother like Lacey. And it seemed like maybe she got him, too. He'd already started into the kitchen to ask the kids to wash up when Lacey called after him.

"Do you love her?"

"Who?"

"Ruth, weirdo."

She'd stood, holding Dahlia crosswise on her belly, and she picked her way across the messy playroom.

"I think so. It's different than it was with Starla. We've got more...breathing room. There's pressure because both families hate the idea, but it's not like we're trying to rush into things. At least, I'm not. I just like her. Like being with her."

"You can be yourself with her," Lacey said, nodding.

"Yes. And I *like* who I am, which is kinda...new."

Her smiled turned sad, and she leaned in and hugged him awkwardly with her free arm. "It's good, Charlie. It's okay to be happy."

"Right. I know." The thought was like peanut butter on the roof of his mouth; it felt pretty weird and out of place. But he wasn't trying to scrape it off just yet.

"Guys. Hey," Jason called, "stop hugging. Let's eat. I'm dealing with a possible mutiny out here." Charlie could hear his children arguing now, Aiden saying he didn't need Emily's help getting out salad dressings, Emily crying because Uncle Jason said she could.

"We're coming," Charlie said, giving her a squeeze as he let go. "We'll get there."

"We will," Lacey murmured, squeezing him back.

CHAPTER THIRTY-FOUR

Ruth

Sunday night, Ruth went over to see her mom. It was going to be a long week, and even though Dahlia would be with Starla and Sawyer, both of whom were taking time off work, she still wanted to be available to support them and Charlie in whatever they needed. When she walked into her family's home, her brothers were all eating cereal on the couch.

"Hello, everyone." To her surprise, Ranger paused the movie they were watching. He jumped up and gave her a big hug, and a little taken aback, it took her a second to hug him back. She hadn't quite recovered when Ryan took his turn, stepping in as soon as Ranger stepped away, and she saw through happy tears that Wyatt and her dad were right behind him.

"This is a nice welcome," she wheezed out, because Ryan was still squeezing the stuffing out of her. Then she noticed Levi was still on the couch, ignoring all of them, reading a book.

"Don't look in the kitchen," her dad whispered when it was his turn, and Ruth chuckled.

"Okay." When she got through the hug line, she glanced at Levi again.

"Hi, Levi." He grunted in response, shoveling more cereal into his mouth. She walked over and gave him a hug over the back of the couch from behind. "Missed you."

He said nothing, but put his hand on her arm in acknowledgment. After a moment, Ruth let him go and straightened. She glanced around the room for the first time and rather wished she hadn't; three overflowing baskets of laundry sat next to the TV. There were muddy footprints on the carpet, and someone had started a woodworking project on a card table in the corner that had dripped yellow wood glue onto the surface and dried there. And worst of all, Duchess was asleep on the couch. She'd had a strict *no ferrets on the couch* rule. *Right. Not my house anymore.*

"Gonna go see Mom."

"You want a cinnamon roll? Levi made some this morning."

"No, I'm good. Thanks, though."

Deborah was asleep when she crept into the room, the quilt she'd been working on sprawled across her lap, light still on. Ruth picked up her hand and rubbed the back of it lightly, and her mom's eyes fluttered open.

"Ruthie!" Her mom sat up and hugged her.

"You're all acting like I've been gone for an age," she said with a laugh.

"Well, it feels like you have," Deborah replied. "Seriously, girl. You have no idea the silly arguments your father's recounted. Took them forever to even find the laundry soap."

"Not sure they have yet," Ruth said, trying not to laugh again. "I'm happy to help if they'd just call me."

"Levi didn't want them to."

Ruth's gaze fell to their joined hands. "Still mad at me, huh?"

"He'll get over it." Deborah squeezed her hand. "Now, I want to see pictures of your new place. And let's plan to have Dad bring me up soon." She'd need extra help and sleep for a few days after that, Ruth knew. Post-exertional malaise was a bear.

"I might get some time off this week," she said, scrolling past selfies of her and Charlie to her house pictures. She'd meant to bring prints; Mom couldn't do a lot of screen time. But Deborah took the phone with a big grin on her face.

"Oh, a little vacation?"

"Sort of. Dahlia's having her surgery."

"Oh, that's right! And that's Wednesday?"

"Yeah."

"How's everyone feeling?"

Ruth rubbed at one of her arms. "Pretty stressed. Even Aiden."

"From what you've told me, he's pretty sensitive to upheaval."

"I think he's trying not to show it, but...yeah. I think it upsets him more than he wants it to."

"I'm glad you can be there for them. It's good." Deborah sounded wistful, and Ruth remembered how many times her mom had taken meals to families having tough times when she was young.

"Learned from the best," Ruth said, lifting her chin, and her mom just glowed back at her, raising a hand to brush Ruth's hair back. "Are they taking good care of you?"

"The best," her mom said with a nod. "Dad's cut back his hours a bit, but we're making it work." Ruth's heart sank. She'd hoped that wouldn't be necessary. But without her around, her dad would be responsible for helping her in the shower, managing her meal prep, making sure her laundry got done...

"I'm sorry I haven't come by more—"

"Nope. Not interested in that sentence. Thanks, though." Ruth scowled at her, and her mom just laughed, then yawned. "I'm fine, Ruth. Really."

"These are the same sheets you had on Wednesday."

"He changed them on Thursday and washed these and put them back on in the interim."

"All right," Ruth said, patting her hand. "Love you. I'll let you be."

"Come by any time," her mom said, yawning again. "I mean it."

"Okay." She got another hug and a kiss on the cheek before she left. She sat and chatted with her brothers, Levi still ignoring her like a doofus, for a few minutes before she headed out. But the woods were calling to her. She paused next to her truck, listening to the low call of an owl. She picked her way through the pear orchard, trying to figure out where it was coming from, and veered west into the woods toward the Miller's property. Strangely enough, for all the animosity between them, they never had erected a fence; that would mean they'd agreed on a property line. Ruth rolled her eyes, just thinking about the arguments that would spark.

The owl hooted again, low and short, and when she heard an answer, Ruth gasped. A pair of them? That might mean a nest, and soon, owlets. She couldn't wait to come back with a better light and bring the kids.

Then another noise had her craning her neck. A shadowed figure sat on the tire swing, looking out over the river, the tree creaking under its weight.

"Charlie?"

The figure turned. "Ruth? What are you doing here?"

She gestured over her shoulder. "Just stopped by to see Mom." She rubbed his back a little. "This is still your thinking spot, huh?"

Even in the dark, she could see one side of his mouth hitch up.

"I guess so. Just dropped them off with Starla."

"Oof. It's hard to be away from her, huh?"

"Is it Wednesday yet?" he joked, but she could hear the pain in his voice. Ruth wrapped her arms around him and just held him as the river sang soothingly to them. When she pressed her nose to the side of his face, he sighed, sounding a little more contented.

He nestled deeper into her arms, and Ruth pressed a kiss to his jawline.

"I feel like all you do is take care of us, Ruth. I wish I could do more for you." That comment had her a little wordless; he should think about his baby girl, not her.

"I'm fine."

"No, really," he said, pulling her closer still, wrapping himself around her arm like it was Em's koala, Coleman. "If you could do anything—anything at all—what would it be?"

"Get my mom an electric wheelchair."

He hummed thoughtfully. "A very kind idea, but not what I meant. Like, what's your dream job?"

An idea floated to her on the wind, beckoning to her as the woods had tonight, and she shivered.

"It's too silly."

"Bet it's not. Come on. Tell me. Please?"

She still hesitated. "Are you going to make me fill out a business plan? Because I don't want to do that."

"You want to start a business?" Charlie's excitement made her cringe.

"Never mind."

"No, no. This is good. I can help with business ideas. I'm great at business ideas."

"I know you are," she said, pulling back, then giving the tire swing a shove to send him away from her. Only he was heavier than she thought, so it was more of a lean than a swing. "But it's not quite a business. More of a foundation idea."

"For people with ME, like your mom?"

"No, actually. For birds." It sounded extra foolish now, saying it out loud, caring about animals when she should care about people. "I thought we could do a fun run, or some- thing. I don't know. It's probably a ridiculous idea."

"Why?" He twisted, catching her hands, and he pulled her gently so that she was leaning on the tire swing. "Lots of people in town like to run."

"But how much could we actually raise? And how much would we even charge? I don't know."

"I think it's a great idea. I really do. And if you want my help, I stand at the ready."

Ruth snorted, then leaned forward and kissed him. "Okay, Chuck."

"What?" he protested. "What's so funny?"

"Nothing," she said through a laugh, even though more happy feelings were bubbling up in her belly. "Just you." She kissed him longer this time. "Being you."

"Whatever that means," he grumbled. "You're trying to distract me with kisses. It's not going to work."

"I think it already has," she said, trailing her lips along his jawline, down to burrow into his neck just below his collar, where she could smell his cologne.

"This is cheating. This is unfair," he breathed, even as his fingers sunk deep into her thick hair. "I want to talk about the Ostrich Run."

"Oh, is that what we're calling it?"

"Is there another bird that runs?"

"Lots of birds run," Ruth said, trying to keep from shaking with laughter.

"Penguin run would be ironic. They slide more than run, I think."

"They waddle."

"Sure. But once we get a name, we can come up with branding and T-shirts and a date and—"

Ruth pulled back. "You're really serious. You want to help with my silly idea?"

"The Organization Fairy is silly. Littering my entryway with cotton balls in the hopes of snow is silly. This is a great idea. And yes, if it's something your heart desires, I want to help. I want you to have dreams. You have such a big imagination, Ruth; it's such a shame that you don't get to put it to work for yourself."

A surge of emotion welled up inside her for this man who was so put-together on the outside and so soft on the inside. She was thankful she got to see that, to treasure it. It felt like the wardrobe to Narnia sometimes, just peeking into his soul.

She put her icy hands on his cheeks and kissed him, too overwhelmed for words.

"You're shaking again," he chided gently. "What did I say wrong?"

"Just cold," she said with a smile. "Walk me back to my truck?"

"Gladly."

CHAPTER THIRTY-FIVE

Charlie

Once he sat down in the waiting area of the hospital, Charlie couldn't stop his knee from bouncing. He clasped his hands in front of him in an attempt to look casual, but the knee was still giving him away. Across from him, Starla and Sawyer sat snuggled, holding hands, but they both looked like they were going to throw up. Nurses and patients bustled around them, but their area of padded chairs stayed still, like the calm at the center of a hurricane. *If only.* At least the chairs were decently comfortable; the tile floors looks like they could use an upgrade.

"You probably know every little thing that could go wrong today, don't you?" Charlie asked, looking at Sawyer.

He nodded.

"Is that what you're thinking about now?"

"Trying not to," Sawyer murmured.

"It's a simple surgery," Starla said, bouncing her gaze between them, her eyebrows in a V. "They said it'll be fine."

"I'm sure it will. This is a good hospital."

"We should've taken her to Doernbecher," Charlie said, letting his head hang down, feeling the stretch of his tight muscles all the way down his back.

"You'd feel the same way sitting at Doernbecher," Sawyer said.

"Let's talk about something else," Starla said, even as she leaned harder into Sawyer. "We only have an hour to kill. How hard could it be?"

They all stared at each other for a minute, then Sawyer chuckled.

"Not sure we have all that much in common, Star."

"Sure we do," she said, squeezing his arm. "How's that motorcycle you bought working out, Charlie?"

"Great. I love it. It was kind of expensive, but..."

"Oh, that's BS, I gave you an amazing deal!" Sawyer griped, and Charlie grinned.

"No, you were supposed to *bond* over this," Starla said, annoyed.

"Yeah, good luck with that." Charlie checked his watch. "Fifty-eight minutes left." But a strange thing happened as they sat in this white waiting room littered with coffee cups and tissue boxes he hoped he wouldn't need. He wanted to drop his guard. And he wanted to do it with these two people, who would understand better than anyone.

"I can't stop thinking about all the things that could go wrong. She's so sweet and small and...precious."

They both stared at him, and he could see the surprise in Starla's face that he'd been so honest. Sawyer just looked like he was going to cry...which was pretty normal for him, as far as Charlie could tell.

It felt like an ocean separated him from the two of them, even though they obviously felt the same way.

"Is Ruth coming?" Starla asked gently, and Charlie shrugged.

"I thought so, she was just going to drop the kids at sch—"

"I'm here," Ruth said, gasping for breath as she squeaked to a stop in her wet tennis shoes on the tile floor. "I'm here. Did she already go in?"

When they all nodded, Ruth cursed softly. "I didn't get to kiss her head for luck."

"I don't think she needs it," Charlie said, tugging her down into the chair next to his. Reading his mind, Ruth grinned and said, "What about you?"

"Maybe just a quick one," he muttered, and his heart finally slowed down when she gave him a long, innocent kiss.

"I brought snacks," Ruth said, digging around in her backpack. "It seemed like the kind of situation where we might be hungry." He hadn't felt hungry all morning, but it was hard to say no to homemade peanut butter cookies. She'd even made them without flour to limit the carbs for him; they were a bit crumbly, but he caught the part that broke off when he bit it with his other hand. Starla and Sawyer both took one, too, and Charlie silently thanked them.

"She is going to feel soooo much better after this. I bet she sleeps a lot, don't you think? Even though it's fairly minor, I think she'll need some time to recover. Maybe I can take the kids to the zoo or something on Saturday, so the house is quiet. Then again, third children often don't mind the noise. I knew one baby who *couldn't* sleep if her sisters weren't bouncing around in the background; isn't that wild? They were both gone to a slumber party one night and her mother said she didn't sleep at all. So wild!"

"Ruth," he said gently, but she didn't even hear him. She just kept prattling on, telling them stories, and the three of them just listened, letting her be a much-needed distraction. He swore she wasn't even breathing, just producing this endless river of chatter. Apparently, his lady was a talker when she was nervous. He thought about going to get her a cup of coffee to make her take a breath, but he was afraid it would just amp her up even more.

His brain wandered back toward Dahlia, and he checked his watch. Still forty-five minutes to go. This was interminable. Charlie stood up.

"Let's go for a walk."

Ruth stood up with him, but Starla frowned. "What if the doctor wants to talk to us?"

"We won't go far. You can text me." Charlie grabbed Ruth's hand and pulled her after him before Starla could argue with him again. He pulled her straight out the front door, and when the cold hit his face, he shivered. He was just intending to circle the parking lot when Ruth pulled him toward the little garden area.

"I don't want to sit."

"We're not going to. There's a secret path over here."

Well, that piqued his curiosity. "How do you know that?"

The smile she shot him over her shoulder was sad. "I spent a lot of time here when my mom started having health problems, trying to keep the boys happy during her appointments."

"Oh." He squeezed her hand, and she squeezed his back. He wished he had the emotional energy to talk to her about that, to hear more about her life, but his brain was still pulsing with Dahlia's name like a heartbeat. It felt like a prayer he was praying without words, and he hoped God understood. "Tell me about that. Distract me," he blurted out, and Ruth slowed down a little.

"It's okay. Let's just walk. I don't have to talk."

"No, it's okay. You can talk, but I can't really respond. Not like I want to. But I can listen."

"That's fine. Maybe it's better. I don't know what I'd want you to say."

"Okay."

She veered behind the building and onto a dirt path that led into the woods. The pine trees smelled good, and he took a deep breath and let it out slowly, trying to keep that delicate smell inside him a little longer. The deeper they got into the woods, the more ferns and branches started crossing the path, and they eventually dropped hands to walk single file.

"Well, I was twelve when she first got sick. They'd just gotten back from some tropical vacation a few weeks before, and they know now that she picked up a virus there. At the time, she thought she'd gotten food poisoning from the food truck they ate at, but..." She sighed. "I guess it wasn't."

She stepped over a big root, and Charlie wished he could see her face.

"They saved up so long for that trip. My aunt came and stayed with us, and I remember thinking that I was so glad my mom was back, because I ended up taking care of my brothers the whole time and it was so much work. And then the work just...never ended." They came out into a clearing, and the path ran along the edge of the meadow, thick with brown winter grasses. "I feel like I've been taking care of other people my whole life."

"Sounds like you have."

"The other day my brothers were talking about me and they didn't know I was listening, and Ryan said something about how I had a right to have dreams, and it kind of just...never occurred to me. I mean, drowning people don't dream, right?"

"Maybe some do. Maybe that's how you get back to dry land."

"Maybe. But I didn't have time to dream. I was too busy trying to make sure they all graduated and didn't get into toxic relationships or drugs or anything. Their dreams became mine."

Charlie just nodded. He understood that a little; she was such a giving, innocent person, he could see how she'd get sucked into someone else's life that way. And in some ways, hadn't she channeled that energy into her imagination, into making amazing experiences for kids? It was no lack of creativity, just opportunity. He made a mental note to think of more ways he could encourage her to dream for herself. If she wanted it, he was going to make that race happen if it killed him.

"And your mom?"

"She does what she can. But that isn't much. I worry that she feels guilty, especially when the boys kind of run roughshod over me."

"Helplessness is always a hard feeling." He was feeling it right now.

"I'm feeling less of it lately. Until right now."

He smiled ruefully. "Yeah, me too."

"We should probably head back. We promised we'd stay close."

"No, *you* promised," Ruth said, poking him in the chest with one finger, and he grabbed her and pulled her into his arms. He spoke his deepest fear into her smooth hair.

"She'll be okay, right? Dahlia?"

"Of course she will," Ruth said, rubbing his back, and even though it was impossible for her to know it for sure, it made him feel better to hear it.

Their conversation on the way back was lighter, and Charlie was able to chat with her a little more. It helped to be moving; he always felt better when he was moving. By the time they got back, his head felt clearer, and they only had fifteen minutes to kill. He wished they'd stayed out there and made out for ten; Ruth was a great kisser.

Sawyer and Starla had gotten coffee, and they were both on their phones; she appeared to be ordering printer paper for the library, and he was answering emails. Charlie would be afraid he'd royally screw something up if he tried to work right now...and really, there was no need. He had Henry now, who was getting better at the customer service side of things. The other day, he showed some customers a car and almost closed the deal. Charlie had been obscenely proud and considered moving him up to salesman instead of being his assistant, but he needed an assistant more. He loved not making his own phone calls.

A doctor stopped at the reception desk, and a nurse pointed toward them. *He's coming over. He's going to tell us how it went.* Charlie was so nervous, he couldn't force a single word out of his mouth to tell the others, so he just whacked Ruth, and she looked up.

"Oh, hello! How did it go?" She sounded like she was picking the kids up from school, not finding out how surgery on his infant daughter had gone.

He smiled at her. "Glad you made it, Ruth; I'm Dr. Bowers." He had everyone's attention now. "The surgery went very well. She's still asleep, but you can go in and see her if you'd like. We're planning to send her home with Mrs. and Dr. Devereaux, since our understanding is that it is their week for custody."

He'd forgotten Dahlia wouldn't be coming home with him, where he could check on her through the night, where he could lay a hand on her chest and feel her deep, even breathing, touch her forehead and make sure she wasn't feverish or cold. He was going to have to go home to his empty house and simply wonder. The thought filled him with a sadness so deep, it bordered on hopeless. Ruth was urging him up now, trying to follow the others, but Charlie just stood.

"I think I'm going to head home." He didn't want to cry about it here.

"What? Why?" Her big dark eyes, so wide and confused, made him not want to put her between him and Starla.

"She's safe. She's good. I'll let them have time with her."

"They'll get their time tonight," Ruth said, dragging him across the waiting area after them. "If anyone should leave, it's me; I'm not even her parent."

"I don't want you to leave."

"And we don't want you to leave. So come on and let's go see your girl. You'll feel better once you see her safe and sound."

"You don't *know* that they don't want me to leave," Charlie muttered as she pulled him into the large room with curtains around each bed, but Ruth just scowled at him. The other three crowded in around the small bassinet, but Charlie's feet felt heavy, and he slowed his steps.

I'll just be in the way. This won't accomplish anything. Unfortunately, just as he was about to turn and go, Starla noticed him. She motioned him forward, and between the adults, he could see Dahlia lying there in her small white hospital onesie. He didn't want to see her like that, all small and sick, but he shuffled over dutifully. She looked peaceful, even with the IV still in her arm. Would she be mad about it when she woke up? He would. He hated hospitals. There was no specific reason beyond being expensive and full of sick people. Sick people made him nervous. Was *that* why he didn't want to see her? *Dahlia deserves better. I can do better.* He pushed back his shoulders and leaned forward...but tears sprang to his eyes immediately. If he wiped them away, the rest of them would notice. *But, really,* a little voice whispered, *who's going to care?* The voice sounded suspiciously like Kellan's, and he once again lightly resented the way the man made him question the premise of things he'd believed his whole life. The tears were coming faster now, streaming down his cheeks into his collar, and when he sniffled, the three of them turned to him, surprised.

"Nothing to see here," he said gruffly, but he saw Sawyer's eyes fill, too.

Was he going to hug him? Oh, yeah. He definitely was. It was a side hug, which was more bearable than Charlie'd imagined, but he still didn't want to need it, no matter how nice Sawyer's arm felt around his shoulders.

"She's gonna be okay," Starla said, patting his back awkwardly, and Charlie shrugged them both off gently.

"I know that, I just don't like seeing her so...so..." Words failed. What was the word for feeling like someone had just operated on a piece of your heart? Even if it was a good thing, it still hurt.

"I feel that, too," Sawyer said, his voice thick. "I know." He squeezed him again, and then finally let him go, and Charlie felt a little weightless without the man's anchoring touch. Thankfully, the one person he wanted to touch him snuck in to clamp around his side, and he wrapped both arms around Ruth. He wished she could hold him all night long. After a few minutes of just watching his daughter sleep, he said his goodbyes and gave Dahlia a kiss on the head. She was in good hands. Things would only get better from here. It felt easier to believe now that he'd seen her with his own eyes.

CHAPTER THIRTY-SIX

Ruth

Ruth hurried through the cleanup at the lodge. The kids gave her a wide-eyed look when she hustled them toward homework with ruthless efficiency, ignoring their pleas for leniency due to it being Friday. She *was* getting out of here on time tonight, come crying or complaining. Because they'd gotten everyone through the surgery and initial recovery, and now it was finally her turn to plan a date. Starla would be home any minute, and she wanted to take off immediately; she and Charlie really needed some fun, and she had the perfect thing in mind. As they finally settled down to work, she pulled out her phone.

> **Ruth:** Dress down for our date tonight.
> **Ruth:** Like, do wear clothes, but not nice clothes. Don't come naked.

She was just pressing out the first pizza when Charlie's text came through.

> **Charlie:** So...a tux?

> **Ruth:** Yes. That's exactly what I was imagining. Well done. Please show up in a tux.

She sent a drooling emoji. She'd actually made him blush the other day, and now it was her goal to do it as much as possible. Ruth hadn't thought such a handsome guy—who obviously knew he was handsome—could be so affected by some simple flirting.

Charlie: Seriously, though, what are we doing?
Ruth: I seriously won't be revealing that.

He hadn't told her what they were doing when he planned it, and she felt she was entitled to some secrets.

Charlie: Whaaat

Charlie: This is BS

Ruth: You didn't tell me what we were going to do when you planned it!

Charlie: Next time, I'm going to take you out on the motorcycle and we'll get burgers in Sisters.

Charlie: There, now you can tell me.

That sounded delightful. She could almost feel the wind in her hair...then she remembered she'd probably have to wear a helmet. But that only spoiled the mood a little. She'd never felt trapped in Timber Falls the way some people did, but the idea of going somewhere with Charlie appealed to her.

Ruth: I'm sorry, sir, but with secrets, advance payment is not accepted.
Ruth: Also that sounds like fun and I can't wait.
Charlie: THIS IS BS
Charlie: I WANT TO KNOW
Ruth: You will in a few hours.
Charlie: Grumpy.
Ruth: I see that. Something bad happen today?

There was a long pause, and she didn't know how to interpret it.

Charlie: No, it was a good day.

Charlie: And even better knowing I'll get to see you tonight.

Ruth: You see me all the time.

Charlie: Not this week. I missed you.

Ruth: You missed kissing me or you missed seeing me?

Charlie: Both. And eating your food. And rubbing your back. And laughing about my goofy kids. And watching pointless TV together.

Ruth: I can't believe Rafaella got kicked off!

Charlie: I know, right? She should've joined that alliance with Soren when she had the chance.

Ruth: Totally.

Charlie: I'm going to drive now. I'll see you soon.

Ruth: Not soon enough.

CHARLIE

He sent her a kiss emoji as he started the car. He hoped tonight would be chill; it had been a good day, but he was still tired. He really just wanted to lie on the couch with his body pressed against hers and watch something meaningless. But he didn't want her to think he was an old person. It would be fine; he would rally the energy. They'd had fun at sushi—this would be fun too, whatever she had planned.

He pulled up to her house at exactly 6:55, and he could see her through the window, curled up in the window seat. She jumped up and ran to the door, and when she threw it open, she was wearing...camo?

I do not want to go hunting. Especially not in the dark.

She came bouncing over to the car, and he got out slowly.

"Hi," he said with a grin, despite his caution.

"Hi!" She kissed him briefly. "Where's your tux?"

"Ha ha. What's the plan, Stan?"

She leaned back to see him better, even as she held him around the waist. "Boy, you *really* don't like not knowing what's going on?"

He couldn't deny it, but that didn't make it comfortable to hear aloud. "No."

She watched him for a moment, the cool breeze playing with her hair. "All right. That's fair. I'm sorry I teased you."

"No," he said, kissing her again. "It's fine. I shouldn't care."

"I don't find 'should' to be a very helpful word. Do you?"

It seemed that *should* encompassed most of his life, but he couldn't help but nod.

"In the future, I will keep you informed," she said with a nod, almost to herself.

"Zane..."

"Now," she said briskly, "who's ready to run around in the woods?"

Charlie was sweating. He could feel it seeping into the headband that was holding the night vision goggles onto his face. He thought about taking off the thick canvas jacket she'd given him, but he was afraid it was going to hurt when she shot him. Turned out they were going hunting: for each other. The paintball gun was surprisingly heavy, and he tried to hold it closer to his body as he hid against the tall Ponderosa pine. He could hear her moving, but he couldn't see her, and it just made his heart pound harder.

A brief movement out of the corner of his eye made him jump: it was just a chipmunk. He breathed a sigh of relief and let his shoulders drop. That's when he felt her muzzle in the middle of his back.

"Hands up."

"You're supposed to just shoot me!"

Ruth giggled. "How do you know? You've never played before, either!"

"Well, I know that much," he said, turning slowly with his hands in the air. He thought it might be harder for her to shoot him if she had to look him in his handsome face. It was no secret that she liked looking at him; maybe he could use it to his advantage.

"Throw down your gun," she ordered with faux solemnity.

"Never."

He couldn't see her eyes, but the way she lifted her chin told him that this did not cow her in any way.

"Fine."

She shot him dead in the belly, and Charlie bent over, holding his injury. "Ow!" he moaned loudly, and Ruth mirrored his position as she whispered, "Should've complied when you had the chance."

By the time he straightened to an upright position again, she was off and running, and Charlie took off after her. It wasn't like she could lead him into a trap...was it? He briefly imagined her dad and brothers lying in wait for him and shuddered. She zigzagged through the woods down the narrow path, and he raised his gun to shoot her, but she'd disappeared behind a tree again by the time he aimed.

This was a better workout than the treadmill, that was for sure.

The trail spurred off to the left, and as the wind rustled the ferns and wild grape, he followed it. She was quick, but she could only run in spurts...he'd come around the side and ambush her when she got tired. That's when it hit him—this was fun. He was having fun. He'd whined and complained when she'd pulled out the gear, but he was actually glad she'd ignored him now. First of all, it was a cheap date since Mr. Oberst was letting them use it for free, and he knew she was on a tight budget. But more than that, it was the same burst of adrenaline he got pursuing all kinds of things: a sale, a debate with his dad, a new PR in a workout...that sense of *wanting* that he felt in his veins like it was taking him over. And best of all, he wasn't hurting anyone in the process.

Well, once he caught Ruth, he might hurt her a little bit, but only with the paintball and only because she wanted him to. That didn't count.

He stilled as he heard her heavy breathing ten feet away. He dropped behind an azalea silently and waited for her to get closer.

"Where the heck did he go?" she muttered, and he almost snickered. Almost.

"Charlie?" she called. "I'm cold. Let's go inside."

His snort of derision was even harder to hold in, especially because she was still holding the butt of her weapon to her shoulder, like she was ready to take aim the moment she saw him.

Not that gullible, princess.

Closer. Closer. Through the thin branches, he watched her, something in his heart being mended by this dark-haired beauty who loved to play. Who loved him, even though she hadn't said as much; he thought she did. The wind whispered in his ear that he wouldn't screw it up this time, and he leapt to his feet. He got his shot off before she could even turn around.

"Ha! Suck it, Zane!"

With a grimace, she lifted her weapon to shoot him again, but he stepped forward and slapped it toward the ground.

"Nuh-huh. I thought you wanted to go home."

"An obvious ruse."

"Not obvious enough. And I'm hungry."

"Fine," she said, letting the weapon drop. "Truce?"

He wanted to shoot her again, but now that she was defenseless, it didn't seem fair. He'd have to kiss her instead. He threw down his weapon too and pulled her close with an arm around her waist.

"I can't kiss you with these weird goggles on," he murmured, and she immediately whipped hers off. Charlie chuckled at her enthusiasm as he took his off too and tossed them aside.

"I should make you catch me first," Ruth whispered, and when her cold fingers trailed over the back of his neck, he shivered.

"I already did," he said, nuzzling her with the tip of his nose.

"No, the game was over. That doesn't count."

"I think it does. I want my prize."

Ruth barked out a laugh. "What prize? I got you like ten times!"

"Fine, we can call it your prize, if you like." He shuffled her backwards until she met a lodgepole pine. "Are you ready for it?"

"Better make it a good one, Miller." Gosh, he loved it when she lifted her chin like that, defiant, as if she didn't believe he could make her melt.

"Oh, I plan to, Zane." He slid a hand behind her neck and swept his thumb over her rosy cheek.

"Good. I deserve it."

"You definitely do." As he dipped his mouth toward hers, it wasn't just the wind through the trees above them that made him shiver.

CHAPTER THIRTY-SEVEN

Charlie

Three days later, Charlie finally had the kids back. He'd done a ton of reading and prepped all he could for having Dahlia there, but most of it turned out to be unnecessary.

"Welcome home," Ruth greeted him with a grin on Monday. They'd agreed that there would be no smooching on the job, but he was finding it difficult to maintain the boundary when she looked at him like that. She'd been coming back after the kids were in bed; he didn't think they knew, but one time he thought he'd heard one of them on the stairs. There'd been no one there when he went to check.

"You want to stay for dinner?"

"No, I've gotta check on Mom. Thanks, though."

"It smells delicious."

She beamed. "Thank you. I'll see you later." The meaningful look she gave him told him he'd see her in more like two hours than twelve.

"Can you call Aiden on your way out?" He was too hungry to change his clothes first.

"Sure."

He picked up Dahlia; he didn't even care if she spit up on his work clothes. She'd been doing so much better lately, though—thanks to Ruth. He was so thankful his girl was okay. He just wanted to hold her all the time when he was home. But that wasn't so different from before, now that he thought about it.

"How was your day, Em?"

"Pretty good," she said, not looking up from her tablet.

"Screens off. Talk to me, please." She complied with a sigh and started into a story about some kind of recess drama that Charlie was only mostly listening to.

Ruth appeared in the kitchen, her face perplexed and pinched. "He's not upstairs."

"What?" Those words did not compute.

Emily's eyes were wide. "Who's not? Aiden?"

"I brought him home after school and he went right upstairs. He didn't even want a snack. I haven't seen him since."

"But he's not upstairs now?" Charlie passed Dahlia to Ruth and took the stairs two at a time. Bonus room: empty. Aiden's room: nothing. He even checked his own room and Emily's, just to be thorough, and stopped to quickly change his clothes. Nothing.

"He's probably just out on the trampoline," Charlie said, heading for the back door. "He's outside somewhere."

Emily went running out onto the deck, leaving the door open behind her. "He's not!"

"Look around, Em. Maybe you just didn't see him."

Ruth looked like she might throw up. "Have you ever known him to play outside by himself when you didn't make him?"

"No, but..." Charlie scoffed. "Where else could he be?"

"I don't know. That's why I'm worried," Ruth said quietly, bouncing Dahlia, who was starting to fuss. Ruth was shaking again, and Charlie had to admit that he was feeling a little fragile himself. He wrapped both of them up in his arms for a minute while he tried to think.

"I didn't see him anywhere. Where's his tablet? I wouldn't leave without that," Emily said, coming back inside.

"You're right," Charlie said, pulling out his phone. He felt a little lightheaded as he pulled up the parent app, but the contact with Ruth and the soft sucking sound from Dahlia's pacifier helped ground him. Ruth must have been feeling the same way, because she gestured to Emily, and his daughter joined the hug, too.

This isn't happening. This is too strange to be real.

Ruth was looking at his screen. "Does that say it's in his room?"

"Yes, but we looked in his room. He wasn't there."

"Did he..." Ruth's lips pursed. "Do you think he..."

"He what?"

"Ran away." She whispered the words, like saying them aloud would make the unthinkable possible.

"Aiden ran away?" Emily wailed, tears immediately springing to her eyes.

"No! No, of course not. There's gotta be some kind of misunderstanding. Maybe Sawyer dropped by and picked him up; they were going paintballing or something. Here, let me call them."

Starla picked up on the third ring. "Hey, Charlie."

"Is Aiden with you?"

"What?"

"Aiden." Charlie could hear the urgency creeping into his own voice. "Is he with you? Did one of you pick him up without talking to Ruth?"

"No...why wouldn't we talk to Ruth?"

Emily and Ruth were watching him, waiting for an answer, and when Charlie shook his head, a silent tear ran down Ruth's cheek.

"What's happening?" Starla asked, sounding concerned.

"I..." He was starting to panic now. That wasn't what anyone needed, but it was happening anyway. "I'm not sure. Let me call my folks."

"Do you not know where Aiden is?" Starla's voice was high, shrill, and Charlie winced.

"Stay calm, please. I'll call you right back."

"We're coming over. We'll be right there." Starla hung up. It was just as well; he needed to call his parents anyway. He rehashed the same conversation, but his dad's response was unhelpful.

"Didn't I say? Didn't I say to never trust a Zane? How could she let him run off like that? You've let your guard down with this horrible woman and look what's happened. I never—"

Charlie hung up. He braced himself on the kitchen island. "Do you want food, Em?"

When she nodded, he served her a bowl and took Dahlia back...the lavender scent of her baby wash calmed him down a little, and he rubbed his cheek against her soft head, then got her a bottle. She should be in bed right now, but that was a problem, not a crisis. He just needed to think. Aiden wouldn't run away. He was too smart for that, wasn't he? It was still pretty cold at night. How far could a twelve-year-old have gotten, anyway?

"My dad and brothers haven't seen him," Ruth said, letting her phone fall from her ear. "Neither has Cord's mom."

"He's hiding somewhere in the house," Charlie said, his voice soft. "I'm sure of it. He has to be. He's curled up in the attic or something with *City of Ember* having a good laugh about this."

"But if he's not…"

"He is," Charlie insisted. "He has to be."

"Charlie, don't you think we should call Lizzie?"

"No." Deputy Painter wasn't necessary. Not yet.

A few minutes later, when Charlie had searched the outside of the house himself, the front door flew open, and all heck broke loose. Starla was already crying, and then Emily started crying harder as she ran to her, babbling incoherently about what they'd done so far. Everyone was asking questions over each other, positing scenarios. Strangely enough, the only person who seemed truly levelheaded was Sawyer.

"Give me the baby," he directed, holding out his hands. "Y'all split up. Search every inch of the house, and then we'll move outside."

Even with four people, the room-to-room search of the house turned up nothing—they even searched the tiny attic.

"He didn't take his bike," Starla called.

"His backpack's gone, though!" Emily shouted from the laundry room. *So he'd planned this.* The idea had his heart threatening to seize up.

"Did y'all eat dinner?" Sawyer asked as Charlie wedged his boots on.

"Kids ate."

"You should, too."

Something broke inside him, and he whirled on the man. "My son is missing!" Charlie roared. "I'll eat when he's found!" Everyone froze, and then Dahlia started crying.

"I just meant," Sawyer said softly, "you'll be able to search better if you have your basic needs met. That's all." He handed Charlie a flashlight. "I'll hold down the fort here. My mama and Paige are fanning out from Riverside. If he's downtown, they'll find him." The coffeeshop was central and therefore a good place to start from.

"Tell them to check the library," Charlie muttered. How Aiden would've gotten that far, he had no idea, but it was a place he liked, felt safe. That was how they needed to think.

"I'll call Lizzie," said Ruth. "Do you remember what he was wearing today?"

"His red hoodie, I think."

"That's what I thought, too. And his black track pants."

"Yeah." Charlie eyed the food on the island, but his stomach was already cramping just thinking about it. He stalked through the entryway and opened the front door just as Mr. Zane was lifting his hand to knock. The two stared at each other for a stunned moment, then Ruth's dad cleared his throat. "We're all here to help. Just tell us where to look." And when Charlie lifted his gaze, Levi, Ranger, Wyatt and Ryan stood behind him, coats and hats on, their faces pinched with concern.

Quick, crunching steps sounded behind them, and Charlie's mom and dad stepped into the light. "What's going on? Did you find him?"

"No, not yet. We were just organizing our search," Charlie replied.

"We don't need their help," James said, climbing the steps.

"Yes, Dad, we do. If we ever needed their help, we need it now." Charlie's voice cracked on the last word, and he felt Ruth's hand on his arm.

"Charlie's right. It's all hands on deck." She seemed to have recovered somewhat from the shock, and he was relieved she could take charge.

"I get to help search, too?" Emily asked, her eyes edged with tears, but Charlie shook his head.

He bent to whisper in her ear. "You stay here with Papa. He'll need your hugs. That's an important job, too." She looked conflicted, but then she turned and ran back inside.

"We're going to walk the property from the house to the river in a line so we don't miss him," Ruth said. "Lizzie said to start here, and she'll mobilize some folks to look between town and here and start working their way toward us. She said…" Ruth paused. "She said to look in all directions. He may be lying down or up in a tree if he doesn't want to be found."

This is my fault. Tears threatened again, and guilt overwhelmed him. He punched it down, but it sprang back up. *I should've gotten him help. I should've checked in with him more.* A voice in his head reminded him that Aiden had three parents, not just one, but it didn't seem to matter right then. His son needed him; it was time to go find him, and he was going to use every available resource to do so, even if it pissed his father off.

"You heard the lady. Line up, let's go." Charlie pulled the door shut behind him.

His own property had never seemed so foreign to him. He felt suspicious of every shadow, every lump of grass. Hearing Aiden's name echo off the trees was unnerving. And the falling dark had him worried about animals. They didn't often have anything to worry about, but every once in a while, they'd get a curious black bear or a cougar crossing the river, especially this time of year when food was more sparse before the fruits of spring had really started.

Aiden, where are you?

Without his bike, he probably wasn't along the road. But it was getting colder, and he wished he'd brought more than just a sweatshirt. Did Aiden have a coat?

"Here's something!" Ranger called out, and they all broke ranks to see. It was a granola bar wrapper, the healthy kind Ruth bought, and since they were only ten minutes from the house, it was very possible it was from him.

"That could be from weeks ago," Charlie pointed out, and the others nodded glumly. They didn't find anything on the rest of their walk to the river.

"All right," Charlie said as the others circled up. "Let's spread to the neighboring land. Starla, can you help Mom and Dad check their woods? I'll help the Zanes."

"Someone check on Sawyer, too," Ruth called. "Maybe he came home."

Charlie texted, and Sawyer's disappointment was palpable.

Sawyer: No, nothing here, either. You don't think he was making his way up to my house, do you?

The group discussed this, but dread filled Charlie at the very idea. He'd have to cross the highway to do that, and then head up the mountain. If he wasn't sticking to the road, who knew where he'd end up? But if Sawyer drove that route with the girls, there was a chance he'd see him. They decided to send Sawyer home with Emily and Dahlia in case he showed up there and send Ruth back to Charlie's house. But before anyone could move, his phone lit up with another text: Sawyer's mom had added them all to a group text.

Rhea: Nothing in the center of town. Once folks got wind of what was happening, they all spread out to help. Library's closed and Marge hadn't seen him. One group's going up toward the falls now, and the other's going to head toward Sawyer's. Grandpa's going to stay at my place in case Aiden ends up there.

How could this child not realize how many people love him? How could he think he was better on his own? Shame filled him again. This was what he'd modeled, wasn't it? That being a man meant doing it on your own, going your own way. Being "tough." He wished he could go back in time and tell his kid how that had worked out for him. How great it had been to have the Divorce Support guys, how much he wished he hadn't pushed people away because of what they might think of him, including his brother. Speaking of...why hadn't he thought to text him before? Panic was addling his brain, and he didn't think he was the only one—they were all still milling around instead of spreading out, like they didn't want to be separated.

Charlie: Are you home? Aiden ran away.

Jason's response was curse-laden and sympathetic and Charlie's eyes welled again.

Jason: What can I do? What do you need?

A voice that's not hoarse from calling my son's name. A better idea to know where he is. A hug from Ruth. He could have one of those things. He turned. "Ruth!"

She'd started toward the house, but she turned around to rush over to him, eyes wide. "News?"

"No." He held out his arms, and she ran right into them, squeezing him tight. "Jason wants to know how he can help."

"Do you think Aiden would go to the shop? Could he check?"

That was ten miles away, but they didn't know when he'd left. He could've had a two-hour head start. But it was a good idea; she was clearly handling this much better than he was. Charlie used speech to text to write a message so he didn't have to let her go.

"This is all my fault," she sniffled into his chest.

Oh. Maybe she wasn't.

"Quit hogging all the blame, Zane. I already called it."

She gave a wet sort of laugh and wiped her nose with her sleeve.

"He wanted to go to Cord's a few days ago, but I told him no, it was easier to take care of Dahlia at home, and

I wanted her to get good rest, since she's still recovering, and—"

"Ruth." He tipped her chin up to look into her eyes. "This is not your fault. No one's blaming you. Kids do foolish things, it's in their programming. If it hadn't been you, it would have been me, telling him to turn off screens or Starla, telling him he can't shoot BBs at the trees around the property. It is *not* your fault."

"That's right, Ruth," Starla chimed in. "It could've happened to any of us." The wind was picking up, and it blew her words to the others. They started chiming in, both sides, to tell her the same thing. And for an odd moment, Charlie considered how hearing a chorus of Millers, Zanes and Devereauxs all agreeing about something was the most unlikely thing to ever happen to him.

CHAPTER THIRTY-EIGHT

Ruth walked back to Charlie's house alone. Sawyer was already gone by the time she got there, and she was numbly impressed by how quickly he'd gotten the girls packed up. She put her keys and her coat on the kitchen island, but left her shoes on. She might need to leave quickly...

A thousand images of Aiden hurt or scared or alone flipped through her mind like the pages of a book, and Ruth closed her eyes. When she'd quelled them enough to function again, she reached for the remote and turned on the TV. It was on that nature channel Aiden liked, which just made her heart hurt more, but she didn't have the energy to change it. She was just spooning some Paleo casserole she wasn't going to eat into a bowl when it hit her.

She knew where Aiden was.

With shaking hands, she pulled out her phone and called Charlie. No answer.

They must be out of cell phone range. It often happened in the woods; most of them had boosters in their houses, but there were plenty of times her dad had been out in the orchard and she hadn't been able to get ahold of him. Ruth hesitated—if she was wrong and Aiden came back here, he'd find an empty house...but she didn't think she was wrong. And furthermore, she was the only one who'd think to look for him there, because she was the only one who knew he'd been there.

She quickly jotted a note which she taped to the front door and texted the group her plan. It started to rain as Ruth neared the woods that spanned their properties, and Ruth broke into a jog, unable to wait to see if her theory was correct. She didn't see her brothers or her dad; they must not have thought to look so close to the river. But when she ran up to the cabin, she noticed a shadow move across the window. Ruth flung the door open.

"Aiden?" The phone on her flashlight revealed fresh footprints, but those could be from her family, checking for him. She stood still and just waited. Then, slowly, the boy stood from where he'd been crouched behind the bed. She held out her arms, and he flew into them.

The rain continued to pitter-patter on the roof and the ground outside as she held him, relief so strong it was almost painful pumping through her veins. She wouldn't get cell service here, she knew. They'd have to walk back toward her house or Charlie's.

"Am I in trouble?" he mumbled into her chest.

Ruth couldn't help the laugh that broke free. "*So much* trouble." She pulled back to look him in the eye. "What was the plan here, kiddo?"

He cast his gaze toward his shoes. "I don't know. I was just mad at you for not letting me go to Cord's, mad at Em and Dad and Mom for other stuff..." He sighed. "But once I got out here, I wasn't so mad anymore. But I didn't know how to fix it. And then I heard people calling for me, and I knew I was going to be in trouble—"

"Deep trouble," Ruth clarified. "Gigantic trouble. Think, like, Mariana Trench trouble."

He sighed again. "I know." He lifted his gaze. "Are *you* in trouble?"

"No, Dad knows this is mostly your fault."

He gave a little nod. "That's good. I only realized once I'd left that you might get fired, and I didn't want that."

"Well, I appreciate that."

"But I also didn't think Dad would fire his girlfriend."

She pulled him into a side hug as they moved toward the door. "Did that make you mad, too? That your dad and I are dating?"

"At first it did. Now I don't care. I just didn't want him to send you away like the others."

"Don't think that's going to happen," she said as they traced the path along the river. "But I guess no one knows what the future holds."

"I do."

She turned to look at him over her shoulder. "You do?"

"Yeah. I'm gonna get grounded for the rest of my life."

Ruth laughed. She texted the group chat the moment she got back into range. There was joy and relief all around that he'd been found, but several people were still beyond cell service, it seemed, so the messages filtered in slowly.

Sawyer was first on a video call.

"First, good work, Ms. Zane. You did us all proud."

"Thanks, Sawyer."

His expression turned stern. "Could I talk to my son, please?"

"Sure!" she chirped, and Aiden groaned as she handed him the phone.

"Hi, Papa."

"Hi, Aiden. Are you okay?"

He nodded. "I'm sorry."

"Not as sorry as you're going to be. Your mom and dad and I will be having a discussion about consequences. We're all very glad you're safe, but you scared the living crap out of us. I've got six new gray hairs."

Aiden gave a rueful smile. "I'm really sorry."

"And yet the gray remains..."

"How do you know they're new?" Aiden joked. "I think Didi put a few in there, too."

"That she did, son. That she did. I'm gonna let you finish your walk home. I love you."

"Love you, too, Pop." The connection cut off, and Aiden handed the phone back to Ruth.

"I'm gonna have to talk about this a *lot*, aren't I?"

Ruth nodded. "You have a lot of people who care about you, Aid. They're gonna have things to say when you screw up. Just remember: that's not a bad thing. I had some classmates who could get away with whatever they wanted, because no one at home was paying attention. That may sound great, but it felt bad. They would've given anything to have half the town looking for them."

Aiden winced. "Half the town? Dad's not gonna like that."

"I think Dad's just going to be glad to see you." She had more to say, but no opportunity, since Starla called next. Hers was just a regular phone call.

"Hi-Ruth-can-I-speak-to-Aiden-please?" She already sounded quite close to tears, and Aiden looked truly chagrined when he put the phone to his ear.

"Hi, Mom."

"AIDEN CHARLES MILLER, DON'T YOU EVER DO THAT AGAIN." It was loud enough that Ruth could hear her even from two feet away from the phone.

Ooh, the middle name. It's serious now. Ruth was allowed a few moments alone with her thoughts as Aiden *mm-hmm*'ed and *yeah*'ed his way through the uncomfortable conversation with Starla. But the worst was yet to come.

Charlie had beaten them back to the house, and he was pacing the gravel driveway out front, hands on his hips, his shoulders high and tight, when they walked up. The minute he spotted them, he took off at a run toward them, and she felt Aiden tense next to her, pausing to see what would happen next. Barreling into him, Charlie engulfed the boy in a hug, pressing Aiden's head to his chest, kissing his hair, tears running silently down his cheeks. There was something about seeing a dad cry over his kids that just broke her, and Ruth put a hand on Charlie's back, intending to comfort him, when she found herself unceremoniously yanked into the hug as well. Aiden was crying now, too.

"Dad, I'm sorry."

Charlie just kept holding the two of them, squeezing them. When Charlie finally let go, he stepped back, wiping his face with both hands, and let out a gigantic sigh.

"Can you say something?" Aiden pleaded, but Charlie just shook his head. He held out his arm, and Aiden went in for another side hug as they walked toward the house.

Then Charlie paused and held out his other hand to Ruth. She took it with a weak smile, deep fatigue threatening to trip her over the uneven ground. There was a lot to unpack from tonight, but at least she thought Starla would probably agree to that counseling now. Charlie let his parents talk to Aiden for a minute, but Ruth wasn't listening. She needed to go home; it wasn't that late, but she was beyond wrung out emotionally and she didn't think she'd be safe to drive tonight for much longer. She paused at the bottom of the stairs in the entryway.

"I'm gonna take off," she whispered to Charlie. "I'll see you tomorrow morning."

Charlie released Aiden then, who was being ushered toward the kitchen by Starla. "Are you sure?"

"Yeah. I think I just need..." Dang, she was shaking again. So annoying. "Downtime."

"Thank you for your help," Charlie said, gazing into her eyes so sincerely that it made her want to cry. "That's twice now you've helped my kids in big ways."

"It wasn't a big—"

Charlie swore loudly. "I'm so tired of you saying that. Just admit it! Admit that it was a big deal!"

She blinked at him, shocked by his outburst. "Fine, it was a big deal."

"Good! Thank you! Now come and eat something before you go." He pulled her deeper into the house before she could argue with him.

Starla was smirking at her when she shuffled into the kitchen, and she handed her a bowl. "He's not wrong, you know."

The food felt like grace, giving her a reason to fill her mouth, so she didn't have to figure out what to say. It had been a weird day. She allowed them to take care of her collectively; her dad and brothers showed up a few minutes later, apparently invited by Charlie. Riverside had donated all their leftovers to the gathering, brought over by Sawyer's mom Rhea, and someone brought Ruth a cranberry scone. She sat on the couch and ate it, listening to the families talk and cry and laugh, sharing their collective relief. Some of Charlie's Divorce Support guys showed up, too, just to give hugs. Only Sawyer was missing, stuck at the lodge with the sleeping girls. Her eyes felt heavy, and she turned and let her head rest on the back of the couch, just for a minute. The next thing she knew, Charlie was shaking her awake.

"Come on, sweetheart. Your dad's going to give you a ride home."

"Okay," she mumbled, and Charlie chuckled.

"You were out hard."

"Told you I needed to go home."

"You were right. Sorry I didn't listen to you. I just wanted you around a little longer. Next time, I will."

"Okay." She yawned. She was already wearing her coat and shoes, and the cold air outside woke her up a little as she kissed Charlie goodbye and got into her dad's truck.

"Your mom said to tell you she's proud of you," he said, as he pulled out on the highway.

Ruth snorted softly. "For losing the kid?"

"No," he said, "for finding him."

CHAPTER THIRTY-NINE

Charlie

Four months later

"We are gathered here today," the dark-haired man with the microphone said solemnly, "to celebrate birds!" The small crowd cheered; they made more noise than Charlie thought 150 people would be able to, especially so early in the morning. He shook out his legs again, jumping in place.

"Welcome to the first annual Race for the Raptors, organized by our very own Ruth Zane!"

She waved shyly as people cheered again, several nearby people patting her on the back.

"I still think Birdrush was a better name," Charlie grumbled, and Ruth grinned.

"No. People like specificity. Now they know what they're running for. Also, hush."

"We're asking," her dad went on, "that the walkers please move to the rear of the pack so that the runners have a bit more space...as long as you have your apps active, it should record your time no matter when you start."

Charlie had to admit that the app the nerdy kid Starla had recruited from the library had written for them was pretty cool.

"Bye, babe," Charlie said, giving her a big kiss on the cheek. "Get that winner's trophy ready for me."

"You're really not going to walk with me?" she asked, and even though she batted those long eyelashes, he didn't waver. He'd been working too hard to throw it all away now.

"Nope. Love you." It was easy to say it now. He'd held off for a long time, not wanting her to think he was trying to manipulate her with the words. He'd waited until he was sure. Until he was sure she'd say it back.

She'd been opening her mouth in example, trying to get the baby to open up for the plain yogurt on the long rubber spoon, but Dahlia just wanted to grab the spoon and chew it. Now that Dahlia was healthy, she'd developed a stubborn streak that Charlie secretly admired...when it was Starla's week, anyway.

"Come on," Ruth had coaxed, moving the spoon away. "You can do it. Open, please."

He didn't know why the feeling had hit him so clearly then. He also didn't know why Dahlia had chosen that moment to spit the yogurt back at the side of Ruth's face. He could've just handed her paper towel instead of bending to tenderly wipe her face clean with a warm rag, letting the baby have the spoon while he worked. He'd wiped it slowly, trying to figure out how to spring the words from where they held back, when she smirked at him.

"How can you look at me like that when I'm disgusting?"
He'd shrugged. "Guess I just love you."

"Love you, too!" Ruth's musical laugh followed him as he worked his way up to the starting line. He glanced askance at Levi, Ranger, and Ryan, who were all lined up together, and they gave him a nod of acknowledgment.

"No Wyatt today?"

"He wanted to make sure Mom didn't get stuck in her wheelchair," Ranger said.

Charlie nodded, but felt a secret glow of happiness that Ruth's mom could be helped because of his gift. He and Mr. Zane had worked it out; they told everyone the insurance claim had finally come through, when really, Charlie had just bought it for them. They both knew Deborah would never have accepted it otherwise. They finally installed the ramps yesterday, just in time for her to attend the race.

"Let's settle down now," her dad boomed, and the crowd quieted. "On your mark..."

"Get ready to eat my dust, Miller," Levi growled.

"Get set..."

"You've got that backwards, Zane."

"Go!"

The Zane men took off as fast as they could, and Charlie chuckled. They'd wear themselves out before they even passed through the middle of town. But he'd let them appear to be winning in order to make Deborah happy. He found he had a soft spot for the lady; he'd walked over to see her often since Ruth had introduced them. His own mom still hadn't apologized, but she had made a large personal donation to his team, the Miller-Devereaux Dragonflies (he was never letting Emily name anything again). Starla and Sawyer were walking with the kids, and they were all so excited to support Ruth. He'd thought about offering to push Dahlia's stroller, but she was getting kind of chunky in a good way, and he didn't want her to slow him down. In a weird way, he considered it personal growth; it was still hard to let her out of his sight sometimes. He went into her room sometimes, just watching her breathe, thinking about how lucky they were that she was totally fine now. Ruth was always quick to remind him that the chance of her being in any real danger was small, but still. Things were good now, and he couldn't help but be thankful for it.

Up ahead, the Zane men were already petering out a mile in, and he waved to Kellan, Tess and Arrow...the boy had a cowbell that he was ringing ardently, and it made Charlie laugh, which made it hard to breathe. Kellan was wincing at the sound, but made no move to stop him. He seemed determined to be a good dad, and Charlie had to respect it. He wasn't sure what the future held for Kellan and Tess, but at least Arrow would have a dad. That was important.

Chase and Christopher Carpenter passed him, running in sync as the route curved along the river, and Charlie picked up speed. No identical blond giants were going to put him to shame. And when they both slowed down to wave at Lizzie and Paige, Charlie sped on ahead. He didn't need to win...just to beat the Zanes. And he was closing on them. Ranger looked like he had a cramp; Charlie had tried to bribe Ruth to make them a big breakfast this morning, but she'd flatly refused. But based on the way he was holding his side, perhaps Ranger had sabotaged himself.

"You okay, man?" Ryan called over his shoulder, but didn't slow down. Levi didn't appear to notice at all. *Jerks.* Charlie slowed down to match Ranger's speed.

"You all right?"

"Yeah," he gritted out, not sounding like he meant it. "I'll be fine. You go ahead."

"You want some water or something?" They were about to pass a table.

"No, I'm good."

"You sure?"

"What I really want is for you to humiliate my selfish brothers, who said we were all going to stick together."

Now that he could do. "See you at the finish line," Charlie said with a grin, giving Ranger a friendly clap on the shoulder.

"Good luck."

"Don't need it!" It was definitely on now. He had express permission from a Zane besides Ruth to run these fellas into the ground, and by golly, he was going to do it. Charlie stretched out his legs and picked up his pace, blowing past them as they stopped for water. *Who needs to stop for water in a 10K, anyway?* Charlie thought it was really more of a "cover your legal bases" situation; he and Ruth had both done a lot of reading about organizing a successful event, but hers had focused more on safety than his.

Charlie heard Levi and Ryan curse as they saw him go by, and he grinned. They dogged his steps for the last mile, but couldn't catch him, and honestly, it felt nice to get a win.

Ruth was cheering wildly at the finish line, and he heard her yell, "Go, Chuck, go! That's my guy!" *Husband. I want to be her husband.* It was too much excitement to ask her today, especially in front of all these people, but he was going to do it. And soon.

EPILOGUE

Ruth

Three months later

"Where did you say this nest was?" Ruth followed Charlie between the rows of apple trees. They were heavy with Rome apples, their dappled surfaces mostly unblighted, but quirky how apples left to themselves tended to be.

"It's just up here." Charlie paused. "Or maybe it was..." He fell into a mumble as he backtracked the way they'd come, pivoting to the left, ducking under the branches, turning so fast he nearly ran into her. "Sorry."

"That's okay," she said, perplexed. He was being weird. They'd been wandering around the orchard for twenty minutes now; no kisses, no handholding...just looking for this hummingbird nest he'd supposedly found. Given the thimble-like size of an Anna's hummingbird's nest, which was the most likely species given that they were residential in these parts and the most plentiful type, and given also that Charlie spent most of his time outside either jumping on the trampoline with his kids, mowing the lawn, or running, she thought it was very unlikely that's what he'd found. Even so, she should give him a chance. It was nice that he'd found something he thought she'd appreciate.

"How did you happen upon this?"

"Oh. Uh." More mumbling. Her smooth-talking guy was definitely up to something. "I was out for a walk with Dahlia."

"When?"

He waved a hand carelessly. "I can't remember. A few days ago, I think."

"Hmm."

More and more suspicious. Dahlia had been fighting a summer cold; there's no way he would've been walking her around so far from the house.

"Well," she prodded, "there's no reason why we have to see it today, is there?"

Charlie stopped suddenly. He spun to stare at her, a move that would make her shrink from anyone else. It only made her smile now.

"Why am I getting the third-degree, princess?"

Ruth shrugged. "You're being weird. I want to know why."

"It's weird to want to go on a walk with my girlfriend?" He was flailing his arms about, a clear sign he was lying. He was out of practice now, and Ruth loved that. *I love him.* The warm, happy feeling that flooded her chest made it hard to breathe. "That's weird? What's weird about that?"

"You're saying the word 'weird' a lot," she pointed out with a smirk, and he pulled her closer.

"Well, I guess I'm just a weird guy, then," he murmured. Charlie pressed a teasing kiss to her cheek, letting his lips wander down her jawline to her neck.

"This is more normal," she said, letting her hands roam over his back.

"Kissing in the orchard is normal?"

"It should be."

"Agreed."

"Why do you smell like work?"

"It's my fancy new cologne. For when I'm trying to make a good impression."

"Why haven't you worn it on a date before?"

She smelled him again, then pressed a kiss to his neck because she couldn't help it.

"Just wanted everything on my side today." He sighed as she continued her kisses. "But in accordance with my attempts to be more authentic, I guess I should let go of perfect and just ask you." Ruth barely had time to register the words *ask you* before he was charging ahead. "And we don't have to do it right away, we don't even have to set a date now, and I don't care if you want to have it in the backyard if it's easier for your mom, but I talked to the kids and they're all happy about it—well, I don't know if Dahlia's happy, but she's always happy, so—"

"Chuck…" she said, but he powered on, like he was afraid he'd lose his nerve.

"And I found a honeymoon trip to Arizona that I think you'll love; there were a ton of birds that don't live around here. I found a service that can send a nurse to care for your mom if your dad needs help while we're gone, and Starla said she was happy to keep the kids—"

"Chuck," she said, slapping a hand over his mouth, happy tears dancing in front of her vision. He frowned as one escaped.

"Is that a no? You're not shaking. I decided to hold you to cut down on the chances of you shaking. That's the only reason I'm not on one knee. And I guess I lost the ring for the moment. Please say yes anyway."

She started shaking then, having finally caught up with his rapid-fire non-proposal, and she struggled to get the words out smoothly.

"Gonna give me a reason?" The 'r' clanged, and she didn't flinch. She just stared at him, barely able to believe this was happening. That this boy she'd been curious about since childhood had grown into a man who wanted her.

"Aiden said I should 'lock it down.' Is that what you mean?"

She shook her head slowly.

"Emily wants to call you 'Mama Ruth' and has her heart set on being our flower girl, even though she's far too old. She said she could walk down with Dahlia. How's that?"

Ruth whacked him. "Be charming for just one minute. This is an instance when it's okay to use your schmoozing powers for good!"

"Okay, okay," he laughed, holding her closer to keep her from hitting him again. Charlie cleared his throat, and Ruth decided that if he told another joke, she was really going to let him have it. But when he sobered, she wasn't sure she was ready to hear the actual proposal.

"My reason is the way you flip your pancakes gently so the bubbles don't pop. My reason is your very sketchy opinions about cars, which you will clearly need a lifetime of education to reform. My reason is the way you remove me from reality with your creativity and ground me in reality with your wisdom about kids and life and what matters. My reason is how good you feel on the back of my bike with your arms around my waist. My reason is how when I ask you what happened to all my socks, you just say, 'Gnomes,' like that's logical. My reason is that when you care for others so selflessly, it makes me want to make sure someone's taking care of you all the time. And I don't deserve it, Ruth—"

"Don't."

Charlie clenched his jaw for a moment. "Fine, I don't *feel like* I deserve it, but I want to be the one to take care of you, the way you've taken care of us. And I'm not going to mess it up this time. I'll do better, I'll—"

She kissed him then, not because she didn't want to hear his promises, but because he'd already proven them to her over this last year, and it was more important that he feel her *yes* in every bone of his body. Then a sudden thought made her laugh.

"If you did screw it up, my family would kill you."

"Extra incentive, but unneeded, I assure you." He gently brought their heads together. "You're all I need, Ruth. We've got this."

"I think so, too." She wiped her eyes, trying to get her heart rate under control. "I don't know why I didn't expect this."

"I don't know why, either. Ranger's been texting me for months now, asking why it hasn't happened."

"I don't think he understands what it's like to have kids."

Charlie chuckled. "That might be it. I had a heck of a time finding the right ring, too."

"And then you went and lost it?" she asked with a laugh. "What did you do, stick it in an old nest?"

"Yes! Hawk nests turned out to be impossible to get to. It was supposed to be romantic!"

"It sure will be when we find it."

"We better find it," he grumbled. "I'm going to be paying for it for a long time."

"You're sure?" she asked, caressing his face. "About this? About us?"

"Completely. Please marry me, Ruth."

"Okay," she whispered, still trembling, but this time, with joy at what the future held.

"Also, all the families are back at my house, so we should probably go before they kill each other."

She rolled her eyes. "I don't think killing is a possibility anymore, but a maiming isn't out of the question. And you don't have to taunt them by putting your Run for the Raptors trophy on the mantle, you know..."

"I'm just proud of my beautiful future wife's accomplishments," he grinned, taking her hand to lead her back to the house. "And I'm proud of what we've built together. We're gonna soar so high."

Would you please leave a review?

Small businesses like mine thrive on honest feedback! Indie publishing is my dream job, but I want to be sure I've done it well. Your review lets other readers know if they'd enjoy Charlie and Ruth's story and helps give my work credibility in a huge sea of options. Thank you in advance!

Get access to your Timber Falls bonus library now!

Newsletters subscribers have access to seven exclusive short stories starring your favorite Timberites! (Including a steamy one for Charlie and Ruth coming soon...) What are you waiting for? Find a screen, go to http://www.sub-scribepage.com/timberfalls and sign up now.

Don't miss a moment of Timber Falls fun!

Could Be Something Good (Daniel and Winnie)

Must be a Mistake (Kyle and Ainsley)
Right Back Where We Started (Martina and Carter)
More Than We Bargained For (Starla and Sawyer)
Just Getting Started (Lizzie and Chase)
No Time Like the Present (Greg and Tharushi)
Never Say Never (Charlie and Ruth)
Don't Push Your Luck (Christopher and Paige)

Also by Fiona West
Rocky Royal Romance (sweet fantasy romance)

Chasing Down Her Highness: a chronically-ill princess who fled from her responsibilities is forced to face the fiancé she abandoned and journey across a magically-unpredictable continent. Can she keep the life she's given up everything to build?

#

Breaking Up the Royals: a king caught between love and legality...can Abbie and Edward's relationship survive engagement and the opposition who wants to tear them apart again?

#

Serving Side by Side: a security professional finds herself paired with a shy, sensory-sensitive man on the night watch. Can their friendship blossom into something more?

#

Bringing Down the King: a single mother gets her dream job as a journalist, only to find herself caught in royal scandal, opposing her son's new mentor. When forced to choose between love and her career, can she still come out a winner?

#

Winning Back the Duke: a doctor takes an expedition with her brother's best friend that has life-changing results. Can she resist the underlying attraction that's been there for years?

\#

Working Under the Warlord: an expert magic user is being slowly overtaken by magic, and his apprentice is the only person who can help him. After years of emotional isolation, can he trust her with his secret...and his heart?

Acknowledgments

To my writing Discord: Thank you for listening to my fears at strange hours of the night, helping me rework trouble spots, and gasping over little revelations when I share snippets. Y'all are the best.

To my sensitivity reader, Kristin Houlihan: No one knows better than you how to help me craft a book with characters with realistic illnesses. I know you enjoy my work, but I also know that it cost you spoons (and naps and energy) to help, and it is deeply appreciated.

To my sensitivity reader, Justin Gross: How vastly you underestimate what you've contributed to this book, I'll never know, but I'm thankful you said yes when I asked for your help! You're such a caring friend, and Charlie would be lucky to be as self-aware and transparent as you.

To my beta readers, C.M. Caplan and Liz Schandorff: Thank you for helping me take the work deeper! You pose wonderful questions and make great suggestions, and I appreciate you both.

To my copyeditor, Reina at Rickrack Editing: Your insights and sensitivity truly help me send out a better story! Thank you for your wonderful touch on the work.

And last, but certainly not least, thank you to my CFO, my partner in life and love. Your encouragement is truly what makes this possible. Thank you for being the pumpkin spice to my latte.

Connect with Fiona!

Thanks so much for taking the time to sample my work. I hope you enjoyed reading it even more than I enjoyed writing it, though I doubt that's possible. Being an author is a dream come true, and getting to share my books with delightful, thoughtful readers like you just adds to the sweetness. Drop me a line and let me know what you thought or leave a review on Goodreads!

Sign up for my bi-monthly newsletter, The West Wind, for freebies, deleted scenes, book reviews, and insight into my writing process at https://www.subscribepage.com/timberfalls.

On Twitter as @FionaWestAuthor[1]

On Facebook as @authorfionawest[2]

On Instagram as fionawestauthor[3]

On Goodreads as Fiona West[4]

Or email me at fiona@fionawest.net.

I love talking to fans!

---

1. https://twitter.com/FionaWestAuthor

2. https://web.facebook.com/authorfionawest/

3. https://www.instagram.com/fionawestauthor/

4. https://www.goodreads.com/author/show/18433825.Fiona_West